INTO THE FIRE

NUCLEAR DAWN BOOK 4

KYLA STONE

PAPER MOON PRESS

Into the Fire

Copyright © 2019 by Kyla Stone All rights reserved. This book or any portion thereof may not be reproduced or used in any manner whatsoever without the express written permission of the publisher except for the use of brief quotations in a book review.

This book is a work of fiction. Any references to historical events, real people, or real places are used fictitiously. Other names, characters, places, and events are products of the author's imagination, and any resemblances to actual events or places or persons, living or dead, is entirely coincidental.

Printed in the United States of America

Cover design by Christian Bentulan

Book formatting by Vellum

First Printed in 2019

ISBN: 978-1-945410-39-0

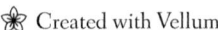 Created with Vellum

1

DAKOTA

Dakota Sloane was prepared for battle. She gripped her Sig in one hand, the AR-15 slung over her shoulder, the extra magazines tucked into a pouch at her belt.

"Let's go," Logan Garcia said gruffly. He carried his rifle, the Glock 43 tucked into its concealed holster at the small of his back, his combat knife strapped to his belt. "You ready?"

She nodded tightly. She was as ready as she'd ever be.

The group followed Dakota across the road. They hiked into the dense, dark forest with only the two small penlights to see by. Dakota had one; Julio de la Peña, the other.

An owl hooted overhead. Unseen creatures scurried through the leaves.

Anxiety scrabbled up Dakota's spine. Doing this at night was a terrible idea.

But they had no choice. If Ezra was in trouble, he'd be dead by morning. If anything happened to him, she'd never forgive herself.

They couldn't wait. They had to reach the cabin tonight.

Ominous shadows crouched all around them. They kept tripping on roots and vines. Mosquitoes whined in their ears. The air smelled dank and damp, peat mixed with rotting vegetation.

Half-jungle, half-swamp, the Everglades was a land of haunting beauty. Wild and foreboding, primordial and ancient—here long before humans, and probably long afterward.

Ezra loved this place. Dakota loved it, too.

This mosquito-infested swamp was the only place in the world that had ever felt like home.

She and the others had escaped the radioactive ruins of Miami in search of the safety she knew she would find here. But now Maddox Cage and the Shepherds were threatening everything she held dear.

Her heartbeat quickened, thumping against her ribs.

Almost there.

She was trekking purely by memory, the cabin in the clearing fixed in her mind: the oak, pine, and cypress forests surrounding it. To the north, a wide expanse of sawgrass and brackish water that turned into a million miles of swampy marshlands.

"What are you looking for?" Logan whispered behind her.

She'd explored these woods dozens of times, but not for two years, and seldom at night. Everything looked different—strange and dangerous.

"Ezra has a buried cache near here. If I can find it, I can orient myself and know exactly where we are. Plus, the cache will have more nine mil ammo, and if we're lucky, another gun."

She was searching for a particular live oak tree with the branches locked in a weird, twisting shape that resembled a heart. There were two smaller scrubby pines on either side. The three rocks pushed up against the roots looked natural—unless you knew what to look for...

It was ridiculously hard to see in the dark. Shadows wavered just outside the penlight's halo. The moon still shone high in the night sky, but the trees blocked most of its light.

Twigs and thorns caught at her clothing. She nearly twisted her ankle on a tree root. The others stumbled behind her, Logan cursing softly.

She paused and glanced behind her, making sure Eden was keeping up.

Behind Logan, Julio trudged next to fifteen-year-old Eden, holding her hand to keep her from tripping. She looked so small and vulnerable. The girl had been through so much already. She needed Dakota by her side.

But Dakota had to lead them. She had to reach Ezra first and make sure he was safe. Then she could tend to Eden's needs. Until then, Julio was standing in the gap for her.

Her chest tightened. Julio was a good man. Steady and dependable—a loyal friend.

"I'm too out of shape for this," Julio huffed, but his tone was good-natured and self-deprecating. He rubbed his round, middle-aged belly with his free hand. "Too many *Cubanos*. What I wouldn't give for a delicious ham and cheese sandwich right now."

Eden looked up at him and signed something with one hand. It was hard to tell in the shadows, but it looked like she was smiling a little.

"Count me in." Yu-Jin Park took up the rear, but only slightly. Even with his broken arm, he managed to keep up. "I've never been hungrier in my life."

"We need to stay quiet," Logan reminded them.

Dakota returned to her task. Even at night, the heat was oppressive. She breathed in the dank, familiar scent of moss, peat, and wet leaves. Every passing minute felt like an hour.

Please, please find it...

Finally, her gaze snagged on something familiar.

She rushed forward, fell to her knees, and pushed the stack of three rocks aside. One of the rocks was long and flat, and had three short lines etched into it. It was perfect for digging, chosen by Ezra specifically for that purpose.

The others crowded behind her as she handed Eden the penlight. Eden kept the light trained on the ground where Dakota needed to work. She dug frantically for a few minutes until the rock scraped against something.

She brushed away the dirt, twigs, and leaves, and twisted the top off the five-gallon bucket—one of several Ezra had buried within a few miles of the cabin. This was the closest one on the southwest side of the property.

Ezra always said you couldn't keep your entire stash in one place. You might be returning home when you surprised an intruder. Maybe you'd be forced to flee without your weapons.

Ezra Burrows always had a backup plan.

Dakota reached in and pulled out a Springfield XD-S pistol wrapped in a Ziplock-type bag with anti-corrosion lining, made specifically for long-term firearm storage.

She could've wept with joy. It was close to the same model as her old gun, the one she'd lost with her bugout bag in the moments after the nuclear blast rained hell down upon Miami.

That was almost three weeks ago, but every day felt like a lifetime.

There were two spare magazines for the pistol—both preloaded and wrapped in the protective lining—and a box of 9mm ammo. She handed the box to Logan, who slipped it in his cargo pocket.

She moved aside some packaged protein bars, bottles of water, a small first aid kit, and a tin box she knew contained fire starter tools. She pulled out a folded tactical knife and held it out to Eden. "Take it, just in case. Keep it in your pocket."

Eden obeyed without protest.

Dakota handed a second, smaller pocketknife to Park. He stuffed it in his pocket with his good hand. The last item she took was a pair of binoculars.

She closed the lid, but didn't rebury the bucket. It would piss Ezra off—he was fastidious about stuff like that—but there wasn't time. She'd come back later and take care of it.

Suddenly, it was hard to breathe. It felt like some giant hand squeezed her heart. She hoped he'd be pissed at her. It meant the ornery old bear was still alive.

Dakota climbed to her feet, brushing the dirt off her knees, and slung the binoculars' strap around her neck. She handed Park the Sig, who returned the Glock to Logan. Dakota kept the XD-S.

"Point and shoot, remember?" she said to Park.

Park took it gingerly. "Okay, yeah. Got it."

"Now you've got a gun and a knife. Never bring a knife to a gun fight, they say, but when you need stealth and surprise in close quarters, it still works."

Park nodded soberly, his face round and pale in the shadows.

She held her finger to her lips. No more talking. They were close.

Within ten minutes, she'd led them safely through the woods and past a tripwire, the thin wire invisible in the darkness. But she knew it was there.

Ezra didn't use fishing line. Rather, it was a low-stretch, high-strength cord he'd previously sprayed with a flat, grayish green spray paint to dull the shine and blend in with the foliage.

She suppressed a tight smile. Everything was the same. Just as if she'd never left.

Her heart lifted with a hope she hardly dared believe. Maybe Ezra was safe. Maybe everything would be fine.

When she glimpsed the glint of the fence ahead, she scanned the area for a tree to climb. She gestured for Logan and the others to remain where they were, then swung herself up on the low branch of a live oak.

Swaths of Spanish moss tickled her skin. Tiny bugs crawled up her arm, but she couldn't brush them away. She grunted, muscles straining, bark scraping against her belly and arms as she clambered into a sitting position, then carefully stood, leaning against the trunk for balance.

Her pulse hammering in her ears, she peered through the binoculars. Ezra's cabin squatted in the middle of the wide clearing. There was the big shed, the chicken coop, the garden, the well, and the outhouse buildings, with the dock and the fishing boat in the distance.

Ten yards in front of the cabin, Ezra's familiar pristine 2004 Dodge Ram SRT-10 pickup sat in the dirt driveway. But two other trucks were parked in the drive. Strange trucks she didn't recognize.

The front gate was dented, hanging half-open.

Her heart stopped beating and her mouth went dry. Her hands were trembling, but she forced herself to keep looking. To see it all, no matter how terrible.

Three dead bodies littered the driveway. Dark, unmoving blobs in the moonlight. None of them were him—she was sure of it.

Two trucks meant more people. More enemies, more danger. They were inside. With Ezra.

Her worst fears had come true.

The Shepherds were already here.

2

DAKOTA

"What's the plan?" Logan asked. They'd turned off their penlights and gathered behind the cover of several large, leafy trees. He scanned the trees around them, his eyes hard and alert. His unkempt black hair curled around his temples, his bronze skin darkened by the tattoos spiraling up both muscled forearms.

He glanced down at her. "We're not going in half-cocked."

Dakota nodded tightly. Of course, he was right—though every cell in her body thrummed with a desperate desire to do just that, to turn and run straight to Ezra, shooting anything that got in her way.

"Seems like our best option is to take them by surprise," Julio said. "We don't know how many are in there."

"How do we get close?" Park asked nervously. "What about the electric fence?"

He pointed at the fence line in front of them, the rusted metal sign that read, "Warning: Electric Shock."

Dakota shook her head. "It takes too much electricity to actually run the thing. The fencing keeps most of the critters out of the hen house and gardens, and the sign itself scares most would-be trespassers away."

Park looked dubious. "So...you're saying it won't electrocute us to death. You're absolutely a hundred percent positive on that?"

"I am." She remembered the first time she'd crossed into Ezra's property, a wounded Eden in tow, her heart thudding, frantic with fear and blind determination, willing to risk anything to save someone she loved.

Just like now.

"Park?" Julio asked. "What's wrong?"

Park shook his head, his eyes wide and panicky. He was staring at the Sig in his hand like it might bite him. "This is real. The guns, those dead bodies. This isn't a roller coaster ride where I scream my head off, but really, I know I'm safe. Anything could happen. Ten minutes from now, I could be dead."

He clenched and unclenched his good hand at his side, clearly shaken. "I thought I was fearless. I really did. But I'm not."

"No one is," Dakota said. "We do it anyway."

"All this time, I was just play-acting. I had no idea. No freaking clue."

Dakota pushed back her impatience. His false bravado was slipping. It was finally real to him. All the skydiving and bungie jumping in the world meant nothing when you were facing down the muzzle of a gun. *Well, join the club.*

"Harlow was the first person—" He swallowed hard. "The first dead body I ever saw..."

"You're about to see some more. And if you keep it together, it'll be their dead bodies, not yours."

Julio shot her a reproving look. She thought he was going to coddle Park with some *it's all gonna be okay* nonsense, but he didn't. He put a gentle but firm hand on Park's shoulder. "Don't overthink it too much. You'll only psych yourself out."

Park gave a tremulous nod, his eyes still terrified.

Dakota gritted her teeth. He was going to be worthless in a gunfight. Maybe worse than worthless.

"The plan," Logan said, drawing them back to the point—how the hell to save Ezra and regain control of the cabin.

Dakota's mind raced. "We're coming in perpendicular to the property on the western side. The cabin faces south, with the water behind it, to the north. On this side, there aren't any trees or other cover close by, other than the shed and the cisterns, but that's one hundred yards from us and still about fifty yards from the cabin."

She chewed her lower lip. "We can't go in guns blazing, not with Ezra inside. The cabin walls are thick concrete, but we might still hit him."

"So, we sneak in," Julio said. "Get in close and aim through the windows once we can see inside?"

"We can try," Logan said, "but that's a lot of open territory to cover without anybody seeing us. Especially if they have a watch posted."

She didn't see a watch, but that didn't mean there wasn't one. She glassed the property again, searching the darkness, zeroing in on the cabin. The window glowed with a dim light. Shapes were moving inside. One head, then a second one.

"I see two hostiles, but there could be more."

She felt every passing second like a ticking bomb. The Shepherds were in there, doing who-knew-what to Ezra. Probably torturing him. And if they didn't get what they wanted, a bullet to the brain.

She couldn't let that happen.

Dakota handed the binoculars to Logan. "There's a trapdoor hidden under the small palmetto, the one about fifteen feet or so from the west-facing cabin wall. It goes to a shallow tunnel I can crawl through to get inside the bathroom. There's another hatch beneath the tile and a bath rug."

Julio raised his brows.

"I told you he was prepared."

"Or paranoid," Park muttered.

"Doesn't seem so paranoid now though, does it?" Her nerves were strung taut. It was hard to breathe properly. "If I can sneak in and surprise them, I can take them out before they know what hit 'em."

"Maybe," Logan said. "Especially if we start firing once you get inside. It'll distract them, and you can shoot them all in the back like they deserve."

Dakota gave him a tight smile. "I like that plan."

"Can you provide covering fire?" Logan asked Julio.

Julio squared his shoulders. "I'm no marksman, but I've shot a gun before. I'll do my best."

"Good. I'll cover Dakota until she gets to the shed. Then I'll follow her. Once I'm at the shed, too, then I can cover her while she heads for the trapdoor. If anyone starts shooting at us from the cabin, aim and fire. Just make sure you don't shoot us in the back."

Park handed the Sig to Julio. "You'll be better at this than me."

She wished they had more than the two AR-15s. She wished they had grenades and night vision goggles. Hell, she wished they had a tank.

"Eden, you and Park stay back here."

Eden shook her head, starting to sign some furious rebuttal.

"I need to know you're safe, understand?" She pulled Eden into a quick, fierce hug and murmured into her hair: "Remember, I'll never leave you. Never, ever."

Eden's shoulders slumped, but she hugged Dakota back.

"We've got this," Julio said, gripping the Sig firmly. "Don't worry about us."

Logan turned to Dakota, his eyes white in the shadows. He scratched at his scruffy jawline, frowning. "Our clothes are dark, but you're too pale. We need camouflage."

Eden tugged on her arm.

"What?" Dakota asked.

But Eden was already reaching for Dakota's pack. She pulled out the water bottle, squatted, and pushed aside a thick sludge of decaying leaves, twigs, and damp soil. Using the water, she made a muddy paste to smear on their faces and hands.

Peat and calcitic mud—or marl—would've been better, but they needed to be closer to the marshes for that. Like Ezra always said, *Look around you. Use what you have.*

"Good idea, Eden," Julio said.

Eden grinned at him.

"At least we've got the darkness on our side," Julio said. "There's a light on inside the cabin. Our eyes are adjusted to the moonlight—theirs aren't."

Dakota swore softly. "Oh, hell."

"What?" Park asked.

"The security lights. They'll switch on with any movement within twenty yards. They're attached to the cabin and the shed."

Logan grunted. "We can shoot them out, but that would defeat the purpose of stealth."

"They're 360 degrees…" she bit her lip, grasping at dim memories she hadn't considered in years. "But there's a blind spot on the southwest corner."

"You sure?"

"Yes. The southwest corner. But once you step out of that blind spot, you'll be lit up like a Christmas tree."

"So we can reach the shed in the darkness, at least," Logan said. "Once the lights come on, I'll just have to keep them busy and distracted. Or maybe we'll get lucky and kill them all right then and there."

A noise came from the cabin—someone screaming in pain. *Ezra.*

Dakota stopped breathing. They had to move now.

3

LOGAN

Logan moved out from the treeline but south of the shed, shuffling half-bent and crouching, rifle banging against his shoulder. The only sounds were the trilling of crickets and his own panting breaths.

He was covering Dakota, a dark shape running ahead of him amidst a sea of dark shapes. There was just enough moonlight peeking through the clouds to see by.

Almost there.

Come on, come on.

She'd nearly made it to the shed when the night burst into bright white light.

Logan's heart plummeted. Ezra had fixed the blind spot. Damn him.

That fast, their entire plan went to hell.

Men poured out of the cabin, shouting in alarm. The cabin's motion sensor lights clicked on, bathing the yard around the cabin in more bright light. Three hostiles plunged off the porch, semiautomatic rifles swinging toward the light—and the shed.

Dakota was caught in the spotlight, still fifteen feet from cover.

Logan's adrenaline surged, his heart a wild thing in his chest. If he didn't do something immediately, she was dead.

Still in shadows, he dropped to one knee, aimed the rifle, and opened fire. They fired at Dakota, but their shots were wildly off-target. They'd been caught by surprise, still blinking against the harsh white lights and heavy black shadows as they scrambled back behind the safety of the cabin wall.

Dakota sprinted for the shed, bullets slamming into the ground a few feet behind her. She made it, pressing herself back against the western wall of the shed with a muffled curse.

She peeked out and exchanged fire with the three Shepherds crouched behind the front wall of the cabin. Dakota was trying to be careful not to fire a stray shot that might penetrate the cabin's western windows, but the Shepherds had no such qualms.

One of them nudged his entire head and shoulder out behind the wall, the Shepherd so intent on nailing Dakota he didn't take his own exposure into account. Or heck—maybe he saw his attacker was a girl, and got smug.

Either way, Logan was taking him out.

Just as he got the scumbag in his sights, the guy's head jerked back in a spray of red. He flopped to the porch, his neck bent at an unnatural angle.

Dakota got him.

The two remaining hostiles disappeared around the front corner of the cabin, out of sight. They peeked back around much more warily this time, only the muzzles of their guns showing. They'd learned their lesson.

Smiling grimly to himself, Logan took the opportunity to slink back deeper into the shadows. They still didn't know he was there. He needed to take advantage of that. Crouching, he scanned the yard.

The moon slipped behind a cloud. The motion sensor lights blared from the shed and cabin, but outside their bright halos, it was pitch black—to them, not to Logan.

Beyond the reach of the lights, he just glimpsed the hunched dark shapes of the Shepherds' two trucks parked in the drive.

The shed was set fifty yards southwest of the cabin. The two trucks angled along the dirt drive were just to the left of the front of the cabin, giving Logan line of sight to both Dakota and the Shepherds.

He could circle around the front of the cabin, stay low, reach the trucks. From there, he could more easily pick the guys off. It'd give him a clear shot, especially if their focus remained on Dakota.

It was a risk—they could have someone circling out there or lying in wait, but somehow, he doubted it. They seemed sloppy, reacting instead of proactively attacking or working as a coordinated unit.

It was a calculated risk, but one he was willing to take.

Dakota had warned him where the booby traps were located, but it hardly made him feel any better. One wrong move and he'd get taken out by the very guy he was trying to save. Best not to overthink it and just move.

He ducked into a crouch and scurried across the open yard, feeling exposed and vulnerable, his pulse a roar in his ears.

He skirted the cabin, giving the lights a wide berth.

The exchange of gunfire between Dakota and the two Shepherds made plenty of noise. No one heard him. No one saw him.

He didn't bother to try shooting while he ran. His aim would be poor at best. And every time he fired, he risked exposing his location with his own muzzle flare.

He wouldn't risk it unless it counted.

He reached the first truck—parked sideways with the passenger door flung open—and sank to his knees behind the protection of the engine block. His heart was pounding, his mouth dry, but his head was clear.

The rat-a-tat of gunfire stilled for a moment. Logan eased forward, staying low and protected, gravel digging into his knees, and peeked around the grille.

He had a good view of both men's backs. They were focused on Dakota; they had no idea he was there.

Slowly, carefully, he rose a bit higher, adjusted the rifle against his shoulder and braced it against the hood.

Abruptly, the hairs stood on the back of his neck. It was hard to hear anything with bullets flying, but he felt it. Someone out there, watching him.

He whirled around, peering into the night. He could barely make out a silhouette running across the grass toward him from forty yards away—large and thick. Not Dakota.

A muzzle flash sparked. The bullet struck the rear passenger side window of the truck, spidering the safety glass. Another round zipped overhead. Errant shots clunked and pinged against the truck.

He aimed and squeezed the trigger. It was too dark to tell whether he'd hit his mark.

He adjusted ever so slightly to the right and squeezed the trigger again.

There was a grunt in the darkness. The sound of something large falling into the underbrush.

He fired again, just a little lower.

A scream and a howl. No more muzzle flares.

He'd hit his target.

Two down. Likely, only two left.

He turned back to the cabin. Stilled himself, steadied his breathing. Mosquitoes buzzed in his ears. The drying mud smeared across his face itched.

He aimed, exhaled, and squeezed the trigger in two rapid-fire double taps. Moved slightly, did it again.

The first Shepherd crumpled. The second started to turn, reacting to his partner's sudden fall, but it was too late. Logan's rounds punctured his chest. The man dropped his weapon and slid down the wall, grasping wildly at his chest, mouth opened in a startled O.

A third shot drilled through his skull ended his suffering, not that

Logan really cared about that. He just wanted the scumbag dead. Now he was.

Everything went quiet.

The ringing in his ears gradually faded as the night sounds returned—an owl hooted from somewhere, the occasional splash out in the water, the buzz and trill of crickets, frogs, and cicadas.

"Logan?" Dakota's voice came out of the darkness, low and strained. "You good?"

He stood slowly, rifle still ready to fire, and eased his finger off the trigger. "We're good."

4
DAKOTA

"The bodies," Dakota said.

Logan nodded stiffly. He remained on high alert, scanning the woods and the clearing for another threat to come leaping out at them. But there was nothing.

Swiftly, Dakota checked each body to make sure they were actually dead. She examined their faces with a penlight, her anxiety growing with each one that wasn't him. She recognized a couple of them, but none of them were Maddox Cage.

He wasn't there.

Was he dead after all? Had he made it back to the compound, managed to tell his father about Ezra, only to die from the radiation?

No. She didn't believe it. Not Maddox. He was too tenacious to die so easily, as indestructible as a cockroach.

If he were dead, she would know it, would feel it somewhere deep in her bones, like a release, exhaling a breath held for years.

Something had prevented him from coming. She knew with absolute certainty that if he had the choice, he'd be here doing the dirty work himself. He was many things—but a coward wasn't one of them.

Maybe Logan was right. Maybe Maddox was sicker with radiation than she'd realized. Or maybe Solomon Cage had prevented him from coming for a reason she didn't yet understand.

She counted seven dead Shepherds: the three Ezra had managed to kill in the driveway and the four they'd just dispatched. They were definitely the Prophet's 'Chosen ones', but they were so damn young, their faces still pocked with pimples.

She bent next to the last Shepherd—a skinny black kid with a slack, blood-stained face and wide-open eyes staring at the sky. He couldn't have been a day over seventeen. The Prophet had sent his young, untested soldiers, figuring they could cut their teeth on an easy mission—capture and torture a harmless old man for information, then kill him.

The Prophet had underestimated them. The man's arrogance set her teeth on edge. Each of these kids believed their duty was of a divine calling—but to the Prophet, they were simply expendable.

Now, though, he would be angry. Maddox would come, and there would be hell to pay.

A groan came from inside the cabin.

Ezra.

5

DAKOTA

The cabin was exactly the same as she remembered it: drywall over concrete block walls, a scarred wood floor, small white-cabinet kitchen, the round homemade table, the brown leather couch and colorful knit rug, the black-and-white nature photographs lining the walls. The furnishings simple but clean, everything in its place; neat, precise, and dusted to within an inch of its life.

The only difference sat tied to a chair in the middle of the living room, bloodied and groaning.

"Is it clear?" she asked him, her rifle up and ready, her muscles taut, her gaze scanning for movement, for anything out of place. "Anyone else in here?"

Ezra struggled against the zip ties around his wrists and ankles, pinning his arms and legs to the chair. "There's no one else."

Though everything in her screamed to go straight to Ezra and release him, she needed to be sure. No surprises. Ezra himself had taught her that.

She stood to the side of the hall, rifle slung over her shoulder, pistol up and ready, and moved swiftly, sidestepping so the hallway came into view nice and slow.

She shuffled down one side of the hallway, kicking open the bathroom door—clear—moved to the first bedroom, the "ham shack" she and Eden used to sleep in, and pushed the door in.

She swept it, checking the closet, behind the stuffed chair, and under the desk—clear. She moved to the door at the end of the hallway—the master bedroom. Clear.

Satisfied that the cabin was empty, she holstered her pistol, wiped at her still-muddy face with the back of her arm, and hurried to Ezra.

His grizzled face was bloodied from several deep cuts on his cheeks and forehead. Ugly purple bruises swelled his right jaw and left eye, so puffy it was nearly sealed shut. His top lip was split open. His gray T-shirt, worn jeans, and boots were spattered with red stains.

Dakota's heart ached to see him like that—hurting and vulnerable and weak. Her whole body thrummed with rage. She wanted to revive the Shepherds and kill them all over again, this time much more slowly—and painfully.

She pulled out her knife and sawed frantically at the zip ties. The Shepherds had cinched them so tightly that Ezra's wrists were raw and bleeding. His left hand was swollen, the fingernails of three of his fingers had been ripped off. One of his fingers was already turning black and bent at a horrible, unnatural angle. So was his left pinkie.

A hammer lay on the floor a yard from her feet.

They'd smashed his fingers.

He stared up at her with his one good eye. "Dakota," he said hoarsely.

"I'm here, I'm right here," she said, aghast, swallowing back the acid rising up her throat. "You're safe."

They'd tortured him. They'd tortured an innocent old man because of her, because he'd sheltered her, because she was still alive and they wanted to unleash their outrage on someone, anyone.

But then, they hated anything they couldn't control or understand. She knew that all too well.

Her own burn scars itched and prickled. They'd tortured her, too.

She cut the last zip tie and held out her hand to help him to his feet. He brushed her hand away and rose unsteadily to his feet. He spat a glob of blood on the floor. "What the hell are you doing here?"

"I'm so sorry. They came because of me. This is my fault. We tried to get here in time, but—"

"We?" His sharp blue eye narrowed. "What do you mean?"

The door opened, and Logan stepped inside. Julio and Park crowded behind him, weapons lowered but drawn. They'd wiped the mud off their hands and faces, but there were still smears and smudges. They all looked fierce and dangerous, especially Logan.

Ezra's swollen, distorted face contorted in disbelief—and anger. "You brought outsiders here? To this place?"

The *how could you?* was unspoken, but she still felt it like a slap across the face.

"I can explain—"

"Don't bother." He hobbled to the kitchen, his broken hand cradled against his chest, and grabbed a clean towel with his unhurt left hand.

He wiped the blood from his face and split lip, tossed the stained towel in the sink, and turned on the faucet, his back to Dakota. "Seems to me you made your choice not to be here two years ago. Don't see how that's changed."

"I'm sorry, Ezra," she choked out, "but we needed somewhere safe to go. And then when I heard the Shepherds were coming here—"

"You don't belong here."

"She saved your life," Logan cut in.

With a grunt, Ezra placed his injured hand beneath the running water. His broad shoulders stiffened. Dakota could only imagine the pain he must be feeling.

"I didn't need saving," he muttered, "nor do I recall askin' for it."

Logan snorted. "It sure looked like you did from here."

Ezra spun, water droplets flying, and glared at him. "I didn't give you permission to speak in my house. Get out."

Logan glanced from Ezra to Dakota, confusion on his face. She understood why. She'd promised him a joyful reception, not an old man spewing bitterness and resentment.

She'd known this was a possibility, feared that Ezra would turn her away and send them all packing. She wasn't stupid. She knew Ezra's stubbornness better than anyone.

Besides, he was right. He had every right to be furious. She'd left first. She'd taken Eden and fled without a backward glance. She'd never written him or tried to contact him. To him, she and Eden had disappeared without a trace.

"We're very sorry to have intruded," Julio said quickly, acting as the peacemaker, like always. "We don't wish to be a burden on you."

"Well, you already are."

"Let me get the first aid kit," Dakota said, practically begging him. "You're hurt. Let me help you take care of your hand, at least."

"I don't need your help," Ezra growled.

"They broke two of your fingers!" And they would've kept going until they'd completely broken him—fingers, hands, arms, legs—and his spirit.

Only after hours of torture would they have finally put a bullet in his brain. Or maybe they would've left him there to bleed out on his own living room floor.

Ezra gave a brusque shrug. "Not my trigger finger. That's all that matters."

"Do you want me to—"

"I want you to go."

She felt like crying, like curling into an exhausted ball and weeping until there was nothing left inside her—no more pain and grief and regret, just nothing.

After all the suffering and sacrifice to get here, to get home, and she wasn't welcome. She was homeless. Without Ezra, without this place as her anchor, she was an orphan again: parentless, unmoored in a chaotic world where danger and death lay in wait around every corner.

"Ezra..." She didn't know what to say. She had nothing to say in her own defense.

"Just go!"

A shuffling noise came from behind her as someone else entered the cabin.

Ezra's eyes widened as he looked over her shoulder. "Eden."

Dakota half-turned to take in her little sister. Her golden curls were tangled around her shoulders, her clothes dirty, her face still smudged with mud she hadn't fully wiped off, a couple of scratches from thorns marring her arms.

But none of that mattered. She was as beautiful as always, with a round, full face featuring a snub nose, rose-bud lips, and big blue eyes.

She smiled shyly, held up her new notebook, and showed Ezra one of her drawings—a vivid sketch of a heron caught in midflight over a sea of sawgrass, the sun setting behind it. Ezra had always loved her drawings; he'd told Dakota once how they'd reminded him of his late wife's wildlife photographs that adorned every wall of his home.

His stony expression shifted, an almost imperceptible softening. She knew that look, knew him. He might be ornery and bitter enough to kick out Dakota and her friends, but he'd never force Eden to leave.

"We don't have anywhere else to go." She hated herself for begging, for showing weakness when they both despised it, but she didn't have any other choice. The world was falling down around them—this was the only sanctuary she knew.

"Why don't you two talk privately for a bit," Julio said briskly. "You have a lot of catching up to do. We'll just be waiting outside."

Logan threw her a sharp glance, clearly hesitant to leave her here by herself, but she shook her head. Julio had good instincts. Her best chance at reaching Ezra was with him alone. He'd never let his guard down with strangers invading his house.

Logan set his jaw, but he turned and followed Julio, Eden, and

Park out of the cabin. "Stay on the driveway," she called after them. "Don't wander around."

The door shut behind them with an awful finality. A lone fan spun from the ceiling. An electric fan whirred and rattled in the corner. There was no A/C, but the thick concrete block construction kept the heat from being oppressive.

The room still felt oppressive. She waited, her nerves on edge.

Haltingly, Ezra opened the fridge, dumped ice into a plastic bag, and wrapped it with a strip of cheesecloth. She longed to jump in and help him, but he wouldn't accept it. It'd only make him more irritated.

He held the ice gingerly against his broken fingers and turned to face her. "You have ten minutes. Talk."

6
DAKOTA

"We just saved your life," Dakota said again. She stood in the center of the cabin, hands balled into fists on her hips, staring down Ezra with as much fire and grit as he threw back at her. She could be just as stubborn as he was.

"I'm plenty capable of taking care of myself," he growled.

"You were tied up! They were torturing you. They would have killed you."

Ezra grimaced. "I had it handled. They...took me by surprise, is all."

Two years ago, no one would've taken Ezra Burrows by surprise.

In her memories, Ezra was a grizzled mountain of a man, unhampered by age. Here in front of her, he seemed fragile—and old. He was still broad-shouldered, but those shoulders were stooped, his wizened leathery face lined with a network of wrinkles, more white than gray in his bristly beard.

He must be well north of seventy, maybe closer to eighty. She didn't really know. Was it just time that had stripped him of his vitality, or something else?

You broke something irreparable when you left him, a voice whispered in the back of her mind.

Guilt pricked her. She shoved it away.

"It doesn't matter now," she said. "You're alive. But Ezra, they're going to come back. You know they are. We just killed seven Shepherds. The Prophet won't let that go. You can't protect this place against a dozen armed fighters. Let us help you."

He snorted as he sank into one of the hard wooden chairs at the kitchen table. "Don't think I don't see what you're doing. Trying to turn this around like you're doin' me a favor when it's you should be begging on your knees for scraps."

She couldn't sit down at the table next to him. She was too nervous. She unballed her fists and held out her hands, beseeching. "You want me to beg? I'll do it. For Eden, I will."

His gaze dropped at the mention of Eden.

"You're right. We came here looking for help. Miami is chaos. And it's spreading. Nowhere is safe. Nowhere but here."

"What makes you think this is your home anymore?"

She winced. "I deserve that. I deserve all the anger and resentment you want to throw at me, old man. But Eden doesn't. Those people out there don't. I know you don't know them, but they're good people. Logan saved my life, and I've saved his. Julio rescued Eden and saved all our asses. Park's willing to pitch in wherever he can."

"You wanted to leave, girl, you could've said so at any time. I wasn't keepin' you here against your will."

Dakota sucked in her breath. Here it was. "You're angry because we ran."

He just stared at her, eyes steely. No matter how his body had changed, his gaze was as intelligent as ever, still as sharp and penetrating.

"We didn't want to leave," she said, shifting uncomfortably. "We had no choice. That day we went shopping for clothes for Eden...you were getting supplies from the tractor and feed store. We came out of the store and he was right there in the street, Ezra. Maddox Cage. He was about to go into some bank, but for some reason, he turned and stared straight at me.

"I—I was terrified. I knew what they would do if they got Eden back, what they would do to me—" she shivered involuntarily, the scars riddling her back burning. "If they saw you, they would know. They would come after you, too.

"I didn't know what else to do. I grabbed Eden's hand and we ran. We just ran and ran. For hours, maybe. I don't know. We hitched a ride to Miami with a trucker who didn't look like a perv. I still had the knife you gave me. I knew I could defend us.

"Once we got to Miami, everything was different. There were so many people. Everything was so loud and crazy after so long in the Glades; it was overwhelming. I didn't know how to get us food or a safe place to stay.

"I found us one of those teen emergency shelter places, but they were overfilled so often that we had to sleep on the streets sometimes. Eden would sleep and I would stay up all night, holding my knife so hard my hand would ache in the morning, my eyes so gritty and tired. But I couldn't let my guard down for a second."

She took a breath, stared hard at the nicks in the old table so she wouldn't have to meet the judgment in those eyes. "I wanted to contact you so many times. I—I was ashamed. Because we just took off without saying goodbye after everything you'd done for us...I hated Miami and hated that we were scared and homeless, and I didn't want you to see us—me—like that. And because I knew we couldn't go back to you, no matter how much I wanted to."

She waved her hand without looking at him. "Because of this. They would find out you'd harbored us eventually. Then they'd kill you. I was selfish for letting us stay as long as we did. I put you in danger."

There was a long silence. The clock on the wall tick, tick, ticked.

She could hear the hum of the cicadas outside, the night sounds of the creatures and insects that called the Glades home.

"You should have told me," he said finally.

"I know."

He sighed, let out a curse, and banged the table with his good fist. "I don't have room for five additional people."

"Eden and I can sleep in the ham shack room like we used to. The others can sleep on the couch and the floor—"

"They're not sleeping in this house."

"Yes, they are. They can sleep on the couch and roll out a few sleeping bags. They won't get in the way."

He rubbed his grizzled chin and sighed. "*One* night. That's all."

Something released inside her. She felt her chest expand. She took her first full breath in what felt like weeks.

He hadn't forgiven her, she was sure of that. But he was letting them stay the night. It was a start. She could wear him down from there.

"I'll take care of the extra blankets and the sleeping bags," she said.

"No, I will."

She rolled her eyes. "With that hand? Let me get the first aid kit. We need to splint it."

He stared at her. "You remember what to do?"

"You taught me, didn't you?"

He didn't smile, but at least he wasn't scowling.

"You really need a hospital, but that's out of the question right now."

"I heard as much over the ham. Things as bad as they're sayin'?"

"Worse. Entire cities are burning. Everything is falling apart. Miami was...hell. There's no other way to describe it."

He nodded to himself, like he'd been expecting the end of the world all along. Of course, he had. That was who he was.

"I'll fix up your face and your hand. And get you some antibiotics. You still have that fish amoxicillin, right? Then we'll figure out what we need to do about the Shepherds. Be as furious at me as you want, but they're a threat we can't ignore. They want Eden. They want to kill the both of us, too."

Ezra removed the icepack and glanced down at his ruined fingers with furrowed brows. He gave a heavy, resigned sigh. "I reckon so. Solomon isn't a man who accepts defeat."

A shiver of dread ran up her spine. "Neither is his son."

7

LOGAN

"What do you think's going on in there?" Park asked.

"Who knows?" Logan kicked a stray chunk of rock on the gravel road and rubbed the back of his neck. The sling of the AR-15 dug into his shoulder.

A dull ache radiated from his skull down his spine: whiplash from the insane car chase earlier that night. His muscles were weak and trembling. His entire body was one big bruise. He was drained and exhausted, and the night wasn't over yet.

The radiation sickness symptoms had mostly receded, but they'd return with a vengeance in a few weeks. It was a strange and disconcerting thing, to know you were sick but couldn't feel it. Like a cancer, a rot just beneath the surface of things.

As they walked, Eden and Julio shone their penlights a few feet ahead of the group. After several minutes of waiting for Ezra and Dakota to determine their fate, they'd all decided to walk the two miles or so back to the truck hidden in the underbrush.

This time, they could simply use the road instead of taking the long way through the dense woods.

They'd just saved the crazy coot, and he wasn't just ungrateful—he radiated rancor and indignation, like *they* were the intruders.

Logan already disliked him intensely.

Dakota had sold him on the cabin safehouse, hook, line, and sinker. He hadn't stopped to think whether the old hermit would accept them. Dakota was convincing, if nothing else.

He wanted to be angry at her, but he couldn't. Either one of them could've died tonight. He was just grateful they were both still alive.

Somehow in their struggle to survive, stumbling from one near-death disaster to the next, he had connected to this tough, smart-mouthed girl. It was a thin and tremulous thing, something that might break if he looked at it straight on.

So he did what he did best: he ignored it completely.

"Dakota will get it sorted out," Julio said.

Logan only grunted. From his end, things didn't look too great. "We can always sleep in the back of the truck, I guess."

Park slapped at several mosquitos buzzing around his face. "And get eaten alive by bugs? No thanks."

"How are you doing?" Julio asked Eden. "Are you holding up okay?"

She gave a small shrug of her shoulders but kept her head down and focused on the road in front of her. She looked so small and young and vulnerable. Her eyes were wide and scared, like a rabbit's. Like prey.

Some people were always the victims. Good and kind but too trusting, too easily manipulated, too weak to do the hard stuff.

She was lucky as hell she had Dakota.

"It's almost over," Julio promised the girl. He gave her a comforting pat on the arm. "You'll be sleeping in a cozy bed tonight."

Logan had his doubts, but he kept them to himself.

Though it was the middle of the night, the temperature had to be over ninety degrees, the muggy air like a furnace. Logan wiped sweat from his forehead and swatted away a swarm of bugs.

He hated the swamp.

Trees towered on both sides of the road, steeped in shadows. He hated not being able to see clearly, hated all the darkness. The strange, eerie forest sounds had him twitchy and on edge.

Every rustle, every scrape and scratch and breaking twig had his heart jolting, his hand reaching for his rifle. He felt the comforting press of the Glock's concealed holster at his back. At least he was armed.

"You ever been out here?" Park asked him.

Logan was a city boy, through and through. First in Richmond, Virginia where he'd grown up, then Miami after his stint in prison. The Everglades was a protected national treasure, but to him, it was a waste of space—just an endless boggy marsh to get lost in, a glorified swamp bursting with venomous snakes, giant toothy lizards, and other creatures who wanted to eat you.

Logan shook his head. "What for?"

Park snorted. "I prefer the beaches, myself."

Something crunched in the woods. A dozen yards to the right, leaves rustled and shifted.

Logan whirled around, heart thumping double time, and peered into the darkness. "What was that?"

His eyes couldn't make out anything more than dim, indistinct shapes, a few trembling leaves. The shadows were deep and thick, his brain automatically imagining the lurking forms of predators and enemies.

"Just an animal," Park said, but there was a nervous tremble in his voice.

"Racoons, probably," Julio said.

Logan kept his eyes on the spaces between the trees. "It was something big."

"A boar, maybe? I think there's some in the wild out here."

Logan unslung the rifle, snicked off the safety, and gripped it in

Into the Fire

both hands. No way was he getting taken out by something as lame as an oversized pig.

Not after surviving a nuclear bomb.

"Walk faster," he said brusquely.

Park chuckled. "I guess it's nice to know you're capable of fear, just like the rest of us."

"I'm not afraid," he insisted.

"Uh huh. Sure thing, buddy."

"Don't call me buddy."

Eden tugged on Julio's arm. She pointed the penlight ahead at an indistinct shape looming out of the darkness along the road forty feet in front of them.

"Is that a car?" Julio shone the pen flashlight ahead as a black Mitsubishi parked along the curb slowly materialized.

"They were probably fleeing the city and turned up this road for help, is my guess," Park said. "Maybe they ran out of gas, like all the other cars we passed."

Eden shook her head and pulled harder on Julio's arm. She huffed loudly to get their attention and jabbed the air with the penlight.

Logan paused and glanced at her. "What is it?"

She gestured emphatically at the car again.

"Wait—" Julio said, "is that someone in the driver's seat?"

Park took a faltering step backward, nearly bumping into Julio. "What if it's another Shepherd? A lookout or something?"

Logan tensed. "Everyone, stay here. I'll find out."

8

LOGAN

With his rifle at the ready, Logan inched around the rear of the car, past the rear door to the driver's side door. "Don't move!"

The figure didn't move.

Logan waited, his mouth dry, pulse thudding in his throat.

Still, the figure didn't move. Logan caught a whiff of something rancid. He made out the shadowy form of slumped shoulders, a head leaning back against the seat.

Logan didn't lower the gun, just in case. "Julio, bring up the light. Everyone else, stay back."

With the penlight, they saw what Logan had suspected. The figure didn't move because he was already dead. The harsh white light revealed a garish face pocked with huge blisters, the flesh burnt, boiled, and melted—as if acid had eaten away at him from the inside out.

Not acid. Radiation.

"He made it out of the city, but it didn't matter," Julio said quietly, his hand over his mouth and nose to mask the pungent stench.

Logan closed his eyes briefly. The horrors radiation had wrought upon the man's body were too terrible to look at.

He and Julio made their way back to the group and explained what they'd found.

Julio pursed his lips. "I hate the thought of just leaving him to rot like that. Whoever he was, he was someone's son, someone's husband, someone's father."

"There's nothing we can do about it tonight. Come on." Logan turned to Eden. "Good eyes, kiddo."

Her face was in shadows, but she lifted her head toward him, like maybe she was beaming with pride. Good. She needed to be skilled at something, to feel like she was contributing.

They kept walking. Where was that damn truck? Walking two miles in the dead of night in the middle of nowhere while getting eaten alive by bugs was no one's idea of fun.

About twenty minutes and fifty mosquito bites later, Eden stopped and pointed again, this time into the woods.

"What is it?" Julio asked.

She signed something. Everyone stared at her blankly.

She stepped to the edge of the gravel and aimed the light at the ground. Logan made out the faint mark of tire treads veering off the road before disappearing into the underbrush.

They'd reached the F150's hiding spot.

"Good job, Eden," Julio said. "I would've walked right past it."

Logan, too.

Another sound splintered the night air, this time from behind them. Twigs cracked. Leaves shook.

Logan whirled again, searching the woods across the road. The hairs on his arms and the back of his neck stood on end. "Turn off the lights."

"It's nothing—" Park started to say.

"It's not nothing," Logan said in a low voice. "Not this time."

His body thrummed with adrenaline. He had that feeling again—

like someone, or something, was watching them.

Maybe an animal predator. Or maybe something else.

Either way, he was on high alert.

Eden watched him with wide eyes. Julio put a comforting arm around her shoulder. "What do you want us to do, Logan?"

"Move fast but quietly. Get in the truck. I'll cover you. Whatever it is, I doubt it's friendly."

They hurried into the forest, making far more of a racket than they should've. Logan took up the rear, facing the road and straining over their shuffling movements for any sounds that didn't belong.

The moon broke free of the clouds, illuminating the darkness in shades of silver.

Something crashed through the underbrush across the road. The dark shapes of small trees shuddered as twigs and branches cracked under foot.

Logan raised his weapon, shifting back and forth, wildly scanning the trees. He had no clue where to aim.

A large deer ploughed through the trees and darted out into the road. It turned and dashed into the forest not twenty feet from them, white tail high in the air as it plunged through the underbrush and swiftly disappeared.

The sounds of its flight faded into stillness.

Logan sucked in several deep breaths, willing his heartrate to return to normal.

"Told you it was nothing," Park said, his voice squeaking. "Just nature. Totally harmless."

With his free hand, Logan swiped at a mosquito attached to his forearm and killed it with a satisfying *splat*. He wiped the smear of blood on his pants. "Nature is *not* harmless."

A twig cracked. Then another.

Logan turned toward the sound.

Park sighed. "Just another deer—"

A loud, booming voice shattered the muggy air. "Stop right there!"

9

LOGAN

"Don't you move a muscle!"

Logan froze, AR-15 half-raised.

Not fifteen feet away, a Caucasian man strode out from the trees across the road. His features were shadowed in the moonlight, but Logan clearly made out the shape of him—he was huge, with shoulders broad as a doorway, a barrel chest, and arms bulging with muscles the size of footballs.

He gripped a hunting rifle in his massive hands, the muzzle pointed at Logan's chest.

"Holy hell," Park whispered beside Logan.

The man gestured with his rifle. "Put down your weapons and come out onto the road before I shoot you dead."

Logan cursed. But he didn't drop the gun.

He should just shoot first. It didn't matter if the other guy was the one doing the threatening; whoever shot first always won. Almost always.

He could drill this thug right through the center of his giant forehead with a .556 round before he could blink...

A second, shorter man stepped out from behind the giant. He

looked like the first guy, but he was slimmer and shorter, dressed in a green camo shirt, dark cargo pants, and a leather vest marked with an insignia unreadable in the dark. His long brown hair was pulled into a ponytail at the base of his neck.

He aimed his shotgun at Julio's head.

If Logan was by himself, he'd risk it. Maybe he could make two headshots before either of them could react quickly enough to pull their own triggers.

But he wasn't alone. He had the others to think of, to keep alive.

Helpless anger flashed through him. He'd *known* they were being watched. And now he couldn't do a damn thing about it.

"Move. My brother's not gonna ask twice," the pony-tailed man said.

Logan cursed again, this time silently. Resentment mingled with the adrenaline surging through his veins, but he obeyed.

So did the others. Logan, Park, Julio, and Eden lined up along the edge of the road. They lowered their weapons and raised their hands. Logan didn't remove the Glock, still in its concealed holster at his back.

It was a risk, but one worth taking.

"Kneel down," the giant instructed.

They knelt. Gravel dug painfully into Logan's kneecaps. He inhaled the scent of wet leaves, damp soil, and the sharp tang of his own nervous sweat.

He glared up at his captors, seething.

The two men stood less than ten feet away. It'd be hard for them to miss if they decided to take a shot. At least they didn't bother to frisk their new hostages. Amateurs.

When the opportunity arose, Logan would be ready.

"We don't have anything of value." Julio shifted his body so he partially shielded Eden. "We don't want any trouble."

The huge guy flashed white teeth beneath a thick, bristling beard that reached his chest. "Yet here you are, skulking around like thieves."

Into the Fire

"I assure you, we're not thieves," Julio said calmly.

He was the natural negotiator, so Logan let him do the talking. If Logan said anything, it'd be hurled curses and insults through gritted teeth.

Or maybe he'd just take his chances and lunge at them both, take them by surprise, tackle the smaller one and wrestle that shotgun away...

Ponytail cradled the shotgun in the crook of his forearm and lifted a walkie-talkie to his mouth. "We've got them. Come on in."

The distant rumble of engines filled the air.

Logan felt Julio twisting to look down the road, but Logan kept his gaze lasered on the giant. The giant stared back at him, grinning, like he could read every thought in Logan's head and was relishing the opportunity to blow his head off if he made a wrong move.

Three motorcycles roared toward them. They came to a sharp stop twenty yards away. Three men jumped off and strode up behind Giant and Ponytail.

They were a rough bunch, all in their thirties or forties, worn lines creasing their hard, bearded faces, their expressions grim. They wore leather vests with baseball caps or red handkerchiefs on their heads, rifles slung over their shoulders.

A biker gang, come to rob them or worse. They were probably riding the Tamiami Trail back and forth, waylaying unsuspecting refugees just trying to escape the chaos of radioactive Miami.

"Don't do anything rash," Julio said under his breath. "We can talk this out."

Logan rolled his eyes. "You're thinking of Dakota, not me," he muttered. "I'm never rash."

"Uh huh."

"What's going on, Archer?" asked a broad, heavy-set man with a goatee, thick scowling features, and sly eyes. Aggression poured off him in waves. Logan knew his kind—dangerous and shifty, the type of man who'd slit your throat for the hell of it.

"More thugs," the giant—Archer—said to the others, eyeing Logan's tattoos.

He had no room to judge; his group had plenty of their own ink. If anything, they looked more vicious than Logan's group did. Julio could hold his own, but Park looked about as threatening as a toy poodle.

"You're the thugs," Logan said. "You're the ones holding guns to our heads."

"We're just passing through," Julio said over him. "We're fleeing the radiation and trying to reach Naples. We'll give you whatever you want that we have, though it isn't much. You can let us go."

Julio didn't mention Ezra Burrows' cabin, which was the smart play. These biker gangster wannabes didn't need to know anything about the stash the old geezer had hoarded away.

"Everyone's got a sob story these days," Ponytail said. "Ain't none of our concern."

"They got a kid with them," Archer said.

"So?" Sly Eyes said. "Doesn't make them any less of a threat. The last ones did, too."

The last two men stood a few feet back, both carrying shotguns with handguns holstered at their waists. Logan realized with a start that they were twins—the same burly build and square squat features, wild reddish beards, and forearms so hairy they looked furry.

The first one spat on the asphalt. The second tapped his shotgun with his fingers. "You're trying to tell us you're walking to Naples?"

"It's less than a hundred miles," Park said.

"Nice try," Ponytail snapped. "We've seen your type at least a dozen times already. Thieves and hoodlums taking advantage of the chaos to rob and steal the house right out from beneath a man. That's not happening here, you get me?"

"We wouldn't do that," Julio said.

Sly Eyes gave a dismissive snort. "You, what, got your car stashed around here somewhere, ready to load up on someone else's goodies?"

"No, we don't," Logan interjected before Julio's conscience started bothering him and he confessed the truth. "We don't have a stashed car or anything else."

He'd gotten them wrong, he realized. They weren't the ones preying on others—they were some sort of local patrol, protecting the area from criminals on the prowl.

Not that this made their group any safer, not when they thought Logan and the others were the bad guys. These bikers didn't look like the type to balk at violence, especially when it came to protecting their own.

"We're not who you think—" Park started.

"Got it!" shouted a female voice from a few dozen yards behind them. "A gray shot-to-hell Ford F-150."

Logan's heart sank. *Damn it all to hell.*

10

LOGAN

"Well, well, well." Sly Eyes gave them a nasty, triumphant grin. "Thieves *and* liars. Probably murderers, too."

Logan's mind raced, desperate to find a way out of this mess. If they backtracked and tried to tell the truth, it wouldn't go over well.

A woman sauntered out of the woods where they'd stashed the truck. She seemed to glide more than walk across the road. Though she moved with a fluid grace of someone much younger, the fine lines in the bronze skin around her eyes and mouth suggested she was in her early fifties.

She wore a revolver at her hip along with camo hiking pants, sturdy boots, and a loose, long-sleeved black T-shirt. Her long, raven-black hair was pulled into a ponytail.

Logan couldn't remember what Indian tribes Dakota had said lived in the Everglades, but this woman was definitely Native American.

She looked them over, one hand on her hip, her face expressionless.

"Thanks, Maki," Ponytail said. "Good work. You caught them red-handed."

She gave a silent nod but didn't speak. She was the one he'd heard in the woods, Logan realized with a start. She'd been following them, stalking them.

"We're sorry," Julio said quickly, his words running together. "We lied. We thought you guys were the robbers. We hid the truck. We're staying with a friend here to ride out the storm. That's all."

Archer raised his thick brows. "Oh yeah? Who's the friend?"

Julio glanced at Logan for permission.

Logan shrugged. What difference did it make? Things couldn't get much worse.

"Ezra Burrows."

Archer snorted. Ponytail let out a sharp bark of laughter. The other men chuckled in derision.

"Ezra Burrows, a friend?" Archer bellowed. "That ornery old coot never had a friend in his life. Now we really know you're full of crap."

"Why are we wasting time?" Sly Eyes swung his shotgun between Julio and Logan. "Just shoot them."

The sound of a small vehicle came roaring toward them. Several of the bikers looked up, including Archer and Sly Eyes.

Logan studied them, searching for a weakness, a break. Giant was a beast—a full head and shoulders taller than Logan, who was six feet—and too big to take down quickly. Ponytail was the closest to Logan, but his shotgun was still aimed at Julio. The twins and Sly Eyes were too far away to rush.

A four-wheeler exited a dirt driveway thirty feet to the left. The drive was so overgrown with weeds and crowded with underbrush that Logan hadn't noticed it until then.

The driver parked a few yards away and hopped off, leaving the engine running. The headlight beam lit up an older woman with dusky bronze skin and coal-black eyes, dressed in a flowered nightgown, her long gray hair draped around her shoulders.

She strode toward them, a crossbow in her hands. "What the hell are you doing? I could hear the racket all the way back at my place."

"We're taking care of it, Haasi," Ponytail said, turning slightly toward the woman as she spoke. The muzzle of his gun turned with him.

"Clearly, not well enough, *Jake Collier*," she snapped back, saying the guy's name like an insult.

Logan didn't wait for the neighbors to hash it out. This was his chance, maybe the only one he was going to get. He moved.

He leapt to his feet and lunged for the ponytailed guy, the one the woman had called Jake. Logan didn't care what his name was. He was a threat, and Logan needed to take him out.

He knocked the shotgun from the startled man's hands with his left arm as he reached behind his back with his right hand and seized the Glock. He fumbled with his shirt for a moment, the pistol snagging on the fabric as he yanked it free, but he still had the element of surprise on his side.

The bikers' brains were still registering the fact that their quarry was no longer kneeling by the time Logan had spun Jake around, wrapped his arm around the biker's throat, and pressed the Glock against his temple.

Five men and two women aimed their collective firepower in Logan's direction.

"Let him go!" Archer shouted.

"Let them go first," Logan said. "Then I'll think about whether he deserves to live or not."

"No one needs to die tonight," Julio said, pleading. "We're not enemies. There's no reason for any of this."

"You just made a reason," the old woman they'd called Haasi said angrily, her gaze trained on Logan.

Eden, who'd been huddled beside Julio, climbed to her feet. She was shaking, but her chin was lifted, her eyes gazing straight ahead.

"Eden!" Julio grabbed at her arm but she was already taking a step forward, then another.

Haasi caught the movement and swung the crossbow toward Eden.

"No!" Julio cried. "Don't hurt her!"

Park just stared, wide-eyed, too shocked to speak.

Logan's mouth went dry. He was too far away to stop whatever was about to happen. If he moved away from Ponytail, he was dead. They would all be dead. His gun against Ponytail's skull was their only leverage.

He watched helplessly as the girl walked directly into the line of fire.

11

LOGAN

Eden stood there, arms at her sides, chin raised, just a kid in the middle of a group of armed hostiles.

Haasi's gaze narrowed. The crossbow trembled ever so slightly in her hands. Logan half-expected her to pull the trigger and shoot Eden, but she didn't.

"Eden's just a child," Julio said. "Don't hurt her."

"Eden?" Haasi asked suspiciously. "Dakota's sister?"

Eden nodded.

"You know her?" Archer asked.

Haasi gave the slightest nod, a stunned look on her lined face. "The kid who lived with Ezra Burrows for a while. The one that couldn't talk. She's grown but...I know it's her. She's got the same scar."

"We were telling the truth," Julio said. "We're here to see Ezra Burrows. We're not thieves or looters. We pose no danger to you or yours. Please, if we could all put our weapons down and discuss things like civilized human beings."

"Them first," Logan growled. He wasn't putting down a thing.

Haasi didn't lower the bow. She turned it on Logan instead.

Much of his body was hidden behind Ponytail, but Logan was bigger, broader, and taller. Plus, the old woman stood at an angle from the other bikers, which gave her a far better shot.

If she wanted to hit a vulnerable part of him, she could.

"Why'd you hide the truck, then?" Sly Eyes asked suspiciously.

"Because..." Julio glanced at Logan. "Because of the Shepherds. We didn't want to be seen."

Archer frowned. "Shepherds? You mean the Shepherds of Mercy? Those religious freaks at that compound? They got no business being around here."

"They were here tonight. They attacked Ezra Burrows's place."

"Damn it!" Sly Eyes cursed. "We've been patrolling since the sun went down, but we could've missed them while we were down by Monument Lake Campground. We had a bit of an altercation with a couple of aggressive dentists who thought the Kantor place would make a good bugout location—problem was, it wasn't theirs."

"You did miss them," Logan said. "They nearly tortured the old man to death before we stopped them."

Archer cursed under his breath.

"What the hell for?" one of the hairy twins asked.

Jake tried to shift, and Logan jammed the muzzle harder against his temple. He wasn't letting his guard down for anything. He could smell the man's aftershave, his sour sweat, the scent of his fear.

"Don't test me," he said in his ear.

The biker stilled.

"Let our brother go," Archer said, his hands raised like he was attempting to calm a wild horse. "Let's take this back a few notches, how about that?"

"Great idea," Julio said. "Put your weapons away and we can talk. Please."

Logan didn't move. He sure as hell wasn't going first.

The bikers looked at Archer, who looked to Haasi. Though she was half their size, they all seemed to respect her. The old woman nodded her head.

The bikers reluctantly lowered their guns. The other woman, Maki, didn't move her hand from her revolver, but it was holstered. Logan had the feeling she could draw her weapon just as fast as he could, if not faster.

Haasi met Logan's gaze with a piercing gaze of her own, her crossbow still aimed straight and steady at Logan's head. "How about it, cowboy? On the count of three?"

Logan clenched his jaw. He didn't trust these people as far as he could throw them. He'd rather shoot them and know his people were safe for certain than take the risk of trusting strangers with loaded guns.

"Logan," Julio said quietly. "It's going to be okay. You can stand down."

Eden was standing in his periphery vision. She looked tense and nervous but not terrified, not like before. "You and Dakota know these people?" he asked her. "They're good?"

Eden signed something. She nodded.

"I'm counting," Haasi said. "One, two, three."

On three, she lowered the crossbow as promised.

If Eden trusted them, that was something, at least. More bloodshed was the last thing he wanted. Logan released his hostage's neck, pulled back the Glock, and shoved him.

Jake stumbled but quickly regained his feet. He whirled, his eyes flashing dangerously. Without a word, he raised his fist and swung at Logan's face.

12

LOGAN

It was a messy punch, swooping high and wide. Logan saw it coming a mile away. He was willing to make a few concessions to make peace with these people, but taking a punch wasn't one of them.

He sidestepped with ease, seized the guy's thick wrist, twisted hard, and put him down on his knees. He bent the guy's arm behind his back into an unnatural, intensely painful position.

Jake let out a tortured squeal. Maybe he was used to throwing his weight around and getting his way through intimidation, but he clearly wasn't accustomed to a brawl with someone who knew how to fight.

The five bikers growled in surprised outrage. They raised their weapons.

"No!" Haasi commanded.

The men hesitated.

"Jake lost his temper," she said. "That's on him. I'm sure if this gentleman were to release him, his brothers would keep him under control."

"We would." Archer's glare shifted from Logan to his brother, still cowering on his knees.

"Okay, then." The old woman sighed and turned to Logan. "I'm going to ask you to give Jake a pass on this one. The five Collier brothers you see here used to be six. A week ago, a group of hungry, half-dead refugees out of Miami stumbled upon this road and found the Collier place.

"They attempted to break in. They were armed. So are the Colliers, as you can see. In the shootout that followed, the thieves were all killed. But they managed to kill Ford, a scruffy pain in the ass we're all going to miss mightily."

"I'm sorry for your loss." Julio climbed to his feet and dusted gravel off his knees. He helped Park up, too.

"So are we." Archer's eyes were red-rimmed and puffy. His voice was hoarse.

All the men were haggard, like they hadn't slept in a few days. Grief did that to a man.

"Misunderstandings happen," Julio said affably. "I'm glad we figured out we were on the same side before any blood was spilled."

Logan felt anything but affable, but Julio shot him a warning look. With a grunt, he released Jake Collier's arm.

The man staggered to his brothers, cradling his bruised wrist and cursing. He stared back at Logan defiantly, but Archer put a heavy hand on his shoulder to keep him in place.

"You nearly got us killed," Park muttered to Logan, regaining his composure now that the threat seemed to be dissipating. "We were two seconds from getting our heads blown off."

"I had it under control," Logan said.

Park rolled his eyes. "Like hell you did."

"I did."

"Let's start this introduction again, shall we?" the old woman said. "My name is Haasi Long Creek, which is Miccosukee for 'sun'. My family and I are of the Miccosukee Tribe."

She gestured to the woman who'd discovered their hidden truck, who scowled at them, still fierce and intimidating. "This is Maki Osceola. She's Seminole."

Haasi motioned to the bikers. "And these are the Collier brothers. You already met Jake. The big one is Archer. He's a giant pain in the ass, but a pain you want around when it hits the fan. The one with the goatee is Boyd."

Boyd was the sly-eyed one, the one still staring at Logan with suspicion and dislike. He reminded Logan of a fat fox—lazy, but still cunning and unpredictable.

"And those two hairy ones that look like bears are the twins—Zander and Zane. They may not be the smartest crayons in the box, but they're hard workers and loyal to the bone. Just don't ask me which is which."

"Not true," one of them said indignantly.

"Zane's beard is thinner—and shorter," the other one—Zander—said.

Archer snorted.

"The Colliers got sixty acres a few miles from here, along with a passel of wives and too many kids for this old lady to keep track of," Haasi said.

Zane flashed white teeth beneath his beard. "She lies. She knows every single one."

"Sorry to meet under the circumstances," Archer said. "But we can't be too careful. Not after what happened."

He seemed to be the leader of the brothers, or the eldest, at the least. Crow's feet crinkled around his eyes and gray streaked his beard. He appeared to have a solid head on his shoulders. At least, he wasn't a hothead like Jake or Sly Eyes, i.e. Boyd. He might not be too bad.

Haasi handed her crossbow to Maki and held out her arms to Eden.

The girl let out a breath, as if she'd been holding it all this time. She rushed into the old woman's arms.

Haasi hugged Eden close. "Child, you must've been scared out of your mind. I don't know where you've been these last few years, but I bet you've got a fantastic story to tell us later."

Over Eden's head, Haasi's expression turned serious—and hard. "Swing by tomorrow. We need to talk."

13

SHAY

Shay Harris adjusted her square-framed purple glasses with the back of her arm, careful not to touch anything with her gloved hands, and sighed. Her eyes burned. She was swaying on her feet from exhaustion.

Rows and rows of cots overflowing with hundreds of injured and dying crammed each medical tent. The sounds of moaning and weeping filled the hot, stale air. The stinging smell of antiseptic mingled with the stench of burnt flesh, vomit, and human feces.

The types of injuries were widespread—blunt force trauma, fractures and amputations, penetration injuries, pulmonary damage and eardrum rupture from the shockwave, third-degree burns, radiation poisoning...it went on and on.

A sort of numbness came over a person in the midst of so much chaos, pain, and death. The enormity of it was too much for the mind to handle. But it wasn't in her nature to detach.

She was raw with the grief, the suffering, the pain and loss she saw all around her. Each person had a life, a family, a house and pets and a career and friends...hopes and dreams and disappointments...so many futures snuffed out too soon, so many possibilities ended in tragedy and mourning.

The only bright spots in the midst of this hell were those stolen moments with Trey Hawthorne, when he showed up with a shy smile and a box of takeout from one of the still-operating airport restaurants. Sometimes, he brought her a pack of gum, a cup of coffee, or both.

For just a few moments, she could remember that there was life outside the tent hospital's walls, that there were people still living, still surviving, still fighting to rebuild what the terrorists had tried so hard to steal from them.

Dakota, Logan, Julio and the others had been gone less than two days. It still felt like an eternity. She missed them, but imagining them away from all this madness kept her sane. They were safe and happy in the Glades.

"Shay, you're off," said her supervisor, a brisk but tireless surgeon named Dr. Webster. In her early fifties, the woman looked like she'd aged a decade in a week. "Get some food in you and get back here in six hours for your next shift."

"Of course, Dr. Webster," Shay said. "Any more rescues?"

"Not since two days ago," Dr. Webster said with a discouraged shake of her head.

Dozens of rescue units were risking their own health to wade through the rubble in downtown Miami to search for survivors. Even outfitted in the best protective gear the government had to offer, it wasn't enough.

In the first week, first responders brought in hundreds of injured they'd found huddled in half-collapsed buildings. The news stations covered each one, the nation clinging to any bit of hope in the unfolding catastrophe that only got more dire by the day.

As the days ticked by, the rescues had slowed to a trickle.

"Dr. Webster—" Shay started, but another doctor hurried up to the surgeon, gesturing emphatically and commanding her attention.

Shay gave up and headed to the contamination ward. Her legs felt like lead, and her head was throbbing again. She'd ignored it as long as possible, but she'd have to take more Percocet. The bullet wound was healing well but still hurt.

She hated taking painkillers when there were hundreds—thousands—of patients suffering far worse than she was.

"You won't be able to help anyone if you collapse on your feet," Hawthorne had reminded her. He was right, of course.

She forced herself to pass several beds with patients screaming in agony. One was a child of six or seven—maybe a girl, but it was hard to tell anymore. The hair on the right side of her head was burnt completely off. The skin on her face and arms looked melted.

Someone bumped into her. "Oh, excuse me."

Nicole Williams smiled tiredly at her. She was a kind, plump nurse who'd befriended Shay on her first day. She'd taken the time to show Shay the ropes and gave her more responsibilities as Shay proved she could handle the taxing load—both physically and mentally.

Nicole clutched a container of used, pus-soaked bandages waiting to be discarded. Deep shadows rimmed her haunted eyes.

"Are you okay?" Shay asked.

"I was just...I was..." Her face crumpled. "I can't—I can't do it anymore—"

Shay took her arm gently and led her through a series of tents into the decontamination zone. She sat the woman down on a metal bench in a corner away from the frenzy, the heart-rending cries.

They'd already lost dozens of nurses, doctors, and assistants who'd cracked under the pressure and extreme toll of tending to thousands of the dying and the dead.

Shay resisted the urge to say it was all okay, that things were better than they were. It was in her nature to think positively, to focus on the solution when everyone else only saw the problems, to believe in hope when things seemed the most hopeless.

"There's—just—so much death." Nicole rocked back and forth, staring numbly down at her hands. "We could save so many of them if we just had the supplies...we're running out of everything. The army keeps flying more in, but it's not enough. We don't have the facilities to treat these burn victims. What are we supposed to do? There are, what, one hundred and twenty burn centers? Maybe eighteen hundred burn beds in the entire country? We have that many patients right here, plus all the other hospitals in greater Miami, in Florida, in the other twelve attacked cities..."

Shay felt the same paralyzing despair, the pit of crushing hopelessness yawning at her feet. The sheer numbers were staggering. They were utterly overwhelmed. People were needlessly dying everywhere she looked.

She slid off Nicole's gloves, then her own, and tossed them into the biohazardous waste disposal container. She took Nicole's hands in hers and crouched in front of her.

She said the words as much to herself as to her friend. "We're doing everything we can. We aren't giving up. We *are* saving lives, even if it doesn't feel like it. You're making a difference."

Nicole didn't respond.

"When is the last time you got some sleep?"

"I...I don't remember. A few days, maybe. And before that? I don't know."

"How long until your shift ends?"

"Two hours." Nicole raised her weary head and gazed at Shay, but her eyes stared straight through her, not seeing Shay but some other horror. "My husband is dead. Did you know that?"

Shay sat back on her heels, stunned. "No, I didn't."

"He worked in finance at Miami Tower. Ground zero. I kept hoping they'd find him, that he'd be one of the survivors...But that's a foolish hope now, isn't it? It's been almost two weeks." She inhaled a ragged breath. "Every life I save, I imagine it's him. Maybe that's terrible."

"No, no it isn't."

"It's crazy, I know it is, but I keep thinking, keep imagining, if I save fifty lives, that'll be enough to tip the scales of fate, you know? If I save one hundred lives, then I'll have earned him back, I could save him..."

"I'm sorry," Shay said. "I'm so sorry."

Tears streamed down Nicole's face. She gripped Shay's hands so hard her nails dug into Shay's skin. But Shay didn't pull away. Her friend needed this.

Shay's mother had never grieved after her father took his own life. She'd continued on like everything was fine, just like she had before he'd died.

When he'd stopped taking his meds. When he'd cheerfully given away his favorite signed Dolphin's jersey, along with his fishing gear and the high-end Bose speakers he'd loved. When he'd retreated to the dark, sour-smelling cave of his bedroom and simply gave up.

Grieving was good. Grieving was part of the process. Pretending when the truth was right there staring you in the face was the definition of insanity.

With the satellite phone Hawthorne had given her, Shay had managed to get ahold of her mom, who was stranded in Tallahassee, a few days ago.

Her mother was alive and well, staying at an overcrowded hotel that was fast running out of shampoo, soap, and fresh towels, and experiencing intermittent blackouts. Her mother kept insisting things were fine.

"It's very tragic what happened," her mother had said in her tight, nasal voice, "but thank God it didn't happen here. We're fine. I'm fine. Things are a bit...tense, but Governor Blake says everything will be okay soon. The power will come back. Grocery shelves would be full if all these crazy, paranoid freaks weren't stocking up on everything under the sun like it's Armageddon or something. I had to pay twelve dollars—in cash—for a box of Fiber One yesterday. Can you imagine?"

"Mom, I think—"

"You should come here, Mishayla. It's fine here. It'll be fine.

They've got martial law. The soldiers are keeping order. I want you to be safe. You need to be here."

She'd tried to explain why she couldn't, why she felt compelled to help in any way she could, but as usual, her mother had stopped listening. It was an exercise in futility.

At least her mother was still alive, which was more than most of these people could say.

"Go get some rest," Shay said gently. "I'll finish your shift."

Nicole blinked. Her eyes were dull with grief. "Are you sure?"

Shay managed a weary smile. She was supposed to meet Hawthorne after her own shift ended, but he would have to wait. She had a feeling that he was the kind of man who would understand. "Don't worry, I've got this."

14

DAKOTA

Haasi smacked open the sagging screen door with her hip. She wore sandals, a long white skirt, and a colorful blouse like a patchwork quilt. Several layers of clay beads draped her neck and clinked around her wrists. Her long gray hair draped loosely around her shoulders.

Her gaze was strong and steady—as was the crossbow she aimed at their heads.

"Whoa!" Park muttered, stumbling backward and nearly tripping.

Julio raised both hands. "We come in peace."

Dakota repressed a smile. It'd been two years since she'd last seen the woman, but Haasi was the same spitfire as she remembered.

"You told us to swing by, remember?" Zander said.

"Could've used your walkies to warn me *when* you were coming," she growled at the twins.

They shrugged their burly shoulders.

"Forgot," Zander said good-naturedly.

"Archer and Jake on patrol?" she asked.

Zander nodded. "Boyd had some things to take care of on the homestead, but he'll be out later."

"I expect you'll be wanting a meal. That's why you came at lunchtime."

"We don't expect a handout," Dakota said quickly.

"Good, 'cause I'm not offering any." Haasi hung the crossbow on a hook just inside the door and wiped her hands on her skirt. "But you can work for it."

"We wouldn't expect anything less, Haasi," Zander said.

Haasi's sharp gaze traveled over the group. "No Ezra?"

Dakota shook her head.

Zane and Zander had swung by the cabin around noon—greeted by Ezra via gunpoint —and asked them to come out to Haasi's. Ezra had categorically rejected the offer, but the rest of them had piled into the truck and followed the twins' Harleys down the road, leaving Ezra to keep watch.

Before they'd left, Ezra had given Dakota a two-way radio so they could communicate if there was trouble.

They were still exhausted from the attack yesterday—and from lugging the bodies of the seven dead Shepherds deep into the swamp, leaving them for gator food—but they went.

Now they stood in a large dirt clearing surrounded by oaks and cypress trees. Before them was a plank house with faded paint, a trim little porch, solar panels on the sagging roof, and a screen door propped open with a rock.

Twenty yards to the left of the house squatted a chickee—an open pole house with a palmetto thatch roof, built on a wooden platform on stilts. A small fire burned in the center, and smoke drifted up from a hole in the thatched roof.

An old Chevy pickup was parked in the shade beneath a mossy oak tree. Goats and chickens scampered freely around the property. A shaggy, black-and-white spotted goat trotted up and bumped against Dakota's legs, nosing at her pocket for something to eat.

"Hey!" Park's eyes lit up. "Son of a motherless goat. Literally."

Dakota rolled her eyes and pushed the goat away. "Go bother Park. He wants you to."

"Shoo!" Haasi waved her hands. "Git, Dot."

The goat gave her an indignant *baaa* before trotting off toward a clump of overgrown weeds.

Two older kids sporting long, raven-black hair, bronze skin, and big dark eyes came running around the house, followed by a huge dog that looked like a cross between a German Shepherd and a Rottweiler.

The girl was about twelve, the boy maybe ten. Dakota only vaguely remembered Haasi's grandchildren, but Eden let out an excited gasp and dashed across the yard to greet them.

They hugged her, chattering incessantly while the dog circled them, tail wagging, barking exuberantly.

Dakota's chest tightened to see her happy.

Once upon a time, a better and happier time, Eden had spent many a summer afternoon here. After the girls' first three months at Ezra's passed without incident, they'd all let their guard down a bit.

A girl needs another girl to talk to, Ezra had said gruffly. Once or twice a month, he'd arranged for them to ride their bikes the few miles down the road to Haasi's place to do some chores, socialize, and bring back some goat's milk. Dakota hadn't minded; it'd been good for Eden.

Haasi gestured at the children. "You remember Peter and Tessa."

"Hello there," Julio said.

"You're covered in skeeter bites," the little boy said to Julio with a wide grin. He had big ears, bright inquisitive eyes, and a mischievous expression.

Julio scratched at several red, swollen bumps on his cheek but managed a good-natured grin. "I think they like me a little too much. I've got twice as many bites as anyone else."

"Your blood must be sweet," Tessa said. She was tall and lanky, with defined cheekbones and sleek black hair tied in a braid that reached the small of her back.

Julio raised his eyebrows. "Is that it? I'll be sure to tell my wife. She'll get a kick out of that."

"You can't go a second without protection," Tessa warned. "Here we've got skeeters big enough to put a saddle on."

"Trust me—I've learned my lesson."

Park scratched at several bumps of his own with his good hand. "Me too."

Maki came to the screen door. She said little but watched everything with a sharp, analytical gaze. Dakota remembered that about her. She was one of those still-waters-run-deep kind of women.

"We'll give you some skeeter paste before you leave," Maki said.

"Thank you," Julio said with a wry, grateful smile. He put his hand over his heart. Several more bites swelled on his hand and arm. "You're saving my life."

Peter giggled.

"Used to be, moonshiners and poachers kept swarms at bay with smoke pots and cheesecloth sack netting," Haasi said. "Our people used to smear rancid alligator fat on their exposed skin to keep the insects away."

Peter and Tessa squealed in disgust. Eden scrunched up her face and pretended to gag.

"And everyone else, apparently," Park said with a grimace. "Please tell me there's a better option. I'm running out of DEET."

"The old ways of doing things are mostly gone," Haasi said. "When I was a girl, we would crush beautyberry leaves in our hands and rub them all over our skin. That still works, but now I strain the crushed leaves in rubbing alcohol, add a few drops of lemon eucalyptus, and put it in a spray bottle. The skeeters hate it. It's natural and just as effective as all those expensive, toxic chemicals. I'll give you some to take with you."

"Thank you," Park and Julio said at the same time.

Haasi used to make and sell their herbal remedies, poultices, and tinctures at the Little Cypress farmers' market. Maybe she still did.

Little Cypress wasn't really a town but more of a small settlement, like the old days of the Wild West; made up of a gas station, a family-owned grocery store, a tiny post office, and a cluster of squat houses and mobile homes on cement blocks.

"I'll give you some ground mangrove leaves for Ezra," Haasi said. "Mangrove trees have great anti-inflammatory and antibiotic properties."

"He needs it," Dakota said. "Thank you."

Haasi turned to the children. "Kids, weed the garden and feed the chickens. Then if there's still time, you can go hunting and rustle up some Muscadine grapes to make that jelly Tessa likes before the storm hits."

She gestured up at the sky. On the horizon across the vast sawgrass plains, dark clouds thickened. The trees rustled in the growing breeze. The temperature had lowered several degrees in the last few minutes.

Tessa rolled her eyes and grabbed Eden's arm. "Come on, we can get it done fast. Then we can listen to music and you can draw a new portrait of me, if you want. I still have the drawing pad and pencils you kept here."

Eden nodded eagerly and hurried after her, trailed by Peter and the dog, all of them happy and grinning.

"Eden—" Dakota said, concern already tensing her stomach.

Eden turned back to her with an embarrassed frown. *I'm fine!* She signed. *I'll be okay.*

"Typical teenager," Haasi said.

Eden wasn't a typical teenager. She grew up oppressed, restricted, and abused, her voice stolen from her in more ways than one.

Haasi put a reassuring hand on her arm. "They're fine. All of them. They know to stay close. That dog may look like a mutt, but he's smart as a whip. Nokosi's trained to protect those kids with his life, and he will. 'Nokosi' is Seminole for bear. He's fierce as one, too."

"Okay." Dakota took a breath. "Okay. You're right." She gave Eden a tight nod, an ache in her chest.

Eden waved while simultaneously rolling her eyes and disappeared out the door.

"I know I am." Haasi was straightforward to a fault, a tough no-nonsense woman. Anyone who chose to live out in the unforgiving wilds of the Everglades had to be. She took no flak from anyone, but underneath her impatience and sharp tongue, she had a big heart.

Dakota had seen it in the way she took Eden under her wing, no questions, no judgment.

Good people have to watch out for each other, she always used to say.

But with actual lives on the line, Dakota wondered if that were still true. Generosity and nice platitudes were fine when everything was normal, when your own kids were safe and warm.

For most people, when the world went to hell, the rule was to protect your own first, second, and last.

How long would Haasi remain kind and generous? How long would anyone? Not long, Dakota suspected. Not long at all.

15

DAKOTA

Haasi motioned to the rest of the group. "Boys, one of the solar panels has been on the fritz. Why don't you get the ladder and toolbox from the shed? Maki will finish with lunch. Wild boar stew, fresh tomato and spinach salad from the garden, and fry bread."

"Sounds delicious," Julio said. "I love a good fry bread. I'm happy to help in the kitchen, but I'm not bad at fixing stuff that's broken, either."

"A man of many talents," Haasi said. "Useful skills are always welcome around here."

Park raised his good hand. "I'll help Maki. Can't do much with this broken arm."

"Good. Get to it." Haasi turned to Dakota as Park followed Maki into the house. The twins led Logan and Julio toward an old, weathered shed in the back. "I'll make a poultice to ease some of Ezra's pain. Come with me."

Dakota followed Haasi around to the back of the house. Haasi kept up a steady stream of conversation, pointing out the water filtration system and the beehives buzzing with honeybees, easily covering the awkward silences while Dakota fumbled for something worthwhile to say.

Haasi motioned proudly at the goats. "The girls each produce about ten pounds of milk a day for most of the year, and they're a lot easier to care for than cows. Goats get a bad rap, but they're lifesavers."

"You still sell goat's milk at the farmers' market?" she asked absently.

Haasi's face darkened. "Not the last few weeks. We heard there was rioting, desperate people stealing from each other. Best to stay away from civilization for a while, even the rural places."

"Good idea."

Dakota paused beside a heavily pockmarked cypress tree. She touched one of the hundreds of holes and raised a questioning brow at Haasi.

"Here's where I practice my marksmanship when I get pissed off." The woman grinned proudly. "It happens a lot. Good thing with the crossbow is I get to reuse the bolts. I hang a target up and don't stop until it's ripped to shreds."

"I know the feeling."

The sweltering heat baked her bare shoulders. Sweat dampened her hairline beneath the brim of the baseball cap she'd borrowed from Ezra. The afternoon thunderstorms couldn't come soon enough.

Haasi followed her gaze toward the clouds billowing over the vast river, the capillary network of mangrove creeks and canals, sawgrass islands, a copse of spindly swamp pines. In the distance, a great blue heron glided across the darkening sky.

"It's beautiful," Dakota said.

"While it lasts. Snowbirds and damn tourists coming down here with their mobile homes and campers and speedboats. They don't know South Florida. They don't know it at all."

Haasi turned her head and spat on the ground. "And all these developers chopping bits of the Glades away, dredging and developing and building their steel and concrete monstrosities, ruining the best parts of the land for nothin' but money. Pretty soon, there won't be anything left of all this. I was born here, and it might all be destroyed by the time I die."

"I hope not."

Haasi shot her a sideways glance, her gaze sharp. "You miss the city?"

"No. Not at all. I...I never wanted to leave here in the first place."

She followed Haasi into the chickee hut. The smoke from the center firepit kept the mosquitos out. Haasi took a stone pestle and mortar from a low shelf and placed it on a narrow wooden counter a few feet from the fire pit, along with a small vial of natural oils.

She dug around in a stout wooden cupboard and pulled out some fresh green leaves and another vial filled with a brownish sludge, which she offered Dakota. "An extract of the mangrove root, for pain relief. I'll need to make a fresh poultice from the leaves."

"Thank you."

"Always use the fresh leaves if you can—they're more effective than dried. Both the bark and the leaves'll work for all kinds of skin disorders, boils, cuts, and wounds. The Seminole have been using it for hundreds of years. It'll heal Ezra right up."

Dakota's throat tightened. "Thank you, Haasi. I mean it."

Haasi bent over the pot of water boiling over the fire and scooped out a cupful of water with a ladle. With a large spoon, she doled just enough boiling water into the mortar to cover the leaves. She mashed them with the pestle while Dakota watched.

"What's it like out there?" Haasi asked. "We've heard things on the radio. We've seen the refugees fleeing, even seen some of the really sick ones. Archer says there are dead bodies littered all along 41—most of them blistered and burned, covered in horrible sores, missing their hair...we've already had to fight a few of the ones well enough to want to steal from us."

"Whatever you can imagine, it's worse." Dakota closed her eyes, reliving the initial terror of the shockwave, the blinding light so bright it'd gouged her eyeballs like fingernails, the poisonous mushroom cloud rising above the devastated city. The screaming and panic. The shattered buildings and burnt bodies. The children weeping over dead parents.

For the first time in days, she thought of the survivors they'd left behind at the theater: mild-mannered Rasha and her husband, Miles; Fierce Zamira and her listless granddaughter, Isabel; and little Piper, who Dakota had dragged from the street moments before the lethal fallout descended.

They would have left the theater by now. Were they okay? Had they reunited with their families, found shelter and safety? She hoped they had, especially Piper.

"Whatever people say about the hard living out here, at least we have everything we need," Haasi said. "My people learned not to trust the government for anything a long, long time ago. Out here, we make our own food, water, shelter, and electricity. We never depended on anyone to give us a thing. We've done this all on our own. And we can keep doing it for the rest of our lives."

"As long as the outside world doesn't come in wanting to take what you have."

"There's that." Haasi's face hardened. "We'll be ready for them. We're prepared."

Dakota wasn't sure anyone could be prepared enough for what was coming.

16

DAKOTA

Dakota licked her dry lips, suddenly nervous. Haasi had never asked her about what it was like in the compound, though Dakota was certain Ezra had told her where they came from. "I should tell you about the Shepherds and the attack on Ezra's place."

Haasi gave her a sharp, appraising look. Though age and sun had crinkled the bronzed, earthy skin around her eyes, with her high cheekbones and the proud jut of her jaw, she was still an incredibly handsome woman. "Yes," she said. "You should."

Dakota explained the facts. Haasi kept mashing the mangrove leaves, remaining silent other than a few occasional grunts. Dakota hesitated, wondering if she should say more. Trust was too big a word to use, but she liked Haasi; she always had.

Maybe *trust* was exactly the right word.

"Ezra is angry at me," she said haltingly. "He doesn't want my friends to stay. He wants us all to leave—me included. But the Shepherds will come back. There's no way they won't come back."

"For someone so smart, he can be stubborn as an ass, can't he? Some of us have been meeting for several years, forming a community group to protect each other. We need it now more than ever. We never turned away anybody needing a bit of help if they were willin' to help themselves. But these people, they're only interested in what they can take."

Across the yard, one of the Collier twins broke into raucous laughter. Dakota glanced over.

Julio was squatting up on the roof, bent over one of the solar panels with a wrench in one hand. Zander was three-fourths up the ladder leaning against the house, holding the toolbox and offering plenty of unsolicited advice.

Logan and Zane were lounging at a picnic table beneath the shade of several live oak trees. Zane had set three jugs on the table and was handing one to Logan. Snippets of conversation drifted her way: Zane was describing the merits of moonshine over conventional alcoholic beverages.

Last night, Archer had explained how during Prohibition, their great-grandfather had escaped to the Glades to make and sell moonshine in peace. The twins—Zane and Zander—still made corn whiskey moonshine with an ancient but working still on their property.

All five Collier brothers worked construction—often traveling over an hour each way to various construction sites in Everglades City, Chokoloskee, Immokalee, Orangetree, and East Naples. Or at least, they did until the bombs.

They were staying away from towns and cities, now. Maybe for a long time. But Archer insisted they'd be fine. They were the hardy types who prided themselves on their ability to live off-grid.

"150 proof—it'll put hair on your chest, that's for sure!" Zane bellowed, laughing at his own joke as he poured booze into Logan's flask.

She frowned. She hadn't realized he'd managed to keep the flask during their decontamination screening. Most people lost all their personal belongings in the process, mostly because FEMA, the Red Cross, and the National Guard didn't have the time to decontaminate millions of items. Their only focus was saving lives.

Because their group had saved Trey Hawthorne and his men, they'd received special privileges. Nonporous items were much easier to decontaminate. It was why Dakota still had her knife, and they had their guns back.

Zane finished filling Logan's flask and held it out to him. Logan shook his head and said something, but Zane ignored him. Zane gestured, laughing, and Logan finally acquiesced and took a swig.

Dakota turned away in disgust—and disappointment. With everything going on, all she needed was Logan too drunk to be useful. Was she right to depend on him? Or was she making a huge mistake?

Haasi cleared her throat, bringing Dakota's attention back to their conversation. Haasi frowned, staring down at her pestle and mortar. The leaves looked well mashed, but she kept working at them. "You know, Ezra was heartbroken when he lost you."

Dakota's throat tightened. There *had* been a stoop to his broad shoulders that she didn't remember. He walked like his joints ached, pressing a hand to the small of his back when he thought no one was looking, grimacing when he sat or stood, a permanent scowl on his face as he fought the betrayals of his own aging body.

Her throat tightened. Old age happened to everyone—but this was different. She hated to see him like that. She hated the realization that she had something to do with it even more.

She sniffed, trying to play off the sudden surge of emotion stinging the backs of her eyes. "Does Ezra even have a heart?"

"You know he does, girl." Haasi worked in silence for several moments. "When Izzy, his wife, was still alive, she used to bring their vegetables to the farmers' market every other week. Made the best Muscadine grape jelly in all South Florida. He'd go with her, smile and chat with the customers. They came to the Colliers' barbeques, and Ezra helped my husband, Minco, install our well before he died.

"Ezra was a different man before she passed. Something inside him broke without her. He couldn't believe that it was cancer that did it, in the end. All that planning, all the years of effort and work that went into creating his safe little self-sustaining world, and it couldn't save the one person who mattered."

Haasi's eyes were bright and glistening—like she was holding back tears. "And then you and that girl showed up. You changed that man's life."

Dakota realized with a start that this woman cared deeply for Ezra. Probably she had for years. But Ezra's heart had been too hardened to let anyone in—until Dakota and Eden.

They'd repaid his kindness by abandoning him without a word. It was the last straw. He'd never risked opening up to anyone else again, not in friendship, and not in love. It only made sense that his feelings toward Dakota—and everyone else—were filled with bitterness, resentment, and anger.

A fresh wave of shame washed through her. Part of this was her fault. Too much of it.

"He saved our lives," she said quietly. "But now he won't let us save his."

Using a spoon, Haasi transferred the poultice into a small glass jar and sealed the lid. She handed it to Dakota. "The paste can be applied directly to the skin and covered with a piece of clean cloth, preferably something thin and light like gauze. Cover the cloth with plastic wrap to hold in the moisture, and change the poultice every three or four hours, or whenever it dries out."

"Thank you."

Haasi wiped her hands briskly on her skirt. "Did I ever tell you what happened to my family?"

"No."

"Tessa was two, Peter almost one when it happened. Their father was out of the picture—and wanted to be—shortly after Peter's birth. I was babysitting them while my husband drove Hachi—my daughter—to Everglades City, to a used car dealership to see about getting her a more dependable car. They were broadsided by a moron texting on his phone at seventy miles an hour. My daughter died instantly. Minco suffered for two weeks before he passed."

"I'm truly sorry, Haasi."

She shrugged off the sympathy. "It could've killed me, that much loss. But the way I saw it, I had two grandbabies who needed me, so I had to fight through somehow, some way. And I did. A few years later, Maki came along. She's Seminole, not Miccosukee, but I've forgiven her for it."

"You've built a good life out here."

"I have. But make no mistake, none of this came easy. It was the bravest thing I ever did. I miss my husband and daughter every single day. But that doesn't mean I haven't carved out a bit of peace and happiness."

Haasi pressed her lips together and shook her head ruefully. "Ezra couldn't face the pain of his past. He allowed it to eat him up him instead. The way he is now, he'll die alone."

"I hope not," Dakota said.

"He made his own choices, don't forget that. We all do."

Haasi was right. Ezra, as much as she loved him, was a miserable man. Rather than risk his heart for the possibility of something more, something better, he'd chosen a safe, solitary life of loss and loneliness.

Dakota turned her head quickly, blinking back the sudden stinging in her eyes. Guilt and remorse pierced her—for Ezra, but not just Ezra.

Maybe she couldn't do a damn thing about how Ezra chose to live —or not live—his life, but she could deal with her own crap.

Silently, she vowed to tell Eden the truth at the first opportunity. Her secret had been festering between them for far too long. She dreaded confessing, but that didn't give her a pass to push aside her own responsibility.

She'd seen firsthand what that did to a person.

She didn't want to turn into Ezra. She didn't want to hurt the people she cared about most in the world.

If she'd learned one thing in the last weeks, it was that the next minute wasn't promised to anyone. The terrorist attacks had obliterated hundreds of thousands of people, every single one brimming with plans, dreams, goals—all turned to ash, their secrets buried with them.

But first, she had to convince Ezra to let them stay.

"Ezra is a hard, stubborn man who can't admit when he's wrong," Haasi said. "You just have to be more stubborn than he is."

Dakota cradled the jar in her hands and managed a small smile. "That, I can do."

17

DAKOTA

"I'm not leaving." Dakota flung open the door and marched back to the cabin. She planted herself in the middle of the worn but fastidious kitchen and stared down Ezra with her hands on her hips. "And neither are my friends."

Ezra shoved back his chair and stood, glowering at her. Old newspapers were spread across the kitchen table, topped by a handful of guns in neatly ordered rows and a well-organized cleaning kit. "If you think—"

She cut him off. "I know they make more mouths to feed, but they make more hands for working, too. And in case you've forgotten, you can't take care of this whole place with one hand. We'll all help. We can maintain the garden, take the boat out and fish, keep up with the rabbits and the chickens."

Ezra only grunted.

"And you and I both know the Shepherds aren't done with us. We're not leaving you to defend yourself on your own. We're going to finish this. I'm going to finish this."

Ezra stared at her.

"After that, if we haven't earned our place, just say the word and we'll leave. Until then, we're staying."

He turned his back to her and fussed with his guns, fumbling with his one good hand, the splinted fingers of his left hand making him clumsy and slow. He moved stiffly, like his joints were causing him pain. Or maybe it was the beating he'd just taken.

She waited him out. Ezra Burrows was incredibly stubborn, but so was she.

Several long, tense minutes passed.

She shifted impatiently, balling and unballing her fists against her thighs, her teeth gritted, staring at the white streaking his thinning hair, his broad stooped shoulders, at a round liver spot on the back of his neck.

Her frustration dissolved, replaced with something that felt a lot like sorrow. He was getting old. She hated that thought with a loathing that made her stomach hurt.

Everything she loved was falling apart.

But not this. Not yet.

She wouldn't let it.

She was strong enough to keep this place together, tough enough to keep the people she cared about alive and well and safe here for as long as they needed.

There was so much more she wanted to say, but the words clogged in her throat like stones. She didn't speak. She waited.

If she lost him now, she might lose him forever.

Finally, he relented. His shoulders sagged. "You're bossier than I remember."

"I was taught by the best."

He gave a soft snort.

When he turned to face her, his eyes were shiny, but she pretended not to notice. He held his splinted left hand up close to his chest. Puffy, purple bruises distorted his features. "Everyone works their asses off."

"They will," Dakota promised, keeping her expression even, fighting back the triumphant grin daring to break across her face.

Someone knocked on the front door. Logan stepped inside. He glanced from Dakota to Ezra. "We have a lot to do to prepare for the Shepherds."

"You don't know the half of it." Ezra gestured at the kitchen table with his good hand. "Bring everyone here. I have a plan."

18

MADDOX

Solomon Cage stormed into the infirmary. The Prophet followed him, his hands folded at his waist, his face grave.

"They're all dead!" Solomon snarled.

Maddox sat up swiftly, his heart hammering. He'd been in bed resting while Sister Rosemarie changed the dressings of the sores pocking his chest and upper arms, sores from the radiation sickness. He was still weak and lethargic, but at least he wasn't vomiting.

The medical clinic was simple, with a wooden floor, plank walls, and a low ceiling. A row of cabinets was set against the fourth wall beside a stainless-steel cart containing scalpels, trauma shears, rolls of gauze, and other medical supplies.

His father jabbed his finger at him. "Seven of our best men! We sent them out yesterday to take care of your screw-up. None of them returned. We've heard nothing all day. No contact. They're dead."

Maddox knew for a fact that they hadn't sent their best men. His father had sent new Shepherds, young and relatively inexperienced, who'd never shot at anything more threatening than a target tacked to a tree.

He pursed his lips but said nothing. To say so would only invite further wrath, and his father was already boiling with rage.

"This is because of *you*." Solomon's expression was stony, as if his features were carved from granite, his eyes a cold, cruel glacial blue. Though his sandy blond hair and beard were peppered with gray, he was still a fit, powerful man. A hard man.

"Are you really my son," he snarled, "or did your mother whore herself out to a cowering dog? Are you really that worthless?"

"No!" Maddox cried, his own anger flaring. "I wasn't even there!"

Outrage thrummed through him. It was her. Dakota did this to him. Without her, Eden would still be here.

Maddox should be one of the elite Chosen alongside his brother, Jacob, setting the world right with nothing to stop them. No one would look down on them ever again. They would rule everyone and everything.

Maddox would have the power. He would be in control.

"And why weren't you there?" Solomon spat on the floor. "Because you're weak."

Maddox bit down on his tongue. Excuses wouldn't matter. To defend himself just made him appear weaker than he already was.

God's will—the Prophet's will—didn't have to make sense. Their duty was to bend to it without question. To question the Prophet was to question God, a blasphemy of the worst kind.

Beside the bed, Sister Rosemarie stiffened. She dropped the cool compress she was holding to the bowl on the medical cart beside her. "Your son is still recovering. He needs peace and quiet—"

"I'll decide what he needs!" his father roared. He turned his scornful gaze back to Maddox. "You know who never wavered? Jacob never doubted. *Jacob* never failed me."

Maddox flinched from the sting of his father's barbed words. *He failed when he allowed a girl to kill him.* But he didn't dare say the words aloud. Thoughts of his perfect, dead brother brought a snarled ache of love and resentment, bitterness and pain.

"I—I have faith," he said instead.

"Solomon," the Prophet said, the faintest reproof in his voice. He had been silent until now, patiently waiting while Solomon burned through his rage.

The instant he spoke, Solomon went stiff and still, like the Prophet had tugged an invisible leash.

In his mid-fifties, the Prophet was a slim, tall man with a long, narrow face and wavy yellow hair to his shoulders. An unremarkable man at first glance. His power was in his eloquent words, his charisma, and the unnatural sway he held over every single one of his devoted followers.

"You know what you must do," the Prophet said calmly to his father. "Sparing the rod is a mortal sin."

He watched his father's jaw work silently, his eyes savage with fury. He spoke like the words were choking him. "The Lord could judge you harshly. Instead, he has spread his hands of mercy over you. Come, *my son*, to the mercy room."

"His body can't handle it!" Sister Rosemarie stood quickly, moving closer to the edge of Maddox's bed. "He's still recovering! He was exposed to radiation—"

"God will give him the strength," the Prophet said. His voice was quiet but as commanding as if he'd shouted. "In our weakness, we are strong."

"But—"

His father shot her a scornful look. "Be careful, Sister, lest you question God's will."

Sister Rosemarie took a step back and lowered her head. "Forgive me, Prophet."

The Prophet patted her shoulder. "Blessings be upon you, dear Sister, for your compassionate heart. Do not allow it to lead you astray."

"Of course not," she murmured. She reached her hand toward him, her head still bowed meekly. "Blessings."

Into the Fire

"Of course." The Prophet held out his hand with an indulgent flourish and let her kiss it. "I bless you, my soul."

She glanced at Maddox, her eyes full of concern—and apology.

It wasn't her fault, but he felt a stab of resentment anyway. She was here, witnessing his humiliation. He hated her for that.

The Prophet gestured at Maddox. "Lead the way."

Maddox gritted his teeth, his legs like lead, dread coursing through him. But he held his head high and strode to the mercy room, ignoring the laughter and calls of the children, the gentle song of someone practicing a hymn on the violin.

Volleys of gunshots echoed through the forest. The Shepherds were training hard for something big. The Shepherds were always together, always secretive, coming and going with increased frequency, their expressions tense like warriors preparing for battle.

The last mission, the people whispered, the one that would trigger the end, the Armageddon, the final cleansing of a corrupt and wicked land.

Soon, Maddox would join them. He only needed to endure a little longer.

As they approached, a man came striding out of the mercy room, shoving his young son of maybe nine in front of him. The boy's head was lowered in mortification. His face was wet, his shirt clinging to his back, red streaks staining the rough cotton fabric.

Maddox recognized the kid's lank, corn-colored hair and pinched features. He was a mischievous kid, always telling inappropriate jokes or giggling in church. His parents were the rigid, pious types who couldn't bear the embarrassment of an unruly child.

"Don't shame me further in front of the Prophet, boy," the father snapped. He turned toward the Prophet, his incensed expression instantly transforming to one of adoration and worship.

Trembling from pain, the boy managed to kneel and grasp the Prophet's hand to kiss it.

"Blessings be upon you, Philip," the Prophet said, his voice kind and compassionate, as if he weren't the one who'd ordered the whipping in the first place. "This too shall pass."

He smiled—paternal, benevolent—but there was that faint twist of his lips that felt somehow as menacing as it was magnanimous.

"I swear this will never happen again," the father said fervently. He reached for the Prophet's hand and kissed it, his head bowed in reverence.

"See that it doesn't," the Prophet said, less graciously.

Maddox tried to catch the kid's eye, to give him a smile and let him know he wasn't alone, but the boy didn't look up. He was too upset.

The father pushed him along, the thundercloud of his expression promising whatever punishment the boy had earned wasn't over yet.

Maddox knew well how some people used religion to cloak their acts of aggression and cruelty. It was cunning and clever, really. No amount of guilt or self-awareness could ever pierce the bloat of self-righteous piety.

Once the man and the boy were gone, Maddox entered the mercy room of his own volition, followed by his father and the Prophet. Maddox knelt, stripped off his shirt, and received the whipping he didn't deserve with his head held high.

He'd been lashed because of Jacob or Dakota more than once. He would remember this, would remember every agonizing blow. He'd hold onto his anger, hatred, and resentment and relish every bitter sting.

"Only five lashes," the Prophet said. "Sister Rosemarie's cautious nature shows wisdom."

Every lash struck with a burning explosion of agony. The pain radiated across his spine, his ribs, until his entire back felt like it was blazing with fire.

He flinched but kept himself steady. He didn't groan or cry out. He didn't make a sound. He squeezed his eyes shut and counted each blow, his mind fixed on his goal: the moment he found Dakota, and this would all be worth it.

When the punishment was over, his father was sweating and short of breath. He wiped the whip clean on a towel, wound it, and hung it upon the hook on the wall.

Maddox wanted to collapse on the cool concrete and let unconsciousness take away the pain striping his back. But he didn't.

He climbed shakily to his feet and straightened his shoulders with a wince. "I'll head the next mission. This is my problem. I'll take care of it myself."

"Clearly, you can't be trusted with—"

"I know Dakota Sloane. I know the backwater channels like no one else. I've spent more time out there—" he pointed at the woods, but meant the outside world, "—than anyone here. I'm the man for the job."

Solomon gave a derisive snort.

"We have more pressing concerns," the Prophet said softly.

Solomon's eyes flashed. Nothing was more pressing to him than revenge.

"I need you focused, Solomon. There is a bigger picture, remember? We have much to do. The physicist arrives tonight. I need you here." He waved a hand at Maddox. "The boy has proven himself capable. Give the task to him."

His father would see him for the warrior he was. Maddox would make sure of it. He'd finally have the respect he deserved. The respect his father loathed to give him.

Once the Prophet saw what he could do, his father would be forced to honor him.

Maddox forced a smile. "Give me the men of my choice. I'll deal with these people and get my sister back where she belongs."

"You have them," the Prophet said. "I want Eden at my side by next Sunday at the latest. Everything changes then. The timing is critical. Do you understand?"

That was seven days away. An entire week. Plenty of time for what he had planned.

He ran a hand through his hair. Several strands came out between his fingers. He stared down at the clump of blond hairs for a moment, startled.

It didn't matter. The agony searing his back didn't matter. The sores blistering his skin didn't matter. None of it did.

He was stronger than anything they could throw at him. He was better than Jacob, his father, Dakota—all of them.

He would show them all.

"It will be done," Maddox said.

19

DAKOTA

After everyone had helped with chores around the property and eaten a hearty dinner of fish, potatoes, and cucumber salad, Ezra called a meeting.

Once they were all seated around the table, he brought out a framed 24-by-30-inch map of the property that Eden had drawn to exact specifications for his birthday three years ago.

The drawing was three-dimensional, intricate, and made to scale—the cabin set in the middle of the clearing, the big antenna beside it, the storage shed, chicken coop, garden, the well and cisterns, and the haybale shooting range near the dock, the little fishing boat seeming to bob in the water.

Eden grinned when he set it on the table and carefully squared it so each side was level. Her grin faded when he took it out of its frame and removed the glass. He pulled out a stubby pencil and marked an X across the sketched driveway and another near the cabin, ruining her pristine artwork.

Anger flared in Dakota's gut but quickly faded. Ezra was practical to a fault; he didn't have a sentimental bone in his body. Well, maybe a few small ones, but he ignored them most of the time.

Their task was to keep themselves alive, not preserve art. Besides, Eden was right here; she could always draw another one.

Outside, an early evening thunderstorm darkened the windows. The first splatters of rain struck the roof. With the rain came the cooling relief from the muggy heat—for a few hours. Inside the well-insulated cabin, the air was cooler, at least.

"We need to establish a guard schedule." Logan rested his elbows on the table and leaned forward. "We can break into rotating shifts, four hours each."

"Trip wires already surround the perimeter," Ezra said, "with motion-sensor security lights and cameras covering all directions."

"We should join the neighborhood patrol group," Dakota said. "The Collier brothers and Haasi. Together, we can monitor any intruders, whether it's desperate refugees trying to steal or the Shepherds."

Ezra's lips pressed into a thin line, his eyes flashing. "No."

"Why not?"

"Did you hear anything I taught you, girl?"

Dakota bristled at his condescending tone. "Of course, I did. You can't depend on anyone to save you but yourself. I know that better than anyone." She shot a glance at Logan. She wouldn't have gotten here without him, of that she was certain. "But we're outnumbered. Seems like the more eyes and hands we have, the better off we are."

"They're too soft," Ezra growled. "Too weak. They don't know what's out there. They think because they can skin a coon and live without modern amenities, that makes them strong enough to survive anything."

"Ezra—"

"They're wrong. Men who don't know what they don't know are the most dangerous kind. I don't trust them. Come to think of it, I don't trust any of you, either."

"Hey now," Park said, defensive, "we're not the bad guys here."

His eyes narrowed. "You sure about that?"

This line of talk would only go one direction—downhill. She had to get him refocused on a task. "What about the front gate? Does it need to be fixed?"

Ezra glared down at his broken hand resting on the table. "They ambushed me when I drove back home after a trip into town for supplies. I opened the gate, and they were right there, waiting across the road. Took me by surprise, that's all."

"We can use the Shepherds' trucks to barricade the entrance to the driveway before anyone gets to the gate, so they have to walk up," Logan said. "The heavy treeline on either side of the property will keep a vehicle out."

Dakota nodded. "We can hide our truck and Ezra's east and west along the road outside the barricade, stashed with bugout bags and jerrycans of diesel, just in case we need to escape fast."

Ezra grunted. "We won't need to escape. Nowhere else is as safe as it is right here. We stand our ground."

Logan glanced from Ezra to Dakota, brows raised like, *who is this guy?*

Dakota gave a sharp shake of her head. This wasn't the time. "We still need to plan for all possibilities. That's what you taught me." She considered all the angles, thinking about her and Eden's arrival via boat and desperate trek through the woods three years ago. "We can't forget the swamp as a possible point of entry."

"Fine. We'll patrol the north perimeter, too," Ezra said, his voice dismissive. "But I doubt they'd attempt to navigate the maze of tributaries out there."

"We did it," Dakota said.

Ezra glanced at her, a flicker of pride in his blue eyes. "No one else knows the water like you do."

"Maddox does," Dakota said firmly. "Don't underestimate him."

Ezra flexed his uninjured hand and made a fist. "I'm not underestimating anything."

"Should the kid be here for this?" Park asked, slanting his gaze at Eden.

"This is her life, too," Julio said. "If she wants in, I think she should be in."

Dakota watched her sister carefully, half-expecting her to sigh in relief and escape as quickly as she could. Eden wasn't the best at facing reality.

But instead of shrinking away, Eden sat up in her chair and straightened her shoulders. She made the *I'm okay* sign and gave a resolute nod.

"Are you sure?" Dakota asked, surprised—and impressed.

Eden pointed to her temple and clenched her hands together in front of her stomach, mouthing the words so Dakota understood. *Trust me.*

"We do," Julio said before Dakota could say anything. "We know you'll do your best."

Eden flashed him a grateful smile and signed, *Thank you.*

"We'll work Eden into the watch rotation," Logan said.

Eden beamed at him. He winked at her.

Wincing, Ezra leaned down, grabbed a black duffle bag from the floor, and set it on the table, right on top of Eden's artwork. He handed each of them a whistle to wear around their necks. "One long blast if you need help. Two short blasts if intruders are detected and we're under attack."

He handed a handheld radio transceiver to Dakota, Julio, and Eden. "I only have three extra. They've got excellent range."

Dakota clipped the radio to her belt. Before they'd left Haasi's homestead, Haasi had given her the frequency and the call signs she and the Collier brothers used for emergency communication, just in case.

Julio motioned toward Eden. "What about her? If there's a situation, she can't communicate with us verbally."

Ezra scratched the white scruff at his jawline and frowned. He picked up the radio and flipped it over in his hands. "She could use CW, i.e. Morse code, I suppose, if she's willing to learn."

Eden brightened. She nodded eagerly.

He smiled—a genuine smile, not sarcastic or mocking. "I'll teach you on the ham. And show you how to use it on a handheld in an emergency. But you need a call sign—a code name—so we know it's you."

She scrunched her nose, thinking.

"We can come up with code names later," Dakota said impatiently. "What's next?"

Ezra pointed to the shed on the map. "If you're not in the cabin when we're attacked, head to the storage shed. I built it myself—same qualities as the cabin: thick, twelve-inch concrete block walls filled with poured concrete and rebar and reinforced with Amortex ballistic-resistant fiberglass panels. Fire-resistant roof. Can't be burned out. Oxygen comes from a couple of high slit windows and a pipe from the roof. Some oxygen masks in storage, too, along with enough food and water to outlast whoever's after you. You'll have to poop in a bucket, but there's wood shavings to dull the stink."

He glared suspiciously at the newcomers, like he'd love to kick them out then and there, but when he turned to Eden, his gaze softened. "You remember the tunnel?"

Both Eden and Dakota nodded. Ezra had built a small escape tunnel through the crawlspace beneath the floor in case the front and back doors were ever breached. Digging holes in Florida's shallow, porous soil was precarious business, so it only went five-or-so yards beyond the side of the house and exited beneath the only clump of bushes Ezra allowed anywhere near the cabin.

"The trapdoor's under the rug in the bathroom off the kitchen," Dakota said. "You can flee to the shed bunker or past it into the woods, where there's several caches with more guns and supplies, if they're still there."

"They're still there." Ezra pointed out the perimeter to be

defended and the weakest points where intruders were likely to attempt entry. He drew X's to identify several tripwires, then drew straight lines between the cabin and the sheds and various outhouses.

"The property is booby-trapped, like I told you. We'll make more, too. Don't go wandering around outside these lines unless you're lookin' to be crippled for life."

Park and Julio glanced at each other with raised eyebrows.

Ezra ignored them and continued on. "Anyone turns onto the drive before the gate, an alarm picks up the magnetic field of the vehicle and sends a warning." He explained how the alarm sent a radio signal to a small receiver. The sensor was buried in a length of PVC pipe beneath the gravel driveway which ran to a transmitter box bolted to the far side of a big oak tree so it couldn't be seen from the road.

"All these security measures may be enough to keep out the casual intruders," Logan said slowly. "They'll give up and look for easier pickings. It's not going to be enough for these crazy fanatics after Eden."

Ezra shot Logan a sharp look. He didn't like Logan, Dakota realized. They were both strong, tough, independent men. She'd hoped they'd like each other—and if not like, at least respect. But maybe that was too much to ask.

"I'm well aware." Ezra marked small X's on all four sides of the cabin at the roofline. "There's a sniper's nest in the attic above us. I've got shooting positions set up to the north, south, east, and west, reinforced with sandbags. Automatic gunfire will eventually chew through concrete, so the sandbags are additional protection.

"I've got a load of sand and dirt behind the shed and dozens of burlap sacks we can fill to set up shooting positions beneath each window down here. And razor wire to put around the inside of the window frames to tear up anyone's hands who try to get inside."

Logan nodded. "Good."

"Should we board up the windows?" Park asked.

Ezra shot Park a derisive look. "Plywood won't stop bullets."

Park ducked his head like a chastised puppy.

"What about the front door?" Julio asked.

"It's solid steel in a steel frame," Ezra said. "Five single-cylinder one-inch deadbolts and strike plates. No one's kicking their way in, that's for sure."

"If someone wants in, they're coming in." Logan jabbed his finger at the cabin in the center of the drawing. "You can steel-reinforce your front door, but what happens when they drive an armored Humvee through your living room wall? I mean, they may not get through this particular wall, but there's still windows."

Ezra gave a grudging nod. "Do what you can to deter, but prepare for the inevitable. So, funnel them where you want them. Pick your weakest point and be ready for them there, in a kill zone of your choice."

Logan raked a hand through his rumpled black hair. "I can get behind that."

"Where do we want them?" Park said. "I mean, where is this kill zone?"

"The back door is designed to be the weakest point of entry. The narrow twelve-foot hallway forces the intruders to enter single file, funneling them into a choke point. The attic entry is at the end of the hallway before the kitchen. I'll set up a defensive sniper position with sandbags and take them out from above. Any scumbag stupid enough to invade my home will get exactly what they deserve."

"Ideally, we kill them all before they reach the cabin," Julio said. "Right?"

"They won't get anywhere near the cabin," Ezra said. "They won't get the drop on me again. Trust me."

Dakota shook her head. Ezra was far too confident. "We underestimate them at our peril. They'll be furious that we killed their men. They'll come back hot, with all the fire and fury of hell at their backs."

Ezra absently rubbed the palm of his injured hand, a scowl deepening the wrinkles crisscrossing his face. "And we'll greet them with more."

"We have to be ready," Dakota said, despising the anxiety creeping into her voice.

Logan met her gaze, his expression grim. "We will be."

20

EDEN

"We need to talk," Dakota said. She wiped the sweat from her forehead with the back of her forearm and turned to face Eden. "This isn't a good time. There'll never be a good time. But you deserve to know the truth."

Eden nodded slowly. She knew what this meant. She'd been waiting for this conversation for three years.

This morning, everyone had woken up early, ready to fortify their defenses. Dakota, Ezra, Julio, and Eden were busy shoring up the cabin while Logan and Park patrolled the perimeter. Julio and Ezra worked on the east side while Dakota and Eden took the west side.

Eden knelt on the ground, already sweating at nine a.m. as she hammered long six-inch nails into thin slabs of plywood to create nail boards. Ezra had called it a punji trap, a booby trap commonly used by the Viet Cong during the Vietnam War.

In carefully chosen spots, Ezra and Julio were digging pits two feet deep and the width of a man's foot. They'd already dug a few holes beneath the windows on Eden's side.

"This is like the opposite of baby-proofing a house, you know that, right?" Park had said with a roll of his eyes before he'd left on patrol. She couldn't help herself; she'd laughed silently.

She didn't feel like laughing now. As the sweat dripped into her eyes and the heat sapped her energy, she just wanted to be done. The late-July air was hot and sticky. Clouds of tiny insects swarmed around her, no matter how often she swatted them away.

Dakota looked even more miserable. She wore thick, puncture-resistant gloves to handle the razor wire. She was working to string the razor wire along the inside frames of all the windows, attaching the wire with a heavy-duty staple gun.

Dakota set the staple gun on the windowsill. "If I don't—if I don't do it now, I'll let myself keep putting it off."

Eden hammered in the last nail for the board she was working on and examined it to make sure the vicious-looking nails were perfectly straight and deadly. They were.

With each board, she hammered in five or six spikes, then flipped the board over so the nails pointed toward the sky, fitted it in the bottom of the hole, and covered it with a paper-thin bamboo board. She replaced the top layer of grassy soil and sprinkled small twigs and leaf litter over it until it was completely camouflaged.

No one would guess that savage spikes waited to skewer any unsuspecting intruder's foot, puncturing through the sturdiest boot soles, deep into the flesh and bone. It wouldn't kill the Shepherds, but it'd disable and slow them down long enough for Ezra or Dakota to shoot them.

She forced herself not to shudder at the thought.

Her vision blurred for a moment as she stared at each sharpened nail. A part of her wished she could be doing something else, anything else. She'd rather be back inside practicing coded sentences on the radio.

After their meeting last night, Ezra had showed her how to use the CW key and started teaching her the Morse alphabet. She'd sketched out the alphabet in her drawing pad, just like she did with ASL. The dots and dashes weren't nearly as hard to memorize as she thought they'd be. He'd promised to teach her the shorthand Q-codes as soon as she was ready.

She'd chosen a code name—Rose. It was her foster mom's middle name. She missed Gabriella and Jorge so much that she dreamed about them sometimes. But the dreams always ended in a blinding white flash and a black mushroom cloud of destruction and death.

Nightmares had plagued her for weeks. Vivid, visceral night terrors that took her right back into the horror, to the pain and fear and confusion. Sometimes it was the blast. And sometimes, the nightmares were from before...

Bit by bit, that awful night from three years ago was coming back to her, in jagged pieces like some gruesome puzzle. She was remembering, whether she wanted to or not.

"I did it," Dakota said so quickly that Eden almost didn't hear her. "That night, it was my fault, what happened to you..."

You don't have to do this, Eden signed.

Dakota just stared at her.

Frustrated, she looked around for her notebook to write it down. She was used to her inability to speak, but sometimes it still sucked. She had so many things to say, but writing it all down or signing to someone who barely understood ASL left her feeling overwhelmingly inadequate.

Finally, Dakota shook her head as if she understood. "Yes, I do. I need to do this."

Eden settled back on her knees. The truth was, she was both desperate to know and desperately afraid. There was a simplicity in not knowing. A peace. But it wasn't a true peace. She knew that.

Tell me, she signed, touching her pointer finger to her chin and holding it out toward her sister. *Tell me everything.*

21

EDEN

Eden watched Dakota take a deep breath. "That night, Jacob dragged me to the mercy room. On his own, without orders from his father or the Prophet. That had never happened before. It was against the rules, but he was angry at me—furious.

"That day...I was working in the kitchen, clearing up after the men. He and Maddox and a few others were still finishing up their dinner. Sometimes, they liked to be slow so they could flirt with the girls when no one else was around. They might've been holy warriors chosen by God to rebuild the new earth, but they were still just guys, hot-blooded and horny like all the rest. They just had to hide it better.

"I was mopping the floor a few tables away when I heard Jacob say something about you. Something in the way he said it, like he was letting slip some juicy secret he wasn't supposed to tell—it caught my attention. I stepped in closer, keeping my head down, pretending to concentrate on my work. The guys were focused on Jacob. They were trained since birth to ignore women. They didn't even know I was there.

"Jacob started going on about their family being chosen for a great honor. He was all hush-hush about it, but the guys dragged it out of him. Of course, that was his plan all along, to make them feel special and accomplished, that they were in on the secret with him. It deepened their connection to him, their unquestioning loyalty. Just another way Jacob constantly manipulated everyone around him."

Eden gave an almost imperceptible shake of her head. That wasn't the Jacob she remembered—the laughing, bright-eyed, golden-haired brother who adored her, who told her fabulous stories and always brought her a piece of forbidden candy, a special treat shared just between them.

As if she could read Eden's mind, Dakota frowned. "He was charming for a reason, Eden. And Jacob Cage never did anything without a reason."

Eden pressed her lips together, wanting to argue, but she was resolved to listen to all of it, even the crazy, unbelievable parts, even the ugly parts.

"He finally leaned in, all excited and secretive, and told them the Prophet had chosen you as his seventh bride. That the marriage was some huge symbol bestowed by God Himself to represent the beginning of the Shepherds of Mercy's reign in the United States—but more importantly, it would solidify the Cage family's power as the Prophet's right hand."

She gave a bitter laugh. "Politics will exist in their new world just like it does in the old. They believe this heavenly utopia will be perfect, but they're corrupt humans, so how could they do anything but corrupt it?"

Eden didn't have an answer for that. She'd grown up believing in the Prophet's power, in faith that the Prophet would bring about the new Jerusalem, a Garden of Eden here in America that would birth the New Earth of biblical prophecy.

She'd believed it with her whole heart. And why not? No one had ever told her any differently.

Until she left the compound at twelve, she'd never seen a TV or a magazine, or set foot in a real school, a mall, a playground, a city. She'd been taught that the world outside was pure evil, full of the demon-possessed wicked souls whose only purpose was to corrupt her into the pits of hell—the depraved, the degenerates, the lecherous and deviant.

For months after she'd left, she used to hear the Prophet in her head, booming his dreadful proclamations and prophecies, his sinister warnings of fire and brimstone, the very pits of hell yawning open to devour anyone who strayed from The Way even a little.

At first, she'd been afraid to believe anything anyone outside the compound said. Heathens and heretics lied with every breath. She'd feared Ezra, thought he'd kill her in her sleep.

Later, during their weeks on the streets, the fear had nearly overwhelmed her.

It was only after months of Dakota explaining that everyone outside the compound wasn't evil that Eden began to listen, and it wasn't until her foster parents, Gabriella and Jorge, that she truly believed it.

Still, it was almost a year before she got over her terror of cracking open the spine of a book or watching a show on TV, positive that at any moment, the wrath of God would descend upon her in a reign of bloody fire.

She could still see the fervent, fevered passion in the Prophet's face as he gripped the pulpit, features rigid and drenched in sweat, eyes bulging as he pelted them with dire warning after dire warning of what was certain to become of them if they gave in to the sins of blasphemy, of pride, of arrogance, and selfishness.

They will destroy your mind and rip apart your body, and your soul will burn in eternal hellfire...

She shivered despite the heat. It didn't matter that she hadn't seen or heard him in almost three years. It was like he was right there in front of her, engulfing her in terror, his eyes piercing her very soul, judging her fitness for eternal salvation and finding her wanting.

22

EDEN

Eden watched as Dakota stared off at some distant spot on the horizon, caught up in her own horrible memories.

"When I heard what Jacob was saying, when I realized he meant you were going with the Prophet, that your father and brothers were just going to let you go..." Dakota shook her head. "I lost it. This...rage came over me. I forgot all my training, all the punishments, all the trips to the mercy room meant to break me and remake me into something meek and compliant—it all burned away. I was livid. Furious. More angry than I'd ever been in my life.

"I marched up to them and confronted Jacob. 'How could you?' I screamed. 'How could you do that to your own sister?' The other guys just sat there, shocked.

"Maddox—I remember his face. The way his eyes blazed, but his mouth pinched into a flat line. He had this tight, trapped expression he got sometimes when his father was lecturing him or he was being publicly reprimanded—he wasn't happy about your fate, either, but he was helpless to do anything. And he hated that he was helpless. There's nothing Maddox hates more than feeling impotent.

"But Jacob, though... He stood up, knocked over his chair, infuriated—and embarrassed—at how I'd dared to speak to him. The others were watching to see what he'd do. He grabbed my arm and slapped me across the face. But that wasn't enough. Not for someone like Jacob.

"He was all charm and light on the surface—his father's chosen son, the firstborn, like an angel sent to Earth to save us all. That's how everyone treated him. The Sisters all adored him because he always stopped to chat and reminisce with them. He'd carry a laundry load for a few minutes or wash a frying pan while he flattered their cooking.

"The children worshipped him because he didn't ignore them like the other older boys they longed to emulate. He'd tell them a joke and laugh with them, pick up the little girls and spin and twirl them until they choked on their own giggles. Remember that?"

How could she ever forget? Dakota's assessment wasn't far off. These were all the things Eden recalled with fondness about her oldest brother, too.

"Maddox loved him. Loved him and resented him at the same time. But Jacob treated him like crap, like something he wanted to scrape off his shoe. Though only when no one else was around.

"Those boys, those sons of Solomon Cage, they wore masks, both of them. Maddox to survive that hateful place. Jacob so he could curry the adoration he craved while still feeding his streak for cruelty. They both developed a cruel streak. It was beaten into them, I guess."

It was true that Maddox had been cunning, often snide and deceitful, prone to rages that made him dangerous. He'd struck her more than once when they were young.

But in his own way, he always came skulking back to apologize, offering her candy he'd stolen from Sister Rosemarie's stash to make it up to her.

Jacob, though...

Eden shook her head, wanting to disagree with Dakota, to tell her she was wrong about him, but frenetic images filled her head—Jacob seizing her arm, leaving bruises in the shape of fingers. Jacob leaning in close, hissing, *Look what you made me do.*

Once, Jacob had left a gun outside instead of cleaning it and putting it away; Eden had watched him come inside without it. When it was found in the woods a week later, filthy and covered with dirt, leaves, and bugs, Jacob had immediately blamed Maddox.

Maddox's screams of outrage had done nothing; he'd been dragged to the mercy room, receiving the whipping instead of his brother.

Another memory came to her then: she and Jacob strolling alone in the woods, checking Jacob's traps. She must have been eight or nine, for she remembered wearing the soft daffodil yellow dress that tickled her ankles, an eighth birthday gift from the Prophet.

They'd come across a young gray fox with its bloody paw caught in the metal trap. Blood stained its muzzle; in its desperation to escape, it'd attempted to chew its own paw off.

Eden wanted to ask him to let it go, but she knew better. God gave them the creatures of the Earth to rule over for this very reason—for pleasure, sustenance, and dominance.

"Kill it quickly," she pleaded.

Jacob only smiled. He squatted in a clear spot between two stubby pine trees and watched in fascination as the fox struggled, suffering.

Something about the way Jacob looked—his eyes so bright, his gaze intense, that pleasant smile still on his face, like he was enjoying it—sent a sickening jolt through her, made her stomach churn uneasily and her skin prickle.

Eden turned her eyes away. She was crying, begging him to put a stop to it. He ignored her. After thirty minutes of agony for both Eden and the fox, Jacob finally pulled the hunting knife he kept sheathed at his waist and slit the animal's throat.

"Thank—" Before she could get the words out, he turned and cuffed her so hard her ears rang.

"Look what you made me do!" he snarled.

By the time they'd returned home, he was all smiles, jovial and laughing, the brother she knew and loved again. She didn't tell her father, her stepmother, or Maddox about the fox. She didn't tell anyone.

She hadn't known how to tell them. She knew she'd be admonished for even mentioning it. She did the only thing she could—she buried the awful memory down deep and never thought of it again.

She never asked to walk with Jacob to check his traps again.

Eden looked up. Dakota was watching her. "You remember something."

She remembered everything.

The heat and the bugs and the trees and the cabin disappeared. Everything faded away beneath an onslaught of memories.

23

EDEN

In her memory, Eden was carrying a basket loaded with clean, freshly washed and dried linens from the laundry lines to the single men's bunkhouses to change their sheets—when she saw them.

Dusk was falling. Bats swooped over the trees in the indigo sky, devouring the mosquitos that plagued them. To the south, the water lay still and placid, unbroken but for the occasional splash of a fish. The croaking of bullfrogs and the buzz of cicadas filled the hot evening air.

She was sweating beneath her long skirt and button-up blouse, but at least her restrictive clothing kept some of the bugs at bay. She paused and pressed the basket against her side so she could free one hand to rub her sore, aching head.

Her stepmother, Sister Hannah, had bound her waist-length hair into a French braid as usual. When she was angry or frustrated, which was often, she would bind it so tightly that Eden's scalp would burn all day. Today was one of those days.

Before she could resume her task, something snagged her attention. Across the wide clearing with the firepit, the Adirondack chairs, and the picnic tables, she caught the flash of familiar blond hair and broad shoulders. Her brother, Jacob.

He was striding toward the mercy room, a plain cement block building next to the infirmary. He was dragging someone with him, gripping a hank of her hair. The girl stumbled behind him.

Eden adjusted her grip on the laundry basket, waved the mosquitos out of her face, and glanced around. The clearing was empty. All the adults were in the chapel for Wednesday night prayer meeting, except for the patrols along the perimeter fence and the sentries in the guard platforms at the front gate.

Jacob should be in the chapel, but he wasn't.

She'd seen plenty of people brought to the mercy room for various punishments, but it was always supervised by her father or the Prophet. Not like this.

The hairs on her neck prickled. Something was wrong.

Eden took a tentative step closer, squinting in the gathering gloom to make out the figures, and sucked in a sharp breath.

She recognized Dakota's reddish auburn hair. She was pulling away, writhing and grasping at Jacob's hands like she was trying to escape.

Eden twisted around, looking again for someone, anyone, to give her direction, to tell her what was supposed to be happening, to either stop this or give their blessing to allow it to continue.

A hundred yards away, light emanated from the opened cafeteria doorway.

She recognized the lean, wiry frame of her other brother standing in the doorway, the light glowing around him like a halo. His hands hung limp at his sides.

Maddox just stood there, staring out into the night.

She shifted her gaze back to Jacob and Dakota. Jacob fished his keys out of his pocket—Eden heard the jingle, heard Dakota give a low moan that sent shivers up and down her spine.

Into the Fire

Jacob unlocked the door, hauled Dakota inside the mercy room, and shut the door quietly but firmly behind him.

Eden tightened her grip on the basket. For several long, eternal minutes, she stood without moving, full of indecision. She should go straight to the men's cabins. She should finish her work quickly and hurry to the chapel, where she was expected.

That's what she should do, what she was supposed to do.

This was none of her business, none of her concern.

Her brother was a Shepherd, the chosen among the chosen, set apart by the Prophet and God himself. Who was she to question his actions?

But the sound Dakota had made...

She longed to ignore it, to just walk away. Push it out of her mind like a thousand other things she made herself forget or ignore.

She could get close, just walk by. It wouldn't break any rules. She wasn't doing anything wrong.

Her feet moved almost against her own volition, swishing through the grass still wet from the major storm that had ripped through the Glades earlier in the day. An owl hooted from the cypress trees.

The frogs were in full-throated singing mode. The trills of birds and insects followed her as she crept closer.

The clean sheets in her arms smelled of the lemon soap she'd used to scrub them. Dakota had helped her even though she had her own chores to finish. Dakota was her friend. Dakota looked out for her when no one else did.

Eden shuffled closer, the low concrete building looming larger and larger, menacing and dangerous.

She stood in front of the door and listened to her own rapid breathing. How many times had she watched people enter that door hunched and sorrowful, and exit slumped and weak, trembling and weeping, sometimes unconscious?

She'd never questioned it.

Never, not until now. The way Jacob had moved—stalking angrily, but also furtively, like he didn't want anyone to see. Like he was doing something wrong.

She could still turn away. She could still forget she'd seen anything.

Slowly, she lowered the laundry basket. She reached out and touched the door handle, half-expecting it to be locked.

It wasn't. In his haste, Jacob had neglected it.

Eden turned the handle and opened the door.

24

EDEN

Eden moved silently into the mercy room and closed the door behind her. The stale air stank of sweat and charred coals, bleach and something else, something sharply metallic she could almost taste on her tongue.

Her veins turned to ice as her gaze skipped from bare wall to floor to bare wall, the stoked fireplace, the lantern hanging from the ceiling —her mind lurching away from the brown stains on cement, from the things she was too terrified to truly see.

But she knew.

Of course, she knew.

Hadn't she cared for Dakota a dozen times at Sister Rosemarie's side? Hadn't she seen the stripes scarring Maddox's back? She knew, but she didn't want to know.

Her brain couldn't handle the knowing.

Someone moaned in the center of the room. Jacob was bent over the girl—Dakota. This was happening to Dakota. Her blouse was ripped, the tank top beneath torn, her shoulders and back bare.

Jacob held her face-down against the tall table with one hand, bracing his body against her to keep her in place. With his other hand, he pressed something against the bare skin of her upper back over her left shoulder blade.

A lit, red-hot cigar.

Eden screamed.

Startled, Jacob whipped toward her. His beautiful, angelic face contorted in rage. "Get out!"

"Stop!" she begged him. "Please stop!"

"You don't belong here. Get the hell out!"

Eden kept her gaze pinned on her brother. Fear and dread and confusion tangled in her gut. She couldn't explain it, but she knew. She knew in the deepest part of herself that this shouldn't be happening.

In the corner of her eye, she saw Dakota wrench free of Jacob's distracted grip. She rolled off the table and stumbled to the floor. She crouched, gasping and trembling.

"I'll—I'll tell Father," Eden said, but her voice was weak and hesitant. She was scared, and Jacob knew it. Her threat was an empty one.

"Be careful, sister, what you say." He took a step toward her, bristling with hostility. "Blasphemy is a grave sin."

"I'm...I'm not..." Eden stammered.

Behind him, Dakota rose to her feet. "You can't do this."

Jacob sneered. "I can do whatever the hell I want."

Dakota lunged at Jacob. For a second, Eden thought she was going to shove him from behind, but instead she seized the hunting knife from its sheath at his belt and sprang backward, out of his reach.

She pointed the knife at him. "Stay back!"

Jacob barely acknowledged her. "Put the knife down, little girl."

"You aren't giving Eden to the Prophet. I won't let you."

He only laughed. "And what're you going to do about it?"

"I'll..." Dakota's wild gaze darted around the room, searching for an escape. There wasn't one, not with Jacob between her and the door. Her eyes returned to Jacob. There was something frantic but resolute in her expression. "I'll take her myself. We'll leave."

"And what makes you think we'll ever let her go?" He turned back to Eden and gestured at the door. A shadow flitted behind his eyes, a flash of something cold and dangerous. "Get out of here. You don't want to see what happens next. I'll deal with you later, after I tell Father and the Prophet what you've done."

His words were meant to fill her with shame and terror. They did.

"Don't move, Eden," Dakota said, the huge knife gripped in both hands. "We're going. Both of us. Tonight."

Jacob paid her little attention. She was just a girl, bred to submit and serve. Jacob didn't even see her. Not really. Just like he barely saw Eden.

"Leave or suffer the consequences of disobedience, sister," Jacob spat, more furious than she'd ever seen him, his face red, his eyes bulging. "Or you know what? Maybe you both need to relearn your place."

Eden froze in indecision. Her gaze darted between her brother and her friend. She didn't understand what was happening. The words they spoke were a jumbled confusion in her head. She was only twelve. She didn't understand it.

But she did understand fear. She understood orders.

She moved toward the door.

"Let us both go," Dakota said. "No one needs to know."

"Never."

"I'd rather die than stay here."

"That can be arranged." Jacob took a menacing step toward Dakota, flexing his hands into fists. He didn't have a weapon, but he didn't need one. He towered over Eden and Dakota, strong and powerful and deadly.

He was right. He could do whatever he wanted to. An expectant, almost rapturous look transformed his face, a hard anticipation flashing in his eyes—he intended to enjoy every second of it.

Time slowed. Everything happened in awful slow motion.

Dakota let out a cry like a wounded animal and charged Jacob. He raised his hands in a defensive gesture, surprise registering on his face as he realized too late that she was attacking him.

She raised the knife, plunged it into his stomach, and wrenched it out.

Jacob groaned and staggered back. He looked down at himself, stunned, and pressed his hands against the wound. Dark red blood leaked between his fingers.

"No!" Eden cried.

Jacob was her brother. She loved him. She'd been raised since birth to adore and obey every man in her family. Instinctively, she ran to protect him.

Dakota's expression contorted in a rictus of panic, fear, and desperation. Maybe she saw Eden, maybe she didn't. Maybe in that moment she didn't care about anything but ending the threat standing between her and the door.

Without a sound, she lunged at him again, the blade flashing as she lashed out, the razor-sharp point ripping across his chest, tearing into flesh. Her arm fell back and surged forward, stabbing him again.

Eden heard nothing but the thunder of her pulse in her ears, felt only the ice-cold rush of fear through every cell of her body, had no thoughts in her head but *stop, stop, stop.*

She flung herself in front of her brother.

An excruciating pain seared across her throat. She fell against Jacob. His chest stuck wetly to her back.

Dakota froze, weapon half-raised. She released the knife. It clattered to the floor.

Jacob collapsed and lay still.

Eden collapsed on top of him, sliding sideways, both hands clasping at her neck. It was so slippery. That was her first thought. So slippery. Her finger sliding in the slick blood.

She couldn't get a good grip, couldn't stop it from leaking out.

A throbbing, pulsing agony filled her whole body.

"Eden!" Dakota screamed from far away. "Eden!"

Dakota fell to her knees beside her. She ripped off her blouse, already unbuttoned, and wrapped the fabric tightly around Eden's neck. She tied it in a clumsy knot. "Hold it tight, okay? Don't let go."

Stars danced across her vision. Eden opened her mouth. A wet, gurgling sound came out. *Help me!* she wanted to say. *Don't let me die. I don't want to die.*

"I'm getting you out of here! Just hold on!"

The door to the mercy room burst open.

25

EDEN

Through bleary eyes, Eden watched Maddox open the door and enter the mercy room.

His face went slack as he took in the blood sprayed across the floor, the knife, his brother's crumpled form.

"What did you do?" he asked, horrified.

Dakota knelt on the floor next to Eden, pressing the fabric against her neck. Her gaze darted to the bloody knife lying a few feet away. She closed her own fingers over Eden's, making sure Eden was holding tight. "What I had to do."

She stood on shaky legs and faced Maddox. Her arms and chest were spattered with blood, both Jacob's and Eden's.

"Is...is he...dead?" Maddox's voice filled with despair.

Dakota glanced down at Jacob's body and grimaced. She raised her gaze to Maddox and lifted her chin defiantly, her eyes flashing, fierce and resolute. "Yes."

"You...you killed him."

"Yes."

"Why?"

"You know what they're going to do to her. You were right there.

All the crap that goes on here, all the horrible things they've done to me...to you...what they've done to us..." She sucked in a deep breath. "Not to her, you understand? I won't let it happen to her."

Eden's vision swam in and out of focus. Sounds faded, then returned. She felt the hard cement on her back, smelled the metallic scent of her own blood, tasted the copper on the back of her tongue.

Maddox took a step toward Dakota.

Dakota dove for the knife. She grabbed it and came up in a crouch, her eyes wild. "Don't make me do this! I don't want to do this."

"I trusted you!"

She stood over Jacob's body like a bloody, avenging angel. Eden blinked. Her mind was filling with fog, her vision shimmering. It was still Dakota. But maybe the angels would be coming for them soon, to take them both to Heaven...

"Just turn around and go away, Maddox," she said. "Walk away. That's all you have to do."

He stared at her—anger, grief, and betrayal shadowing his eyes. Conflicted, his hands balled into fists at his sides. For a moment, Eden thought maybe Maddox would kill them both. Maybe it would be a blessing, an end to the pain.

Maddox stepped out of the way. "If I ever see you again, I'll kill you."

Dakota dropped the knife. She crouched beside Eden to lift her to her feet. "I know."

And then everything faded away for good—the mercy room, Jacob's body, Maddox's tortured face, the blood everywhere.

Eden could only recall snatches of their frantic escape: the airboat ride, the struggle through the woods, finding Ezra's place, collapsing on the shed floor. The next thing Eden remembered was swimming up from deep unconsciousness, awakening on Ezra's leather couch to a fiery pain in her throat and the inability to speak.

Now she was back at Ezra's in the middle of the Everglades, kneeling with the grass tickling her knees, hammer in one hand, a pile of nail boards at her feet, the unrelenting heat of the sun beating down on her head and shoulders.

Dakota faced her, guilt and remorse etched across her features. "I could've stopped. Jacob wasn't a threat to us anymore after that first attack. I could've grabbed you and run. But I didn't. I was so angry. So many years and years of abuse and pain and humiliation...

"I...I wanted to kill him, Eden," Dakota said dully. "I lost control. I was so focused on killing him that I didn't think about consequences or repercussions or anyone or anything except what I wanted. I didn't think about you. I didn't remember that you were there until you stepped in front of him.

"My arm was already moving, I couldn't stop myself...I couldn't stop..." She took a deep, ragged breath. "I stabbed you, Eden. And you can't say it was an accident, because I chose to keep going. I chose to murder Jacob when I didn't have to. I nearly killed you. You have that scar because of me. You lost your voice because of me."

Instinctively, Eden's fingers rose to the ridge of scar tissue at her throat. It was true, everything Dakota said.

But at the same time, it wasn't.

Once, she would've hated Dakota for what she'd done. For hurting her, for killing Jacob, for stealing her from what remained of her family and the only life she'd ever known.

But that wasn't fair. Things weren't black and white. There was another side to the story.

She'd lived outside the compound for three years. First with Ezra, then with her foster parents Jorge and Gabriella, two people who'd shown her what life could be like, who truly loved her.

She'd experienced enough of life to recognize the truth from lies.

She couldn't be a confused, frightened kid anymore. She had to grow up, to see reality for what it was. She couldn't cling to the rosy, idealized image of her childhood and family—which she knew in her heart of hearts hadn't been real in the first place.

Jacob, the golden-haired charmer, was a secret sadist. Something ugly had lived inside him, something bad and rotting.

It was inside Maddox, too. And it lurked inside her father, inside the Prophet, and inside everyone who chose to cut themselves off from the world, feeding on hatred and contempt but calling it by another name.

It didn't matter how it disguised its true nature—evil was evil. And sometimes, evil wasn't the thing you thought it was.

Sometimes, people had to do bad things to survive. That didn't make them bad or evil. Those who chose to hurt and control others because they could, because it gave them power over the powerless—that was evil.

Maybe Eden couldn't speak because of Dakota's actions, but she was alive and free because of her. At the compound, she may have been able to speak, but she hadn't had a voice.

Now, she did.

"I would never try to hurt you," Dakota whispered, tears in her eyes. "Never, ever."

Eden stood. She dropped the hammer in the grass and ran to Dakota. She wrapped her arms around her, buried her head against Dakota's chest, and took in the strong, steady beat of her sister's heart.

26

SHAY

"How are you doing?" Hawthorne asked.

"Good," Shay answered automatically, forcing a brightness into her voice she didn't feel.

"Don't give me that B.S. Not a single person in the entire country is 'good' right now." Hawthorne leaned forward and gave a slight shake of his head. "How are you really doing?"

She swirled her French fry in a glob of ketchup but couldn't bring herself to eat it. Normally she loved food, but she hadn't had much of an appetite in weeks. She was exhausted, weary to her very bones.

Surrounded by so much suffering and death, it was nearly impossible to summon the positive energy she usually thrived on. Instead of healing people, she was working an enormous morgue, putting band-aids on gushing wounds and waiting for people to die.

She'd worked back-to-back eighteen-hour shifts, barely eating or sleeping, until Hawthorne had forcibly pulled her away for a bit of respite and a hot meal at the Chili's in Concourse G at the Miami International Airport.

She dropped the fry and pushed her plate away, leaving half a grilled chicken sandwich. She was grateful she had food at all—she'd seen the reports coming in from towns and cities full of grocery stores with barren shelves. And now there were curfews and martial law to go along with the hunger, grief, and desperation.

"I'm sorry again for skipping out on you yesterday," she said again.

"Never mind that." Hawthorne was looking intently at her. Even tired, Trey Hawthorne was still incredibly handsome. He was 6'4, with a lean, athletic body and warm brown skin to go with his chiseled cheekbones, intelligent dark eyes, and wide disarming smile. "You're not okay."

Shay gave a resigned sigh, tucked her thick, springy curls behind her ears, and adjusted her glasses. "This morning, I sat next to a four-year-old boy whose mother had just died a horrific death from acute radiation sickness. His father never made it to the EOC. The kid has nowhere to go. No family to claim him."

"I'm so sorry. What will happen to him?"

"I don't know. DCF—Department of Children and Families—sent someone to pick him up a few hours ago. The social worker said they're overwhelmed with orphans. They don't have enough foster or group homes functioning..."

She inhaled sharply to keep her emotions at bay. If she fell apart, it would be that much harder to put herself back together. "He'll probably have to go to the FEMA camps, like everyone else. He'll end up helpless, completely alone, and traumatized for life."

Sometimes the suffering and heartbreak just became too much.

"I'm really sorry, Shay," Hawthorne said quietly.

"And I have this friend, Nicole. I'm really worried about her." After the shift Shay had finished for her yesterday, Nicole had returned to work, but she'd barely spoken to Shay. The woman did her work mechanically, a numbed blank look on her face, her eyes dulled.

"What's wrong with her?"

Shay had seen that look before, in her father during his dark times. It was a look of hopelessness, of despair. Despondency. "She's depressed. Honestly, I'm seeing a lot of that. People have this look...it's like they're not really there anymore. They're still alive, but they've already given up, you know?"

"The psychological toll. It's not something people talk a lot about, but the mental health fallout from this is going to be horrendous."

Shay nodded. Memories of her father flooded in, painful memories she didn't want to think about right now.

"How are your friends in the Everglades?" Hawthorne asked, to distract her.

"At least they're doing good. I talked to Julio last night. They're at the cabin, though they had to fight some bad guys to make it."

Hawthorne smiled. "I bet they did just fine. Logan and Dakota know how to handle themselves."

"They're survivors. And good people." She already missed them, especially Julio's steady, calm nature. And she would love Dakota forever for saving her life.

She was grateful they had the satellite phone to communicate, especially since regular cell phones were crap right now.

Dozens of cell towers were damaged. Websites took forever to load, if they even did. The servers were located in major metropolitan cities, many of them hot zones of rubble or evacuated ghost cities.

At least there were a few news channels still reporting. The TV screen over the bar ran a constant barrage of horrifying images—footage of massive grave sites, highways crammed with stalled cars and the refuse of thousands of stranded refugees, aid workers combing through rubble, hospitals crammed with dying radiation patients, and armed soldiers and military vehicles rolling through American streets, enforcing martial law.

Hawthorne saw her watching and cleared his throat. "I got a little something for you." He pulled a pack of gum out of his pocket and handed it across the table. "I can't tell you how I scored it. That's a state secret."

She couldn't help it; she smiled. Hawthorne could always make her smile. She popped a piece in her mouth and savored the sharp,

Into the Fire

minty flavor before handing one to Hawthorne. "Spearmint. Great choice. Thank you."

Hawthorne took a piece and scrunched the wrapper into a little ball. He rolled it around on the table beneath his finger. "So, where would you be if you weren't here?"

"What do you mean?"

"Like, if the bombs hadn't happened. What would you be doing? What was your life like?"

A faint smile tugged at the corners of her lips. "I am—I was—a third-year nursing student at the U. I spent most of my time studying, honestly. I was blessed to get a scholarship, though I still worked twenty hours a week in the admin office. What about you?"

"Back in the day, I had an athletic scholarship to Florida State. Had a chance to go pro, even. Then a bum knee knocked me out of the game for good."

"Basketball?"

He grinned. "You'd think so, wouldn't you? No, it was table tennis."

She snorted a laugh around her gum. "What? That's not even a sport."

"Sure is. It's in the Olympics and everything."

"I'll take your word for it."

He shrugged. "It worked out for the best. I finished my criminal justice degree and got stationed in my home state. I love my job. Investigations, surveillance, kicking down doors. Every time I nail another drug or weapons dealer, it's another scumbag off the streets."

"Way better than the Olympics."

He chuckled. "Okay, back to you. How about music?"

"Of course." She flushed. "I actually, um, like country."

"No way."

"Yep. Guilty as charged. I love Tina Turner, Shania Twain, Charley Pride, and Garth Brooks. All the classics."

"Well, hey, I like Shania, too. There you go. Now I'm gonna have to take you to a concert." The light in his eyes dimmed a little. "After things get back to normal, I mean."

A cold chill crept over her. Her gum lost its flavor. "Are things going to go back to normal? I mean, can they?"

"I don't know," he said, growing serious again. "I really don't know."

She looked out the window at all the grounded planes sitting on the tarmac. Dozens of planes just sitting there, with nothing to do and nowhere to go. Tears stung her eyes. It was getting harder and harder to forget, for even a moment, what things were like now.

"How can it get so bad so quickly?" she asked.

"Transportation of goods is the lifeblood of this country," he said. "Without it, everything grinds to a halt. Our major ports are crippled. Most of our highways are still clogged with millions of stalled cars. Heck, in the first week, hospitals ran out of basic supplies. Gas stations ran out of fuel. ATMs and banks are running out of cash or refusing to process transactions. Have you seen the news footage of the garbage mountains piling up in some cities? In three weeks. It's crazy."

"What about the aid from other countries?"

"It's going directly to the FEMA camps full of millions of refugees. But the millions more still living in towns and cities across the U.S. are the ones in serious trouble. Hundreds of manufacturing plants were burned to the ground or contaminated in the blasts. Without a means of production or a functioning method to deliver the goods that hundreds of millions of people depend on, America will slide into a medieval reality."

"But that seems so...impossible."

Hawthorne gave a helpless shrug. "Ask Venezuela how impossible it is."

She pressed her fingers against her closed eyelids, forced herself to breathe deeply, to accept this terrible new reality. "I know. You're right."

"My uncle always said Americans had grown too soft. We've

gotten complacent and too dependent on our comforts. Most people never had to deal with anything like this. They're used to everything on demand at a moment's notice. I'm afraid we don't have the knowledge or the fortitude to adapt to this harsh new world."

She swallowed hard, accidentally swallowing her gum, too. The enormity of the situation was mind-boggling. Her brain kept wanting to shy away from the facts, to believe Hawthorne was exaggerating, to wrap herself in a bubble of oblivion.

That was what her mother had done her entire life. Shay couldn't do the same. Denial only did more damage in the end. If she was going to get through this, she needed to face it head-on.

But that didn't mean she was going to give up, either.

"Then we'll just have to learn." She lifted her chin, her chest swelling with fresh determination. "We'll get stronger and tougher."

Hawthorne flashed her a brilliant smile. "I like the way your mind works."

"We'll make it," Shay said. "There's no other option."

27

MADDOX

"There you go," Sister Rosemarie said.

Maddox sat stiffly on the edge of the bed, angled sideways and leaning forward, his fingers clawing the sheets into his fists as he bit back a growl of pain.

Sister Rosemarie stood behind him, administering strips of cloth soaked in some topical antibiotic over the fresh slashes striping his bare back. Her little apprentice, a quiet black girl named Ruth, was helping soak the cloth.

"Done yet?" he hissed.

"Patience, Maddox," Sister Rosemarie admonished him. "Isn't that what I always taught you?"

"I have a task to accomplish. Haven't you heard?"

Her hands stilled against his back. "I've heard...rumors."

"They're true. I have my orders from the Prophet himself."

"It's only been two days since the mercy room, Maddox. And you have radiation sickness besides. Surely, it's too soon—"

Maddox jerked away from her. Gritting his teeth at the pain searing his back, he forced himself to stand. He would endure it like he'd endured everything else.

His body might be battered and bruised, but he was still standing, which was more than half of Miami could say for itself. His pain made him stronger than anyone else, even the Chosen among the Shepherds.

He raised himself to his full height and loomed over Sister Rosemarie and tiny Ruth, who only came up to his elbows. Ruth shrank back against the Sister's side.

She feared him. Good. Let her be afraid. She should be.

The Shepherds of Mercy were a force to be reckoned with. They'd irrevocably changed the landscape of America forever. And they weren't finished yet.

"This is my God-ordained mission," he said. "The sooner I get Eden back, the sooner the Prophet can marry her and receive the Lord's blessing for the next stage of New America."

The woman looked like he'd slapped her. She stared at him, blinking hard, her lips pursed. She recovered quickly. "You aren't ready yet. Maddox, you're still weak—"

"Don't call me weak!" he screamed in her face.

She didn't flinch. "You need to recover your strength fully."

"Haven't you been listening? There's no time." He still had three days, but there was no reason to tell her that. "The next step is already in motion. Bring me my shirt," he snapped to the girl. She scurried across the room to the counter, retrieved his neatly folded army-green shirt, and brought it to him.

He snatched it from her hands and shrugged it on, wincing. As Ruth reached up to help tug it down, her fingers grazed one of his wounds. Fresh pain seared through him.

Maddox pivoted and backhanded her across the face.

She stumbled back, nearly falling over her long skirt, one hand pressed to her cheek, her mouth a round, startled O. Tears brimmed in her eyes.

"Are you stupid, girl? Don't touch me!" he hissed through his teeth. "Get the hell out!"

Sister Rosemarie steadied Ruth and patted her shoulder gently. "Go, child. Get some lunch and bring me an extra wedge of that delicious wheat bread your mother makes, okay?"

The girl nodded and fled the room, barely closing the door behind her.

"You didn't have to do that," Sister Rosemarie said. "She was just trying to help."

"She deserved worse." He jerked his shirt down and smoothed the wrinkles. "You should train your apprentice better. The next Shepherd in here won't be as kind or accommodating as I am."

Sister Rosemarie bit her lip as though she had plenty more to say, but needed to restrain herself. Finally, she gave a resigned sigh. "When are you leaving?"

"Whenever I choose to do so."

"Maddox, please. Think this through."

For a moment, he softened. As a child, he'd adored this woman. With his own mother dead and his stepmother cruel and dispassionate, he'd sought affection from wherever he could get it.

Sister Rosemarie had always been patient with him, had shown him kindness and mercy—real mercy—on many occasions. She'd endured his cruel streak, his temper tantrums, his reckless disobedience. Even while disciplining him, somehow she'd never made him feel lesser or unworthy.

"Don't make me do something I'll regret," he said softly.

She clenched her hands in front of her long, dusky blue skirt until her knuckles whitened. But she didn't look afraid—she looked determined. "You'll regret *this*, son. I can promise you that."

Anger flashed through him, obliterating whatever warmth and affection he'd just felt. She was just a woman. She had no right to give him advice like she knew better than him, like God and the Prophet hadn't chosen *him* for a special purpose.

Suddenly, the room was too small. The walls were closing in on him. He couldn't breathe properly. There wasn't enough air.

"You don't have to do this, Maddox. You can let them both go. You can figure out a way to let them escape and get your father's men off their trail. You're smart enough. I know you are."

"Don't you dare tell me what to do, woman. Your words are the words of a heretic."

She shook her head adamantly, strands of gray hair slipping from her bun and falling around her worn, weathered face. "God is a god of love. Of love! He would never ask you to do this."

He shot her a derisive glare. "One day, your blasphemy will cost you."

"One day, your arrogance will cost *you*, Maddox. Your pride is getting in the way. I know you know the truth." Her voice lowered, her intense gaze wild with desperation. "You're smarter than this. You've always been too smart to be taken in by pretty words and promises of grandeur. You know the truth about your father, about the Prophet."

He should report her for that. He had every right. More, it was his holy duty.

What would the Prophet do to her? Probably order her to be whipped or scalded to within an inch of her life. She'd never stand straight again.

Part of him wanted to see her get her just desserts for all the doubt and confusion she incited inside him, for the weakness of his own treacherous emotions. "Shut up! Just shut up."

But she didn't. She took another step toward him, determined and relentless. "I helped raise you. I know you better than anyone. There's a conscience inside you."

"You don't know anything."

"I know you still care about what happens to Eden." She reached out and dared to lay her hand on his shoulder. "And Dakota."

He flinched from her touch. Her fingers burned like the radiation, but so did the guilt. His mind flashed to his sister—her soft, eager smile, those blond curls and vivid blue eyes, the way she'd adored him no matter what he did to her.

And then he thought of Dakota. He swallowed the acid stinging the back of his throat. Dakota's fate was sealed. The words of a silly old woman didn't matter. Even if he wanted to change things, the path was set in stone now.

And yet...

No. There was no second-guessing things, no place for doubt. Doubt was a flaw, a defect he couldn't allow himself to tolerate. Not for a Chosen one.

"Maddox," Sister Rosemarie said, a pleading in her voice he'd never heard before. "Please. You know what's right."

She was just a woman. She didn't know a damn thing.

"Shut up!" Maddox took a swift step back, jerking the old woman's hand off his shoulder.

Dizziness washed over him. His gut clenched with undulated waves of sour nausea. He sank back onto the bed, flushed and weak.

He wouldn't be leading any holy missions today. But there was always tomorrow, and the day after that.

He imagined Dakota on the other side of this damn swamp, waiting for him to come for her—stressed, anxious, and terrified, never knowing when he would strike. She'd be thinking of him, every second of every day.

Another day or two might be a good thing. He could take his time, make her suffer. The more stressed and tired she was, the more likely she'd make a mistake. He imagined her defeated, begging for her life, completely under his control.

He closed his eyes—shutting out Sister Rosemarie, shutting out the pain, shutting out everything but Dakota.

28

EDEN

The next day, Eden spent most of the morning checking the ham radio frequencies and practicing Morse code. She was getting pretty good at the code, and she enjoyed it.

Like sign language, it was another way for her to speak without words. Maybe substituting dots and dashes and units of duration for letters came easier when you were used to finding alternative methods to communicate.

After a late lunch, Eden made lemonade with freshly squeezed lemons, sugar, and filtered water from the pump, and brought the tray outside to the others. Beneath the spreading live oak draped with Spanish moss, Ezra, Logan, and Park sat at a picnic table a hundred feet from the dock and the fishing boat.

It was the only big tree Ezra allowed in the clearing. He liked it too much to cut down, he'd told Eden once.

Ezra had covered the picnic table with newspapers and set out their array of weapons for cleaning, inspection, and field stripping practice. His security video monitor lay beside him, the small screen divided into quadrants that showed different parts of the property.

Dakota was across the clearing at Ezra's makeshift range, practicing with the AR-15, aiming at various paper targets tacked to haybales stacked at fifty, one hundred, and one hundred and fifty yards. Her hair was pulled back in a ponytail, a pair of noise-canceling headphones over her ears.

Eden handed out the cold, sweating glasses.

"Thanks." Park sipped his and gave her a thumbs-up sign. "It's good."

Logan swallowed his down in several large gulps.

Dakota took a break from shooting and stalked over for a drink, her headphones around her neck, sweat gleaming on her forehead.

Eden motioned for Julio to come over too, which he did with a tired sigh, the satphone Hawthorne had given him in one hand. "I got ahold of my wife and Shay. Everyone is okay. Things are getting pretty bad out there, though. And Shay's working herself too hard."

"That's not surprising at all," Park said with a roll of his eyes.

Dakota took a long swallow and set her glass down in the center of the table. "Shay's stronger than people give her credit for."

Eden nodded and signed, *I agree.*

Julio crossed himself and closed his eyes for a moment, like he was saying a prayer for Shay. Eden hoped he was. Shay was in the midst of the madness, trying her best to save people's lives. That made her a hero.

Eden waited respectfully for him to finish, then handed him a lemonade glass.

"Thank you so much, Eden," Julio said.

You're welcome, she signed.

Ezra glared at their sweating, empty glasses leaving rings on his newspapers. Eden swooped in and grabbed them up, stacking them on the tray balanced against her hip.

He gave her an indulgent smile. In that moment, with his furrowed brow lifted, his eyes gentled, he looked like a completely different person. Like the Ezra she remembered.

Into the Fire

She beamed back at him. She wanted to be useful, and she wanted him to be happy again. She hated all this tension between everybody.

"It's so hot out here, all I want to do is jump in that lake and cool off," Park said, gazing longingly at the placid, inviting water.

"You could, but you'd be swimming with that gator's momma." Dakota hooked her thumb at the three-foot gator sunning himself lazily on the grassy bank.

Park blanched. "Alligators aren't aggressive, not like crocodiles," he said, but he didn't sound convinced.

"Go ahead and test that theory out," Julio said. "We'll watch you from here."

"There are American crocodiles in the Glades," Dakota said. "They're rare, but we've got them. They're huge and ornery as hell. A giant fifteen-footer almost tipped my boat once."

Park shuddered. "Maybe I'll stay on dry land."

Ezra let out a derisive snort. He glanced up at Eden, and his expression softened. "Eden can draw gators better than anyone I've ever seen."

"Just don't get too close," Park muttered.

Her drawing pad and pencils lay on one end of the table, each pencil lined up neatly vertical in the center of the cover, waiting for her. Ezra had brought them out for her. Only Ezra would care about ordering the pencils.

But she didn't want to draw today.

She walked around the table and studied the mix of shotguns, rifles, and handguns, hesitantly at first, then with determination. They looked intimidating, but she wasn't a little kid anymore. It was time to grow up.

Last night, after she and Park had fed and watered the chickens and the rabbits, Ezra had put her to work in the ham shack, scanning the radio frequencies for updates on the outside world.

She wrote down everything she found, which Ezra reported to the rest of the group at dinner:

More rioting in Chicago, Atlanta, and dozens of other cities as food, water, and power remain unavailable...Nine soldiers and thirty-six civilians killed last night in armed altercations in Greater Miami... A hurricane swirling out in the Atlantic...President Harrington to recall one-hundred-and-fifty-thousand forward deployed troops, many of them stationed in Syria, to aid the recovery efforts and maintain martial law...

None of it was good. They'd been at Ezra's for four days in relative peace, but she knew things were still bad out there, and getting worse.

And she knew who was coming for her.

She wanted to be able to defend herself. She pointed at one of the shotguns and mimed shooting it at the target.

"No!" Dakota said at the same time Ezra said, "Yes."

I want to do my part, Eden signed.

"I can't learn ASL in a week, Eden," Dakota said. "I'm sorry, but I can't understand what you're saying."

Eden grabbed her notebook from the tray and wrote, *I want to help*, underlining *help*.

"It's too dangerous." Dakota shook her head emphatically. "Absolutely not."

Eden swallowed her frustration. Dakota wanted her to grow up and be brave, but when she tried, Dakota held her back.

It wasn't fair. It wasn't right.

Everyone else was putting themselves on the line to protect this place. Eden wanted to do her part. No, she *needed* to do her part.

Julio studied Dakota, his brow furrowed. "She's not as fragile as you think she is," he said gently.

Dakota scowled. "I know that, okay?"

Ezra finished field-stripping his Remington and set it carefully down on the table. He straightened the newspaper beneath it so it was perfectly square. "As I recall, when I took you out for the first time, you weren't much older than she is now. You did just fine."

"That was different," Dakota said without conviction, as if she wasn't even convincing herself but was too stubborn to give in.

"We need all hands on deck," Logan said. "She has every right to learn to defend herself, too."

Logan and Dakota exchanged looks. Eden expected Dakota to be angry at him for butting in, but she wasn't. She looked apprehensive, anxious, maybe a little sad.

Eden wrote, *I can do this*. She wasn't going to give in this time. She could be just as stubborn as Dakota. Even more, maybe. Without waiting for anyone's permission, she dropped the notepad on the table, grabbed the AR-15, and hefted it in her arms.

29

EDEN

Park snorted. "That thing's half as big as you are."
Eden glared at him. She would've signed, *So what?* But her hands were full.

"A .22 will work better for her," Ezra said. "Easier to handle, less kickback."

Dakota gave a resigned sigh. "Fine."

"I'll teach her," Logan said suddenly, rising from the picnic table bench.

Eden and Dakota looked at him in surprise. Ezra's scowl deepened.

He shrugged his broad shoulders self-consciously. "Someone's got to do it. And Ezra's busy. Come on."

He chose a small snub-nosed revolver and traded Eden for the AR-15. "A Ruger LCR 22 revolver. Six rounds, hardly any recoil."

She took the gun and followed him to the range, swatting away a swarm of tiny bugs, more nervous than she'd expected.

Logan was intimidating. He was an expert marksman, a trained fighter. She was just a clumsy girl who'd barely held a gun, let alone shot someone with it.

Logan threw her a rueful grin, like he was aware how uncomfortable they both were. "It's good to try new things, right?"

I guess so, she signed with a shrug.

His smile widened. He wasn't so intimidating when he smiled. She remembered their awkward conversations in the hospital, when he sat for hours by her bedside.

He must've remembered, too, because he said, "Pretend the target is a platter of spaghetti drenched in soy sauce and banana peppers."

She wrinkled her nose.

"Exactly. Nuke that thing from orbit."

Patiently, he instructed her how to stand with her legs shoulder-width apart, how to aim. "Make sure the gun's nice and steady. Make it stable. Make sure you have good sight alignment. Slow your breathing, control your heart rate—that'll help steady your nerves. When you're ready to fire, place the pad of your finger on the trigger and slowly build pressure, continuing to pull through after the shot's been fired. Squeeze, not pull, okay? You don't want to jerk the trigger and miss the target."

She hung on his every word.

"It's your turn," he said with a wry half-smile. "Go for it, kid."

She clasped the grip like Logan had shown her, with her index finger straight and well outside the trigger guard. She knew not to touch the trigger until she was ready to shoot something. She pulled her arms up and joined her hands together, her left beneath the grip to steady her aim.

The revolver was small and comfortable in her hands. She fit her finger in the curve of the trigger and squeezed. She barely felt the recoil. She didn't hit the target, but Logan was right—it was a good gun for her.

For the first hour, Eden mostly hit the haybales. By the end of the second hour, she'd punched several holes in the target.

With each squeeze of the trigger, she imagined herself growing stronger, braver, defeating nightmare after nightmare, until there were no fears left to overcome and she stood alone in the battlefield of her imagination.

They practiced for the rest of the afternoon, taking frequent breaks for more lemonade and copious amounts of Haasi's insect repellent spray. Logan never got irritated or short-tempered the way Dakota did.

"If we had a week, we'd make an expert marksman out of you," Logan said.

She grinned with pride. It felt like her first real smile since the blast.

The rumble of engines broke through the hot stillness.

Logan stiffened.

Eden shot him a questioning look.

"Sounds like trouble." Logan turned toward the noise, his hand already moving toward the pistol at his back.

30

LOGAN

The roar of the engines grew louder.

Logan hurried back to the picnic table, Eden trailing him.

"That must be the Colliers' patrol," Park said.

"They best not show their faces on my property again," Ezra growled.

Logan pulled out his pistol, racked the slide, and made sure a round was chambered. He holstered the pistol and grabbed his freshly loaded AR-15. The rifle was far more intimidating. "We should check it out."

Dakota jumped up. "I'm with you." She turned to Eden. "You stay here with Ezra. Keep practicing."

"We'll keep a close eye on her," Julio said, smiling warmly at Eden.

"Don't let them set foot on my land!" Ezra called after them.

They jogged the few hundred feet to the cabin and then beyond to the dirt driveway.

Dakota rolled her eyes. "He's like an old woman sometimes." She pitched her voice high and whiny. "You kids stay off my lawn!"

Logan gave a hard laugh, but his nerves were strung taut, the buzz of adrenaline coursing through his veins. He was fully alert, listening to the motorcycles drawing closer, aware of the heat shimmering the air, the still trees, the cabin, and the dirt road.

Nothing moved, no obvious threats presenting themselves.

He also found himself fully aware of Dakota only a foot away from him, her auburn hair bouncing in a high ponytail, her eyes shining, the sly, slightly mocking smile she gave him sending a jolt straight through to his core.

He couldn't help it; he liked that, liked her. Liked her stubborn tenacity, her courage, her resilience, her unerring dedication to saving people, even when it put herself in danger. This girl met everything and everyone with a level gaze, with grit and determination.

Dakota was someone you wanted at your side, watching your back.

It didn't matter that they'd only known each other for a matter of weeks—they'd gone through hell and made it out the other side. He didn't know her favorite color or her middle name, but he knew *her*, knew she was made of braver and tougher stuff than anyone he'd ever met.

The mayhem of Miami already seemed like a distant memory. What if they really could leave it all behind? They could survive forever out here, living off the land, keeping to themselves, protecting their own—together.

The thought was as pleasant as it was jarring. He had no business thinking of a future with anyone. Not with the knowledge of who he really was—the monster who'd done monstrous things—trapped inside him.

The one thing you could never leave behind was yourself.

"Hey," Dakota said. "You with me?"

He shook his head clear. Those thoughts were dangerous. That life was out of his reach and always would be. *She* was out of his reach.

The sooner he killed that yearning, the better off he'd be.

"I'm with you," he said, the irony of his words not lost on him.

Weapons drawn, they jogged past the gate and the truck barricade. A quarter mile down around a bend in the road, the Collier brothers appeared. The five burly men sat on their bikes, blocking the road with shotguns and rifles in hand, their backs to Logan and Dakota.

Thirty feet away, a group of bedraggled people huddled together—three men, two women, and two teenagers, a boy and a girl.

Archer hopped off his bike and strode forward, gesturing with the shotgun. "You're a long way from home."

A thick, blocky man with greasy brown hair, a bland pasty face, and a stubby mustache stepped back, clearly intimidated by Archer's imposing form. Sweat-stained dirt and dust smeared his creased khaki shorts, button-up shirt, and once-shiny dress shoes.

He held a Glock 17 in one fat sweaty hand, his finger too close to the trigger.

Not good.

The other two men had hunting rifles slung over their shoulders, and one of the women had a handgun tucked into the front of her waistband. The two kids and the dark-haired Asian woman standing a little behind the others appeared weaponless.

Logan and Dakota moved cautiously up to the Collier brothers. Boyd nodded at them in acknowledgment. Logan nodded back. He kept his gaze focused on the intruders and their hands, just in case.

"We're on our way to Naples, that's all," the man said. "No need to shove a gun in our faces for it."

"You're off course." Archer didn't lower his weapon.

"We—we got lost," the black man next to the first guy said. In his early thirties, small and wiry, the guy gave off a nervous, jumpy energy, constantly shifting from foot to foot, his gaze darting everywhere but at their eyes.

"Lost?" Jake snorted. "Awfully hard to get lost on a straight road."

Twitchy dropped his gaze. The heavy, pale one didn't. He stared straight at Archer, his eyes defiant, hard, and angry—like he blamed them personally for his misfortune.

"It happens," he said sullenly.

"We're hungry," one of the women said. She sported a fading Miami tan and dyed blond hair cut in a once-sleek bob that was ragged and unkempt. Her skinny legs beneath her cut-off jean shorts were covered in scratches and welts from dozens of bug bites.

"We haven't eaten all day," she whined. "The jerkwad who stole our car took everything but the clothes on our backs."

She squeezed the shoulder of the teenager closest to her, a pudgy fifteen-year-old boy with a wide moon face and a dull, stunned expression. He looked shell-shocked, like the trauma of leaving everything he'd ever known behind still hadn't worn off, and maybe never would.

"We've got kids," she said. "They need food."

"He looks like he could do without a few Big Macs and be fine," Zander quipped.

Zane let out a deep guffaw.

It wasn't that funny. The group of refugees didn't think so, either.

The woman's eyes narrowed. "You seem to be doing just fine out here yourselves."

Logan expected Dakota to offer them half their larder. She had a thing for saving people like lost kittens. But she didn't say anything. Her rigid stance radiated tension.

Maybe she'd changed her tune, or maybe there was something about these people she didn't like.

He felt the same way. Something was off about them, a warning niggling uneasily in his gut.

He knew their type. Upper middle-class shmucks with soft suburban lives and softer office jobs; steady, predictable, boring. They spent their lives worrying about inane things like weeds infesting their manicured lawns or whether the Dolphins would ever win another Super Bowl.

They probably hadn't lived like criminals before. Maybe they cheated on their taxes or their spouses, maybe they pilfered from the office expense account or ran red lights, but they didn't consider themselves bad or uncivilized.

But now, they were scared and hungry. They were tired and irritable and in pain.

Which meant they were capable of anything—just like everybody else in this new man-eat-man world.

31

LOGAN

"Let's start over," the hefty guy said. "We're not the enemy here. We're just regular people, that's all." He poked a fat finger at his chest. "My name is Sal. This is my wife, Brenda, and our son. This here's my brother, Vince, his wife, Clarissa, and their daughter. The high-strung one on the end is our neighbor, Terrance."

Terrance raised his hand in a half-wave, half-swiping sweat from his face. "Heya."

"We just need some help, and we'll be on our way." The woman—Brenda—stared hungrily at the Collier brothers' motorcycles. "It's still two days by foot just to reach Naples, if we're lucky."

"What happened to you?" Dakota asked.

"We had an SUV," Brenda said. "It was hijacked just past the International Mall by a crazed soccer mom. People just...they went insane with fear. Even when the radio announcers said our area wasn't contaminated. No one listened."

"Why not?" Jake asked, sounding genuinely curious.

"Are you kidding me?" Terrance scoffed. "The weatherman can't get the weather right on any given day. You think we were gonna trust 'em that the invisible clouds of radiation weren't headed straight for us?"

"We got the hell out," Vince said. "Most people we knew had the same idea."

"We were running low on gas, but all the stations were closed. They ran out or decided it was smarter to hog it all themselves." Brenda cast a glance at her husband, Sal. "When people started realizing there wasn't any more gas to be had at the stations, they started getting creative. They took it from other people—or just took their vehicles outright."

Sal shrugged, his shoulders hunched. "It was get a vehicle or get left behind for the radiation to eat you alive. Didn't leave people much of a choice."

"It was chaos, man." Terrance shifted his feet nervously. "Never seen anything like it."

"And now?" Logan asked. "What's it like?"

"Hell," the other woman—Clarissa—said in a soft voice. Her arms were wrapped around her ribcage. She took rapid, shallow breaths like she was still in panic mode, just like the boy. Her daughter huddled next to her, clearly still terrified.

None of them had adjusted well. Their soft, comfortable lives hadn't equipped them for anything like this. Nothing they'd ever experienced before had prepared them for this.

Guilt pricked Logan. To be honest, everyone had gotten a little soft, even him. Maybe that wasn't their fault, but their actions and choices now certainly were.

"Fights in the streets," Clarissa said. "Traffic jams like you've never seen. People screaming at each other, shooting at each other. People fighting over food and gas like some third world country…"

The Collier brothers exchanged heavy glances. Logan and Dakota weren't surprised. They'd seen plenty of mayhem and madness just days after the attacks.

"The stores are empty already?" Zane asked with raised eyebrows.

"I manage—managed a Publix in Kendall," Clarissa said with a shudder. "No deliveries, no inventory. We were stripped of everything in less than three days. I didn't think it was possible, especially accepting cash-only payments. People stuffed every square inch of their cars with cans and boxes, filling coolers in the back with dairy and meat until the ice ran out. It was like a scene out of a movie. I've never seen the shelves barren like that."

"The big box stores and distribution centers are being guarded by soldiers," Terrance said. "The ones not guarded are already looted or completed stripped."

"We heard Naples was better off," Vince said. "We're gonna take 75 up to Fort Myers, then head to Orlando where we've got family. It's better there."

"Who's saying that?" Dakota asked.

The man shrugged. "It's gotta be better—"

"Of course, it is," Sal interrupted him. "Their city wasn't blasted to hell, was it?"

"Mom?" quavered the teenage girl, a tiny dark-haired slip of a thing. "I don't feel very good. I think I'm gonna pass out."

Beside him, Dakota cringed. She was letting their sob story get to her—that was her weakness. Logan still didn't buy it.

"It'll be okay, honey." The mother put her arm around her daughter's shoulder, drawing her close.

"You gonna help us or what?" Brenda asked, confrontational and almost defiant, as if she already expected them to say no—and was prepared to bully her way to a yes.

Jake didn't like her tone, either. He ratcheted up the shotgun a few degrees. It was still mostly pointed down, but he was prepared.

So was Logan. His pulse quickened. He shifted his feet to widen his stance and tightened his grip on the AR-15.

"We're sorry for your plight," Archer said. "We understand—"

"But we can't help you," Boyd interrupted, his voice stern. "I'm sure you'll be able to find something in Naples."

"Go to hell!" Sal spat. "That's where you belong, anyway."

"Mom?" the girl asked again, shivering despite the oppressive heat.

"These folks could help us, but they won't," Brenda said bitterly. "Guess it's every man for himself, isn't it? You're just as bad as the hijackers and thieves and looters!"

Vince raised both hands in a pleading gesture. "Please, forgive our rudeness. We're desperate and hungry. Please, if there's anything you can do…"

Archer heaved a sigh and lumbered back to his bike. Shotgun pointed at the ground, with his free hand, he grabbed the pack lashed to the rear of his bike, pulled out a large bag, and tossed it to Vince.

"There's four wild boar and goat cheese sandwiches, two smoked largemouth bass, a jar of potato salad, two bunches of grapes, a cucumber, three bottles of fresh water, and some carrots. Just one fork, but I'm sure you'll make do."

"We'll be hungry again by tonight," Sal said.

"We need a vehicle," Brenda insisted. "Or at least a jerrycan of gas so we can fill the tank of one of these cars along the road and get it running again."

Archer, Jake, and Boyd exchanged a look. It wasn't a pleasant one.

It wasn't lost on any of them that these people hadn't bothered to show a bit of gratitude.

"We don't have anything else to spare," Jake said. "We'll escort you back to the highway. You should be on your way."

"Thanks for nothing," Sal said.

The brothers aimed their shotguns and rifles at the refugees' feet. Logan raised the AR-15. "Like we said, you should be on your way."

32

LOGAN

Brenda let out a low curse. Vince's shoulders sagged. The girl stepped closer to Clarissa, who held her daughter tightly, still trembling.

"Fine," Terrance said sullenly. "We're going."

Zane and Zander remained behind with Logan and Dakota. Archer, Jake, and Boyd gave them a personal escort, ensuring the refugees actually made it to the highway.

The tension didn't melt from Logan's shoulders until they were out of sight and the rumble of the Harleys had faded.

Dakota let out a relieved sigh. "It was nice of you guys to give them your lunches."

Zander grinned. "Nah, that was just Archer's."

"He's gotta eat that much or the big oaf loses weight." Zane patted his own well-endowed gut wryly. "Great problem to have, right?"

Zander rolled his eyes. "You've got the opposite problem, brother."

"Don't I know it." Zane settled on his bike but didn't start it. He crossed his burly arms across his broad chest. "Thanks for your help back there."

"We didn't do anything," Dakota said. "Not really."

Zane grabbed a bottle of water from the pack behind his bike and guzzled it down. "They had more people than we did. Sometimes that makes 'em think they can get the drop on us, take our guns and our bikes. They don't have a snowball's chance in hell of that, of course, but it's best to avoid a messy altercation in the first place."

"Just the appearance of strength makes a difference, believe you me," Zander said, the laughter abruptly vanishing from his voice. He stared off into the middle-distance for a minute before speaking. "We've learned a lot of lessons in the last few days. Hard ones."

Dakota shoved a few stray strands of sweat-dampened hair behind her ears and glanced down at her gun. "I wanted to help them, but..."

"Something was off," Logan finished for her.

Her gaze flashed to his, concern in her eyes. "Yeah. There was..."

"Ungrateful schmucks," Zane said. "They got enough for a full meal each, but they wanted more. No matter how much we'd have given them, they would've felt like they deserved it, not us."

"You offer 'em a loaf of bread, next thing you know, they've invaded your house—and kicked you out," Zander said.

"We had to turn them away." A part of Logan wanted to touch Dakota's shoulder or take her hand—for comfort? For solidarity, or something else? He stopped himself. She wouldn't want that, wouldn't want him.

"I know. Doesn't mean I like it, but I know." Dakota kicked angrily at a chunk of gravel. "It's not those kids' faults they have assholes for parents."

"There'll be more like them," Zander said. "You can bet your bottom dollar on that one."

He was right. Next time, the bad guys could boast more people and more weapons. Haasi had the right idea with the 'sticking together' thing. As much as Logan preferred to be a loner, he wasn't stupid—or so stubborn he'd act against his own best interests. In a

SHTF situation, you needed other people you could depend on to have your back. Ezra was foolish to reject their offer of mutual aid.

They weren't trained soldiers, but Logan liked them well enough. They all seemed proficient with their weapons. Haasi and Maki were both fierce, intelligent, and capable. Like Dakota.

Archer was definitely the Collier brother in charge. He seemed like a sensible guy, affable and even-keeled, but maybe too trusting. Zane and Zander were big and jolly, like a pair of hairy redneck Santa Clauses, but they'd been dead serious dealing with the refugees.

Jake was clearly the spitfire, judging by their altercation earlier, though he'd mellowed out once he realized Logan wasn't a threat. He and Boyd were the more suspicious, standoffish brothers, but that wasn't a negative in Logan's book.

He pointed toward the end of the dirt road. "We should cut down trees and plant underbrush to block the entrance—it shouldn't be hard to make it look overgrown and abandoned. From the highway, anyone passing by likely won't notice the road, and if they do, they won't expect to find anything worth looting."

Zander brightened. "Hey, yeah. That might work. But how do we get in and out?"

"We could create a smaller ATV or dirt bike trail further in the woods," Dakota offered.

"Dude," Zane said, "we've got trucks and chains. It won't be nothing to haul aside a few trees if we need access ourselves."

"Great," Logan said. "I can come help first thing in the morning."

Zander grinned and slapped his shoulder so hard he almost flinched. "Great idea, man. Thanks."

Logan faced the twins and took a deep breath. As long as they remained at the cabin, they needed help, whether Ezra would face it or not. "I know Ezra isn't interested in a community road patrol, but I am. He doesn't control me or what I do. I'm happy to help."

"Yeah, that'd be good." Zander grinned and tugged at his beard. "I'll ask Archer about it."

Dakota glanced at Logan with a quick, hard smile before looking away. "Count me in."

The crack of a gunshot took them all by surprise.

33

DAKOTA

Dakota waited, tense and stiff, straining her ears to listen. Three more gunshots rang out. They were coming from the west—from the direction of US 41.

One of the Collier brothers' radios crackled. Zane grabbed his from his waistband. "What the heck's going on?"

"Damn scumbags turned around and shot at us!" Archer's incredulous voice spat from the speaker. "Almost scalped Jake. He's alright, but we're taking fire. Get your fat butts over here."

"On our way," Zane said.

Zander scowled through his bristly beard. "Archer was too trusting, like always. Damn him!"

"They want the motorcycles," Dakota said.

"Those dirtbags aren't getting a thing from us." Zane adjusted the sling of his rifle and headed for his bike. "I'm takin' back those damn sandwiches, too."

Zander stood still. His eyes were wide and red-rimmed. He looked angry—and afraid. "If something happens, so help me..."

Zane turned and slapped him on the shoulder. "Nothing's gonna happen. Come on!"

Dakota already had her Springfield unholstered. She mentally counted her bullets—nine rounds in the magazine, plus the one in the chamber, plus the two spare magazines in her pocket. Twenty-eight. No way to know if it'd be enough.

She pictured the hundreds of rounds of ammo, the dozens of loaded magazines, and the rifles just sitting on the picnic table a quarter of a mile away. Too far to run back and get them with a battle already underway.

She and Logan exchanged a tense glance. Was he on board with the plan? Was he with her on this?

He nodded.

Good. They were in agreement on this one.

"We're coming," she said.

"Let's go!" Zander went to start the engine.

Dakota lifted her hand. "Wait! We need a plan."

"We don't have time—"

"Thirty seconds," Logan said. "We can't go in hot without a plan."

"We can cut through the woods and surprise them," Dakota said.

Zander nodded tightly. "Okay, yeah. We drive the bikes in fast. The engines will hide any noise you make, and their attention will be on us."

"Good," Logan said.

"Just remember you'll get there faster than we will," Dakota warned.

"Got it." Zane twisted and patted the back of his Harley. "Here, ride behind us until just before we get to the highway. It's a few miles, still. Then you can sneak into the woods and do your thing."

Logan was already moving toward Zane's bike. "Got it."

The ride was short and bumpy. Dakota clung to Zander's substantial middle and turned her head to the side, trying not to inhale strands of his wiry, shoulder-length hair as the wind whipped her face.

A minute later, she was off the bike and darting into the woods,

Logan at her heels. Her pulse thudded in her throat, her hands damp, her mouth dry.

She moved with ease through the trees, stepping carefully to avoid roots and twigs and thorns. She was no ninja, but she knew how to keep relatively quiet.

Logan, meanwhile, crashed after her like an oversized elephant.

"Do you have any idea what the phrase 'walk softly' means?" she asked in a low, strained voice.

"I'm a city boy, okay?" he hissed back. "I'm doing the best I can."

He was, so she swallowed a sarcastic comment and pushed back a tall thorn bush so it wouldn't smack him in the face. "Slow down. Try to step lightly, place the heel or toes of your foot down first and roll your foot slowly and gently onto the ground."

He tried. It was marginally better.

"We don't have to do this, you know," she said. "We can turn back."

"I know you want to. And so do I. We've got to protect this place. And that means working together."

She hid her smile. "Watch your step. Lots of pigmy rattlers and coral snakes out here."

Logan let out a muffled curse. "I changed my mind. Take me back."

Before she could respond, a shout echoed through the trees.

Dakota held her finger to her lips. They crept closer. The shouting grew louder. Another gun went off, this one the resounding crack of a shotgun.

Dakota paused between two pine trees, a large live oak with the trunk the diameter of a kids' bicycle tire directly in front of her. Spanish moss dangled from the branches. Glimpses of highway appeared through the foliage on either side of the oak about twenty yards straight ahead.

She held up her hand. Logan halted. Cautiously, they crept forward.

34

DAKOTA

Dakota peered around the massive tree trunk. She squatted a little to peer through the boughs of a scrubby pine obscuring her view.

To the left, three Harleys were laid down on their sides, facing back the way they'd come. Thirty yards north, the pudgy teenage boy lay in the middle of the road.

The boy was on his back, legs splayed, arms flung out. A dark stain spread across his shirt and leaked onto the pavement beneath him. He didn't move.

She sucked in a sharp breath, her stomach roiling. She hated seeing a dead kid. But these people had chosen to attack first. The Collier brothers had every right to defend themselves.

She didn't want to kill anyone today, but that didn't mean she wouldn't.

If they didn't take care of this problem now, the group would head straight back to Mangrove Road, searching the homesteads for loot, including Ezra's place. Ezra could easily defend his property against the likes of these, but why risk it?

Mistakes happened. Mistakes got people killed all the time.

She could visualize what had likely happened. Archer, Boyd, and Jake rode the Harleys a few dozen yards behind the would-be thieves, who acted appropriately meek and chastised while Archer grew more and more overconfident with every passing minute.

After a few miles, Archer waved them off, Boyd offering one final warning: *don't come back or else* or something equally lame. Then they headed back, not waiting for the group to walk out of sight first.

The scumbags had waited for the bikers to turn around. Someone, probably Sal, had whipped around and shot at the brothers' retreating backs. They hadn't wanted to damage the bikes because they needed to steal them. Plus, being soft city guys, their aim was crap.

As soon as the first shot fired and missed, the bikers had whipped around and returned fire, killing the kid. Both sides fled for the cover of the woods, inciting the ensuing stand-off.

And that's where they remained, hostiles and allies hidden somewhere amongst the trees.

She shifted her gaze and scanned the treeline. A few more shots rang out as she caught sight of a color that didn't belong—yellow, a checkered blue-and-white.

Across the road and sixty feet to the south, two men hid behind a large live oak about ten feet into the woods. Terrance and Vince, both facing the road as they traded volleys with the Collier brothers.

As Zane and Zander roared up the road, they shifted to aim at the bikes' riders.

Sal and the women were nowhere to be seen.

She and Logan had a few seconds of surprise while the intruders were focused on the oncoming bikes. They needed to use them wisely.

If they were lucky, the engines would block the noise of the gunshots, or at least their direction, to give Logan and Dakota more time to hit their targets.

There were plenty of trees to seek cover behind, but the other side claimed the same advantage.

Logan gestured silently. She nodded. She would take out Terrance on the left. He would shoot Vince, who was mostly blocked from their view. She considered herself a good shot, but Logan was better.

She exhaled slowly, controlled her breathing, and aimed her weapon. Terrance's head and shoulders were exposed behind the tree. She zeroed in on the back of his head.

It wasn't an easy shot. But maybe it would flush him out, even if she missed.

She squeezed the trigger. Bark sprayed. Terrance ducked, dropping out of sight. Vince disappeared, too.

Mosquitos buzzed around her face. She couldn't slap them away.

Logan lowered the muzzle of the AR-15 a fraction and let loose three rounds. *Bang, bang, bang.*

A scream shattered the sweltering air. Then a crash. Vince appeared again, staggering between two trees. A few shots came from the south, blasting the tree trunks to the right and left of him.

Logan moved one step to the left, exposing himself a bit as he adjusted his aim and fired two rounds in quick succession.

Vince's body jerked once, twice. He collapsed into the underbrush and didn't get up.

"Two down," Logan muttered. "That includes the kid."

Dakota scanned the woods, ready to fire at the slightest movement, but there was nothing. "I lost the other one. I'm sorry."

"We'll find him again."

She searched the road. A tan Ford Escape sat along the near side of the road about forty yards away. The passenger side door hung open.

A figure lay slumped against the tire closest to Dakota—a heavy, middle-aged black woman wearing a flowery housedress and a fuzzy slipper on one foot. Dozens of red, oozing blisters and sores bubbled the exposed skin of her arms, legs, and face.

Cold adrenaline shot through her veins. Dakota inhaled sharply and caught the rancid scent of decay. The woman was dead, and had been for days. She'd attempted to flee the destruction like so many others, but the radiation was already inside her, eating away at her flesh from the inside out.

Dakota was about to turn away, her stomach roiling, when she glimpsed movement. A shadow through the windshield, then another. At least two people crouched in front of the Ford Escape.

35

DAKOTA

Logan tapped Dakota's shoulder and pointed. About fifty feet south of them on their side of the road, a man crouched behind a waist-high clump of Brazilian pepper bushes. He was facing away, his shotgun braced against the trunk of a slash pine. Sweat drenched the broad, stretched back of his shirt. Sal.

A shotgun blast exploded the silence. Several birds took flight from the trees around them, squawking in protest. She couldn't see who Sal was aiming at through the thick foliage.

Two rifle shots blasted back. One round slammed into a tree trunk a dozen yards ahead and to the left of Sal. A few leaves drifted to the ground.

Sal flattened himself behind the bushes. She could still just make out his hulking form in the forest shadows.

Logan pointed at the truck, then gestured south. She nodded, understanding. She'd circle around to the front of the truck to dispatch whoever was hiding there, while Logan went the opposite direction and took out Sal.

She pressed her fingers to her lips. As if a reminder could make Logan any quieter. He rolled his eyes. A moment later, he was gone.

Her gut twisted with worry. He'd be fine. Stampeding elephant or not, Logan could take care of himself. Still, she didn't like this situation. The sooner it was over, the better.

She made her way carefully through the underbrush, skirting trees, sliding noiselessly past saw palmettos and ferns, stepping soft and quiet to avoid giving her position away.

More gunshots cracked behind her.

This could go to hell in a matter of seconds. There were too many of them—all hunting each other in the woods, jumping at every noise, every shadow.

One of the brothers might accidentally shoot her as easily as one of the intruders. Who knew how well-trained they were, whether they were trigger-happy idiots or smart enough to realize the risks of friendly fire?

Her heart lurched into her throat, but she forced herself to remain slow and methodical, the way Ezra had taught her. She controlled her breathing as she scanned her surroundings from left to right and back again, acutely aware of every sound, every movement.

When she was about thirty feet from the rear of the Escape, she froze. Directly across the road about ten or fifteen feet in, the edge of a red shirt peeked out behind a thicket of spiky saw palmetto bushes.

She raised her gun.

The figure shifted. She glimpsed a scrap of leather vest and a hank of long dark hair in a ponytail: Jake Collier.

She exhaled softly. An ally. She still couldn't see Archer or Boyd. Were they on the opposite side of the road, or her side?

A twig cracked ten yards behind her. She whirled, gun up, peering hard into the dappled shadows, the tangled maze of trees and underbrush, roots and branches.

A squirrel scurried up a skinny slash pine, chattering furiously at her.

Her palms were damp. She couldn't wipe away the sweat sliding down her temples.

A volley of gunfire burst through the forest south of her. For a few moments, she couldn't hear the typical forest noises—or anyone attempting to sneak up on her.

Instinctively, she went still, pressing herself against the trunk of the nearest tree, a pine half as thick as her torso. It wouldn't protect her from much.

Something thudded into the trunk above her head. The entire tree vibrated against her spine.

Too late, she dropped to a crouch.

A flash of movement to her right, crashing toward her.

She spun, her pistol rising to meet the threat, sweaty finger slipping on the trigger.

Pain exploded through her hand. The gun tore from her fingers and she was knocked off balance. She tumbled, her back striking the trunk, and slid to the leaf-strewn ground.

What the hell? Had she just been shot? She raised her hand to her face, expecting gushing blood, a bullet wound. There wasn't one.

The skinny, jittery guy—Terrance—loomed over her. He breathed hard, eyes wild and furious.

She twisted on the ground, her whole hand pulsing with pain, and searched frantically for the gun. A large, fist-sized rock lay a few feet from Terrance's feet. The jerk had managed to disarm her with a stupid rock.

He kicked her as she tried to rise, forcing her down on her back.

He aimed the muzzle at her head. "Stay right there."

36

DAKOTA

Dakota stared up into the muzzle of the pistol. If Terrance fired, she was dead. It didn't matter if he'd never held a gun before; this close, it was hard to miss.

She needed to do something, and do it fast.

He was a skinny guy, not very tall, maybe 5'7 and 160 pounds soaking wet. Not that much bigger than she was. If she could get the gun aimed somewhere else, and reach her knife...

"Wait!" she said breathlessly, opening her eyes wide to make her appear afraid—and vulnerable. "I know what you want. I know where the stash is."

He hesitated.

"I'll tell you everything! Please! They've got a year's worth of food. And electricity and hot water. And guns. As many guns as you want. I have the key. I can show you."

His eyes narrowed. "And what do you want for it?"

"Just my life. Me and my sister. Okay? Just don't kill me, please."

"Okay, yeah," he said, shifting uneasily from foot to foot. "Hurry up."

She reached out her left hand, palm open. Maybe it was instinctive to help a woman, or maybe his greed overruled his better judgement. Either way, he underestimated her.

He juggled the pistol to his left hand and bent to help her up. Leaning, his knees bent, he was no longer in a position of strength.

She gripped his hand, tensed, and yanked him toward her with all her might.

He stumbled, falling forward. She went for her knife, jerked it from its sheath at her belt, and stabbed blindly. He tumbled to his knees on top of her, his right knee jabbing into her stomach as the blade sank into his right thigh.

Terrance howled and jerked backward, scrambling off her and staggering to his feet. He hobbled on one foot, clutching at the knife handle protruding from his leg, grimacing and cursing.

Instead of rolling clear, she writhed to one side and aimed a savage kick at his foot. Her heavy boot struck his ankle from the side and knocked him off his feet.

He fell hard, crashing sideways into the bushes.

She scrambled to her feet and dove at him before he could regain his footing. She shoved him flat on his back and landed elbow first, driving the point of her elbow into his gut, all of her 120 pounds behind it.

With a grunt, he stopped trying to pull the knife from his thigh and reached for her throat instead. His bloodied hands closed around her throat. A ring of fiery pain encircled her neck and cut off her breath.

He flipped her onto her back and used his superior weight and strength to choke her out. Stars danced in front of her eyes. *Stupid, stupid.* He'd taken her by surprise. She'd underestimated his wiry strength, much like he'd underestimated her.

It took everything in her not to struggle to pry his hands off her neck. Her chest burned. She had only a few seconds before she lost consciousness.

One, two, three. Breathe. That's how she endured pain. Only now she couldn't breathe.

She reached down desperately, her hand scrabbling beneath the weight of his torso to his legs, until she found the handle of the knife.

She jerked it from his thigh. It came out easily enough, but her grip was wrong, forcing her to hold it like she was slicing carrots, not flipped the other way, better for stabbing.

His body was on top of hers. He was still choking her. The pain was excruciating. Darkness filmed the edges of her vision. Her pulse was so loud in her ears, she heard nothing else. The only thought in her head screamed *stay alive!* over and over.

One more move before consciousness took over and she was dead.

One more move. Better make it now.

She twisted her wrist, brought her arm in close, and slid the blade into her attacker's side, just below his ribs. His eyes bulged, his mouth opening in an anguished scream.

She yanked out the blade as she wrenched to the side. He lost his grip on her neck, collapsing onto her legs.

Gasping, she sucked in a mouthful of precious air, then another and another, her throat raw, frantically breathing in the sweet scent of pine mingled with the hot, tangy smell of fresh blood.

Her fingers dug into leaves, dirt, and twigs as she wriggled free of him, kicking with her waning strength. It felt like swimming in molasses, every movement slow and requiring incredible effort.

She forced herself to her hands and knees, made herself turn and crawl back to him.

Terrance lay flat on his back, moaning, clutching his bloodied side. He stared up at her, wide eyes filled with agony and terror.

If she spared him and he lived, he'd only prey on someone else. She needed to finish this.

She flipped the knife around in her hand, tightened her grip on the handle, and plunged it into his chest. The metallic scent of blood filled her nostrils, mingled with the stench of bodily functions losing control.

He flailed beneath her, his slick hands smacking weakly at her arms, smearing her skin with his blood. His eyes rolled back in his head. Ragged gurgles rattled from his chest.

Finally, his movements stilled completely.

Only then did she allow herself to sag in relief. She pushed herself off the body and scooted back against the nearest tree, breathing hard. Her heart was still a wild thing galloping inside her chest. She couldn't inhale enough oxygen.

Her stomach lurched. She stared down at her trembling hands, at the blood that wasn't hers. A pink, swollen scrape covered her right hand from her wrist to her knuckles from the rock. She felt her neck—it was raw and painful to swallow, and she'd have an ugly bruise for a while, but she was fine.

She'd be fine.

It was never easy to kill another human being, no matter who they were. An image of Jacob bleeding out on the mercy room floor flashed through her mind. She pushed it away.

She didn't want to kill. Hadn't asked for it. But in a fight to survive, to protect herself and the people she loved, she'd kill if she had to.

Every single time.

Gradually, her breathing steadied. Sounds came back again slowly: the buzzing of insects, the creak of branches, the stutter of gunfire.

The fight wasn't over yet.

Logan was still out there. He needed her help.

She blinked rapidly, clearing her vision, and searched for her Springfield. She spotted it beneath a cluster of ferns a few yards away. She flexed her stinging hand as she forced herself off her butt, forced herself to move.

Something crashed through the woods toward her. She lunged for the gun and rose to her feet in one fluid motion, whipping around to face the new threat.

Zane waved his arms wildly. "Hey, don't shoot me!"

She lowered the gun. "What're you doing here?"

"Came to save you." He moved next to her and toed the body at their feet. "Clearly, you needed it."

"He caught me by surprise. Otherwise, he'd have two rounds drilled into his forehead."

"Either way, I'm impressed."

"Who's still out there?" she whispered.

"Counting this one, we got the four males. All dead." He scratched at his beard. "There's still two women and the girl."

She leaned down, pulled the knife from the dead man's chest, and wiped it on a clean section of his shirt. "At least two of them are behind the white SUV up there. You take the right; I'll take the left. Don't accidentally shoot me."

Zane stared at her, wide-eyed. "Yeah, okay. Got it."

Dakota sheathed the knife, checked her pistol, and replaced the magazine with a spare from her pocket. "What're you waiting for? Let's go."

37

LOGAN

Logan watched a round slam into the pine tree not a foot above Dakota's head. She ducked as shards of bark sprayed everywhere. She might not be so lucky next time.

Fury filled him. This wasn't his home. He didn't know Ezra or these Collier guys. He owed nothing to anyone.

Except to her. For her, he'd happily mow down anyone and everyone in his path.

He understood hunger and desperation to survive, even stealing from the dead or from empty homes. But not from the living.

They'd already given these scumbags a second chance. They were shooting at Dakota. Enough was enough.

The world sharpened. Every leaf, every twig. Sound faded away but for the rush of blood in his ears. He tensed, teeth clenched, every muscle coiled and ready.

That cold, hard calm descended. His head was clear.

He barreled through the woods, moving quickly, searching for targets, firing a few warning shots to keep them ducking for cover instead of shooting at him. Aim, exhale, squeeze. Aim, exhale, squeeze.

He went for Sal.

The fat man whirled, his hiding spot behind the bushes useless. He scrambled to a seated position, swinging his shotgun around to aim at Logan crashing toward him like an enraged rhinoceros.

Logan wasn't as accurate on the move as he was from a still, braced position, but he didn't need to be. He had the element of surprise, he was close, and Sal presented a large target.

He fired two quick shots, dodging to the left to avoid a couple of pine trees, then fired twice more.

The first shot missed. The second drilled into the man's belly, the third skimmed his left shoulder. The fourth nailed him dead center in the chest.

The shotgun slid from Sal's limp fingers. He let out a few gargled gasps as he toppled onto his side, his head slamming into the base of a pine tree. He remained that way, slumped awkwardly, his thick neck bent at an unnatural angle, his eyes open and staring.

Logan grabbed the guy's gun, slid the strap over his shoulder, and kept moving. By his count, he only had a few rounds left. It was as good a time as any to reload his own weapon. Still hustling through the underbrush, he released the nearly spent magazine, traded it for a new one in his pocket, and jacked the fresh one into place.

He paused behind a thin screen of skinny trees just before the highway. He raised the AR-15 and scanned the area, searching for movement.

Zane and Archer emerged from the opposite tree line about forty yards south, their weapons up, tense and ready.

A shot rang out. He ducked. So did Zane and Archer.

Archer pointed ahead of Logan, to the north.

Movement snagged his gaze—someone ducking down after firing a shot. It'd come from the abandoned SUV further up the road on his side.

Dakota was supposed to take care of it. Something must've happened.

Into the Fire

Adrenaline surging, he circled around the white Ford Escape. Three figures huddled against the grille.

"Don't shoot!" the blonde woman—Brenda—cried. Mascara tracked down her cheeks.

She raised shaking hands in the air, her desperate gaze pleading, beseeching. "We're women! We've got a child!"

A handgun lay on the ground near her. She'd tried to push it behind her, under the car, but he saw it. She was the final shooter.

The dark-haired Asian woman next to Brenda—Clarissa—ducked her head. She turned to the side, wrapping her arms around her daughter, attempting to shield the girl with her own body.

"We're unarmed!" Brenda said again.

Logan didn't think. He didn't feel. From ten feet away, he aimed the rifle at the blonde woman and squeezed the trigger.

Brenda's head jerked back and struck the Ford with a dull thud. Blood sprayed the two figures next to her in a fine mist.

"Logan!" Dakota shouted from behind him.

He barely heard her. He didn't register anything but the blood, the crumpled body, his own pulse roaring in his ears.

One target down. He swiveled the muzzle to Clarissa.

The woman whimpered but didn't beg for her life. She pushed herself in front of the girl, protecting her. The girl cowered, weeping, her face buried against her mother's chest.

He aimed, exhaled. His finger tightened on the trigger.

"Logan!"

Ears ringing, he heard her as if from far away. But he heard her.

He moved his finger off the trigger.

Dakota jerked his rifle aside and stood directly in front of him, blocking his view of the woman and the girl.

His vision blurred, then sharpened again, slowly focusing on Dakota.

"That's enough," she said, her voice raspy but gentle. She gazed up at him, forcing him to look at her. Bruises in the shape of fingerprints marked her throat. Scratches, bug bites, and streaks of drying blood stippled her arms. "It's over. They're all dead."

She placed her hand on his chest. He registered the warmth, the pressure of her palm, her fingers splayed, her thumb directly over his thumping, traitorous heart.

He stood there, shaking, as he came back to himself.

Behind Dakota, the woman still curled over her daughter, not moving, waiting for the killing blow. She didn't have a weapon. She wasn't a threat.

They weren't a threat to anyone.

He'd almost killed them. He'd nearly shot her in the head and then the girl. It was simple muscle memory, mechanical. He would've done it without a single coherent thought or flicker of hesitation.

Maybe some would say they deserved death for simply being a part of the group, whether or not they'd wielded the weapons themselves. Maybe that shouldn't make a difference.

But it did today.

Nausea lurched in his gut. He staggered back, lowering the rifle. That familiar sick-spinning horror twisted inside him.

Despair clawed at his throat. Despair—and thirst.

Zander came out of the woods behind Dakota, gun in hand. Archer and Zane strode toward them. Jake and Boyd shuffled out from the other side of the road.

"What do we do with them?" Jake asked, tilting his chin at the cowering woman and girl.

"No more killing." Dakota turned toward the brothers, her jaw set defiantly. "Look at them. They won't cause trouble."

Archer sighed. "I agree."

"Then get them the hell out of here," Boyd snarled, "before I do something I regret."

Dakota gestured at Clarissa with her pistol. "You heard him. Run! Now!"

Clarissa didn't speak a word. She stood, pulling the sobbing girl up by her arm, shouldered her backpack, and ran. They fled down the center of US 41, their slamming footsteps and the girl's sobs the only sounds.

The two figures grew smaller and smaller. Neither one of them looked back.

Dizziness washed over Logan. That sour-sick feeling lurched in his gut as white stars exploded in front of his vision. He could barely hold onto the rifle.

The *need* seared him, throbbing through him, dark and pulsing and vicious.

"Logan," Dakota said, concern in her voice. She reached for his hand. "Are you okay?"

But he couldn't accept her comfort.

It was the last thing he deserved.

38

SHAY

Shay finished the last of her protein-and-banana smoothie—not because she was hungry, but she needed the energy boost. It was after midnight, but no one was slowing down.

Organized chaos around the clock—that was life at the Emergency Operations Center.

Outside the restaurant, important-looking people hurried back and forth along the terminal, everyone focused on the task at hand. A prick of guilt stabbed her. She should be at the hospital helping, but she needed rest or she'd be useless to anyone.

Every muscle in her body ached. Her eyes burned from exhaustion, but she didn't want to catch a few hours of restless sleep before returning to work. She wanted to stay right here in this too-hard seat, the lights turned so low to conserve the generators that she could barely see her food, and Hawthorne squished into the booth across from her.

Hawthorne's partner, Kinsey, had met them for a late dinner, then rushed off for some sleep before heading back into the fray. Shay liked Kinsey—she was plucky, brave, and funny—but she treasured these

Into the Fire

stolen moments with Hawthorne. They were what kept her going, not sleep.

"Shay, earth to Shay," Hawthorne quipped.

She blinked at him, her vision going blurry for a second. She was more exhausted than she'd thought. Maybe she was wrong about that lack of sleep thing. "Yeah, um, sorry. I'm here."

He gave her a concerned look. "I've never had a date fall asleep on me before. Not that I'm worried about my record or anything, but maybe we should cut this short."

She flushed at his mention of 'date.' Was that what this was? Is that what she wanted it to be? She twisted one of her corkscrew curls behind her ears and adjusted her glasses to disguise her embarrassment.

She cleared her throat. "I couldn't live with myself if I ruined your record. I'll be fine. Just get some caffeine in me."

He raised his eyebrows. "You sure? This late?"

"Trust me, I'll sleep like a baby as soon as my head hits the pillow. I could sleep through a train wreck."

"Noted." Hawthorne gestured to get the attention of the waiter. "Let's get you that coffee."

Instead of coming over, the waiters turned up the volume on the TV behind them. They kept the television going 24/7 for news updates, but it was usually the same information repeated ad nauseum. This time, it wasn't.

Several people at the bar gasped. Others stopped in their tracks in the middle of the terminal, staring at the screen with alarmed expressions.

"What's happening?" Shay asked.

Hawthorne's mouth flattened into a grim line. "You haven't seen this yet?"

Shay shook her head. "I've been working nonstop all day." She hadn't even had time to check in with her mom or Julio and the others in the Glades. She turned in her seat to watch.

Two news reporters and several important-looking experts and officials sat around a U-shaped table as a grainy video of two Middle Eastern men played on a loop behind them.

The female reporter touched her earpiece and gazed intently at the audience. "The footage released just a few hours ago features two Hezbollah terrorists claiming responsibility for the thirteen nuclear attacks that have claimed the lives of at least a million American lives. They've also claimed that the highly enriched uranium used on U.S. soil was procured through high-ranking Iranian government officials.

"Iranian President Hassan Rouhani quickly and strenuously denounced the charges in a press conference an hour ago. Iran's top officials claim their uranium enrichment program is exclusively for peaceful purposes. However, Rouhani is refusing to allow UN officials or IAEA inspectors to survey Iran's nuclear research facilities."

The reporter turned to a gray-haired woman in a black suit. "How swiftly should the U.S. retaliate, Dr. Bradley?"

"Hezbollah, the Iran-sponsored militant terrorist group, remains the most hostile of any of the global threats to America," the woman said. "That being said, whether Iran even has the nuclear capabilities is—"

"We have our proof," the second expert interrupted. "Bomb Iran to kingdom come! America needs to prove her strength now more than ever. China and Russia already smell blood in the water. I don't care how many tons of humanitarian aid Russia keeps delivering. They'll tear us apart if we don't act, and act now…"

Shay and Hawthorne continued watching for several minutes, along with everyone else in the bar, but the newscasters had no new information to report. They were just talking heads, arguing over the validity of the footage and who to bomb first.

Shay twisted around in her seat and faced Hawthorne. She was wide awake now, even without coffee. "Do you think Hezbollah did it? And Iran's behind it?"

Hawthorne gave a tight shrug. "ISIS claimed responsibility the day of the attacks, remember? North Korea basically said they wished they'd done it first. I know everyone wants someone to blame, but we can't nuke an entire country based on the word of two insane terrorists."

"Do you think Iran has nuclear weapons? They're not supposed to, right?"

"I'm not sure on that point, but they definitely have enriched nuclear material. It's easier to create an improvised nuclear device, or IND, than most people think." Hawthorne sat up straighter, an eager gleam in his brown eyes whenever he got a chance to talk about something that interested him. "I mean, I don't want to bore you or anything."

"I'm not bored," Shay said, her cheeks warming. She liked that about him: his enthusiasm, his intelligence. "I want to hear it. Tell me everything you know."

"Between plutonium and highly enriched uranium, or HEU, HEU is much easier to turn into a weapon of mass destruction. It only takes fifty-five pounds of uranium to make a crude nuclear bomb. Forget Iran for a minute. The global stockpile is over 3.5 million pounds. That's twenty-three thousand nuclear weapons in existence. The U.S., China, Russia, the U.K., France, Israel, India, and Pakistan all have nuclear weapons. North Korea, Syria, and of course, Iran: maybe."

Shay nibbled on her thumbnail, her gut twisting. "Twenty-three thousand nuclear bombs? That's insane to think about."

"There are literally hundreds of locations holding nuclear weapons or nuclear material. And there's no binding global standards for how well these weapons and materials should be secured. For example, over one hundred research reactors utilize HEU. And some of them are in developing countries, where security and safeguards are questionable."

"How do you know all this?" Shay asked.

"We were just debriefed by an official from the International

Atomic Energy Agency, so everything's fresh in my mind." Hawthorne toyed with his fork, a frown creasing his forehead. "Over the last few decades, hundreds of incidents of theft or 'loss' of radioactive materials have been reported. In 2010, anti-nuclear activists broke into a Belgian military base that stored several U.S. nuclear weapons and walked around for an hour, just to prove how easy it was to break in. And four Russian submarines with nuclear warheads sank, but the warheads were never recovered."

Shay raised her eyebrows. "Or at least, that's what the Russian government reported."

"Exactly. But it's not just foreign governments. At least eleven U.S. nuclear weapons have been lost, too."

Shay's jaw dropped. "What? How can someone lose a nuclear weapon?"

"Your guess is as good as mine. Every country's government claims that one hundred percent of known lost or stolen nuclear material is recovered, but the IAEA rep said it's very possible that these countries may have only recovered some of the material, not all of it, and lied to cover it up."

"Like the way that the Soviets lied about Chernobyl," Shay said. "Some countries fear shame and embarrassment so much they'd cover it up at any cost before admitting it on the world stage."

"That's exactly it," Hawthorne said.

"Okay, so say these terrorists got ahold of some of this 'lost' uranium, either by stealing it or through their government—how did they get nuclear material through port security here in the U.S.? Shouldn't that be impossible?"

"I wish it was. U.S. Coast Guard personnel and Customs agents can only thoroughly inspect about five percent of the nine million shipping containers that arrive at U.S. ports every year. They have radiation detection scanners, of course, but they can fail—or be fooled.

"And lots of items have radiation signatures. Bananas, for example. So does granite, bricks, kitty litter, even potatoes. They all contain low levels of minerals that naturally decay. Individually, their radioactivity won't set off Geiger counters or harm anyone. A container or truckload of bananas or kitty litter, though, would set off the sensors."

"So, a shipping container filled with kitty litter boxes that was also hiding small amounts of nuclear material could potentially slip through?"

"Possibly. Any container with detectible radiation is supposed to be individually inspected. Doesn't mean it happens, or as thoroughly as it should."

"Human error," Shay said.

"Right now, Homeland is busy sifting through irregularity reports from every U.S. port of entry from the last three years. If they don't find anything, they'll go back further. There's also the likelihood that whoever did this has people in this country helping them, including port personnel."

"I surely hope not." The thought of Americans colluding to destroy their own country was beyond the pale. But they couldn't discount any possibility.

"Consider the fact that less than fifteen percent of heroin and thirty percent of cocaine is intercepted by authorities worldwide," Hawthorne said. "Seventy to eighty-five percent of illegal narcotics get through. No one wants to admit it. But it's the truth."

The waiter switched the channel from the talking heads, now nearly shouting at each other over which political party was more at fault for not preventing the catastrophic attacks, to the weather.

He turned up the volume. The forecast should've been the last thing anyone was worried about, but this was Florida—the weather was never benign.

Shay twisted around again as they both watched. On the screen, a meteorologist was discussing Hurricane Helen, still looming out in the middle of the Atlantic Ocean. She pointed out possible landfall patterns on a digital map of the east coast from the Dominican Republic up through South Carolina.

"Looks like if it's going to make landfall, it'll hit Cuba or maybe the Bahamas," Hawthorne said. "Not great for them, but good news for Miami."

Shay was determined to cling to every bit of hope she could find. "We need good news. Finding the good in all the horror is what keeps us sane. It's what gives us hope."

"Do you really believe that?"

"I do, with all of my heart."

Hawthorne opened his mouth, closed it, then frowned.

"What is it?"

He mumbled something so softly that she wasn't sure what he'd just said.

Her pulse quickened. "What?"

He cleared his throat, shifting uncomfortably in his seat. "I like you, Shay. There, I said it." He ran his hand nervously over his bald head and gave her an awkward but sweet smile. "I've faced down armed killers without blinking, but I gotta say this is a bit nerve-wracking."

Shay's weariness vanished. Her stomach fluttered, filling her with a happy, giddy warmth. Maybe she should feel guilty for experiencing a bit of joy in the midst of suffering and death, but she didn't. She embraced it with every fiber of her being.

This was life. This was hope. This was the light you held onto in the middle of the darkest night.

She found herself grinning. "I like you, too."

"I mean, um, I *like* you, like you."

"Yeah, I got that part."

"Oh, good. I, um, wasn't sure—"

She stood and held out her hand. "You wanna get out of here for a while?"

Trey Hawthorne shoved his chair back so fast, it toppled over.

39

DAKOTA

Dakota shoveled dirt into yet another sandbag. She swiped damp strands of hair out of her eyes with the back of her arm. Julio worked hard beside her, sweating and dirty, grunting with the effort.

The temperature had to be over ninety-five degrees, the muggy air like a furnace. The sun bore down on them, sweltering and unrelenting. Sweat dripped down her spine, pooled beneath her armpits, and soaked her shirt.

She'd layered on the sunscreen, wore one of Ezra's old baseball caps to shield her eyes, and draped her neck in a damp, cool strip of cloth dunked in ice water, but it still felt like being fried alive.

She kept waiting for the summer afternoon thunderstorms, but so far, there wasn't a cloud in the sky. The radio antenna set several yards from the cabin offered only a few thin strips of shade.

Normally in South Florida, outdoor labor was reserved for the cooler early mornings and late evenings, but they didn't have the luxury of time.

If anyone had doubts, the events of yesterday had hammered it home for everyone—they weren't safe. Not from the desperate refugees pouring out of Miami, and not from the Shepherds.

It had been five days since they'd killed the Shepherds to protect the cabin. Five days without a hint of threat or danger. But that didn't matter.

The stress and tension were taking their toll on all of them. But that didn't matter, either. They couldn't let their guard down for a second. And they had to be prepared at all times.

The worst was still to come.

She took a swig of water from her insulated bottle and glanced at Julio. His eyes were closed, but his mouth was moving.

"You're praying? Now? Out here in the heat?"

"You caught me." He opened his eyes. He looked forlorn for a moment before his expression cleared. "This time, I was actually having a pretend conversation with Yoselyn. Must be the heat getting to me."

Guilt pricked her. "You miss your wife."

"Every second of every day. And my nieces." He paused, breathing deeply, staring off into the middle distance. "I've always been there, you know? And now, when I most need to be, I'm not there."

"I'm sorry. It's my fault."

"No," he said, shaking his head. "Don't say that. It's not your fault. None of this is."

"But—"

"Listen, Dakota. Please. I'm so blessed and grateful that I know she's safe. I'm able to talk to her with the satphone, even though we're separated by considerable distance, even though the cell towers are still down. My sister-in-law is a strong, prepared woman. They stored away plenty of food and water. They'll be okay until I can get to them and take them out of the city."

She could read the concern in his face, even if he tried to hide it. Palm Beach had escaped the devastation of the blast, but grocery stores and gas stations were empty. The government was in shambles.

Law and order were disintegrating. And people were starting to get very, very hungry.

She knew how hard it was to be separated from the person you loved most, to know they were in danger, but there wasn't a damn thing you could do about it.

Julio pursed his lips. "Don't worry about me. Okay? Or her. We have our faith, no matter what. Besides, Yoselyn knows her way around a gun. She's way tougher than I am."

There was no tremor in his voice, no fear or regret. He was steady as a rock.

Just because Julio was gentle, soft-spoken, and had a good heart, that didn't mean he wasn't also strong. A spine of solid steel lurked behind that kind smile.

And who was she to judge what gave him that strength? For Dakota, it was her relentless love for her sister that powered her through the worst times. For Julio, it was his faith.

Maybe his God really was different than the hateful, vengeful deity she'd grown up with.

"I'm going to help you get your wife," she said, "when this is over."

He met her gaze. "I'm counting on it."

She waved her gloved hand around, spraying dirt everywhere. "You sure *you're* okay with all this? With handling a gun?"

"I've handled a gun before. Just a few days ago, if you recall."

"I mean, like, isn't it against your faith?"

Julio shot her a wry grin. "I happen to believe that God is a proponent of self-defense. In Esther, God's people were allowed to defend themselves against those who would murder them. The Israelites certainly defended themselves against all would-be attackers. Don't worry about my soul."

"That's good."

Julio finished filling a burlap bag and tied it with twine. He hefted it into the nearby wheelbarrow. "Mother Mary and Joseph, that's heavy."

They'd spent the morning training on the range and going over their weapons and ammo again, making sure everything was pristine and in good working order. Then they'd practiced intruder drills.

Ezra had insisted every training exercise be repeated at least three times, so it actually sank in. *If you only do it once, you might as well not practice at all.*

Now, as the afternoon dragged on, they filled dozens of sandbags to shore up the walls beneath the windows of the cabin to create protected shooter positions. Eden was working with Ezra on the other side of the cabin, Logan was working in the garden, and Park was keeping watch.

Everyone was tense, nervous, on edge. But especially Logan. She was worried about him. She hadn't spoken to him since yesterday, since he'd shot the blonde woman, Brenda, and almost killed the dark-haired lady and her daughter.

She wanted to give him his space, waiting for him to be ready to talk on his own terms, but she wasn't sure if he ever would be. Just when she felt like there was something there, a connection between them, he'd withdrawn, pulled away from her and gone somewhere deep inside himself.

He was hiding from something in his past. She knew exactly what that was like.

So was she. More than one thing, in her case.

40

DAKOTA

Dakota took a deep breath as the old memories tumbled back in, sharp and painful. The scars on her back prickled. She hadn't slept well the last few nights. Returning to the Glades and fighting the Shepherds had brought everything back again in harsh, vivid color.

She may have left, but the past was still where it always was. The people of the compound were haunting her dreams again, whispering in her mind with desperate voices.

Not only Maddox and the Prophet, but the others—the women and the children who called that place their home, who didn't know their sanctuary was also their prison.

"Can I ask you a question?" she asked Julio.

"Of course. You can ask me anything."

"I think about them sometimes."

"Who?"

"The kids I left behind. At the River Grass Compound."

The people she'd left behind—they were still exactly where she'd left them. The compound hadn't ceased to be. The people who lived there were still as trapped as she'd been, whether they realized it or not.

"There was a woman...she was always so kind to me," she said slowly. "Nothing like some of the other sisters. Sister Rosemarie. She was maybe the closest thing I had to a mother in there. But that's not saying much."

Julio paused, hunched over his sandbag, and waited. He didn't say anything, but he didn't need to. He was listening.

"I remember this one little girl, Ruth. She wasn't that much younger than I was, but she was so tiny. Always wore her hair in braids. She was so smart, so inquisitive. She wanted to learn everything. She was always shadowing Sister Rosemarie and asking questions about medical stuff."

Dakota closed her eyes for a moment, pushing out the sweltering heat and the bugs, the buzz of the cicadas, the dirt beneath her fingernails. "Out here in the real world, she'd grow up to be a doctor or a scientist. But in there...once, they caught her reading the Bible—the real Bible, not the parts about submission, obedience, and hard work they photocopied and allowed the girls to read. They took her into the mercy room...she couldn't stand up straight for weeks after they were through with her."

Julio's round, placid face went ashen. He crossed himself. "Have mercy."

Dakota picked up the shovel and thrust it into the dirt. She practically hurled the dirt into the burlap sack, clods flying everywhere. That old anger was rising in her again, bitter and helpless and ugly.

"That's probably another sin, right? Being so angry I could kill something? Just add it to the list."

"I'm not a priest," Julio said. "You have nothing to confess to me. That's between you and God. But between you and me, righteous outrage isn't a sin."

She shoveled furiously, her palms stinging from the relentless, repetitive strokes. She filled the sack, lugged it into the wheelbarrow, and started on the next one. "I left them behind. All of them. I took Eden and I ran."

Julio took a step toward her then stopped, hesitating. He scratched at the new, gray growth stubbling his cheeks. "Dakota—"

"Does that make me just as bad? I saved myself and left them. All those kids."

"You were a kid yourself. Don't forget that."

"I don't think that matters to the kids."

"You aren't responsible for saving them."

She wanted to believe his words, but she couldn't. She made a noncommittal noise in the back of her throat.

"Oh, Dakota." Julio paused, studying her, his dark eyes gentle and full of compassion. "You can't save the whole world."

Dakota snorted. "I know that. I just...all I wanted to do was save Eden. But the rest of them...those kids are trapped, too, just like we were."

"I'd want to get them out, too, if it were possible. But we can't right all the wrongs of the world. You can't take that on your shoulders. As much as you might want to think you're in control of everything, you're not."

She stared off toward the water, watched the distant fishing boat drifting next to the dock. "That's what Logan says."

"He's not wrong." Julio hesitated. "Listen. What happened to you in that place was evil. Whatever you think, it wasn't your fault—what they did to you, what you had to do to survive."

She looked at him sharply. He was watching her with a strange, strained expression, like he knew everything. Just like Ezra used to look at her—with a mix of pity, tenderness, and barely restrained anger.

"You don't have to tell me," he said softly. "I can guess plenty. Great evil has been done throughout history in God's name. Trust me, God hates it more than you do."

"Maybe," she said, not convinced.

"Those people aren't God, and they don't speak for Him. God, the real God, loves you more than you could ever know. There's nothing you can do to earn it. And there's not a thing you could do to make Him stop loving you."

A part of her wanted to roll her eyes; another part of her wished it was true. "Not a priest, huh? You sure about that?"

"I'm pretty sure a bartender can't be a priest," Julio said dryly, but he was smiling.

She found herself smiling back despite herself.

She cared about Julio, more than she'd realized. The strength of her feelings had snuck up on her, surprised her. But it was no less real. She cared about him, his safety and his family, and she wanted him to be happy.

She didn't have much experience with friendships. With relationships of any kind, really. Not growing up like she had, starved for affection and human connection. It made you so hungry, so full of longing that it was easier to shut down and go numb than endure rejection again and again.

The thought still filled her with a low, humming terror. The more you wanted, the more afraid you were of not getting it. The more you had, the more that could be ripped away from you.

Her chest tightened. Memories of the Prophet and Solomon Cage flickered through her mind, of Maddox with his knife to Eden's throat, that deadly maniacal gleam in his eyes. *The next time I see you, I'm going to kill you...*

"We could die out here," she said abruptly, her mouth going dry. "I dragged you into this. All this—everything we're doing—it's because of me. I'm putting you in danger."

"It's just as dangerous out there. Maybe even more so. Me, Logan, Eden, and Park are all alive because of you, Dakota. So is Shay. Don't forget that. And don't dismiss it so easily."

She finished the sack, tied it off, and hauled it into the nearly full wheelbarrow. She grabbed another sack from the pile and kept working. "I won't."

But her guilt, of her responsibility for all of them still tightened around her heart like a vise. The Shepherds were coming because of her. It didn't matter what anyone said; that was the truth.

If Julio got hurt, or worse, she'd never forgive herself...

"You can still leave," she said. "This isn't your fight, Julio. No one would think less of you for getting the hell out of here and saving your own family."

Julio reached out and grabbed her hand, stopping her in mid-shovel. "Boy, you are a stubborn one, aren't you? Did you not listen to the part about you saving my life?"

"You don't owe me anything," she insisted.

She hated the thought of anyone sticking around because they felt they *had* to. She'd endured enough of that with foster parents and group home workers who gave their fake smiles and their false promises, but it was all just an act.

Sure, there were plenty of foster parents who genuinely cared—Eden had lucked out with good ones. Dakota's experiences had been very different.

She shook her head and attempted to pull away, but he tightened his grip.

He intended for her to pay attention, to really hear him. "I'm here because I want to be. I'm here to protect this place and the people I care about. That includes you."

Dakota's chest filled with a sudden warmth. She looked away and blinked rapidly. She placed her gloved hand over his. "I—I'm sorry. For everything."

"You have nothing to apologize for. Nothing." He squeezed her hand. "I chose to be here. I'm meant to be here. I have faith, Dakota. There is a purpose in all of this. You may not see it yet, but there is."

"You really believe that?"

"I do. God has a purpose for you, too, Dakota. Maybe it's to save Eden. Maybe it's something more. That's for you to find out. But you'll get through this. You will. And you have your friends at your side. Don't ever forget that."

She used to believe she and Eden were safer on their own. She'd been wrong.

Now she had Eden, but also Julio. She had Ezra, and Logan. People she cared about, who truly cared for her. Maybe this was what it felt like to have a real family. To know people had your back and supported you, no matter what. It filled her with warmth, joy, and resolve.

She had more to fight for than ever before.

And more to lose.

She slipped her hands free of his grasp, dropped her gloves in the wheelbarrow, and straightened her shoulders.

Julio shielded his eyes from the sun and looked at her. "Where are you going?"

"There's something I need to do."

41

LOGAN

Logan paused and rubbed his sore back. His body wasn't meant for all this kneeling. He was supposed to be weeding the garden inside the enclosed greenhouse, but he was doing a pretty crappy job at it.

All the green stuff looked the same. He couldn't tell a ripe tomato from a cantaloupe. Eden had been working with him, showing him which green plants were weeds and which green plants were going to grow carrots, snap peas, lettuce, et cetera.

She'd taken a break to run back to the cabin to refill their water bottles from the pump.

He was alone. He licked his cracked lips, his mouth as dry as a desert. He was thirsty, but not for water.

For the hundredth time that day, he felt the need. The *wanting*. To feel that familiar, welcoming warmth buzzing through his veins. To finally numb the constant, tortured whispers of the monster lurking in his own mind.

Instinctively, he reached for his flask.

He hesitated, his hand hovering inches from his cargo pocket as he fought his own worst instincts. It was pointless to resist, anyway. What good had it done him? What was the point of all this, of any of it? There was no meaning to any of it, only death and destruction and more death.

"Hey," said a voice from behind him.

He whirled around, adrenaline pumping, the flask forgotten as he reached for his pistol. Dakota grinned down at him with a slow, lazy wave.

He wiped sweat from his brow, willing his thumping heart to still. She was good at sneaking up on people. It was disconcerting, to say the least. "It's you."

She tilted her head, studying him, but her steady, enigmatic gaze gave nothing away. That she was willing to speak to him at all was the truly surprising thing.

She must hate him. He hated himself.

"I want to show you something," she said.

He needed to escape the damning whispers inside his own tumultuous head. And his gut was still roiling from the events of yesterday. Right now, anywhere was better than here.

He dropped his gloves in the dirt. "Yeah, sure."

"Ezra will kill you if you leave them like that. Put them in the plastic tote by the door after you wipe them off."

He obeyed, wiping soil from his knees and then the gloves and putting them away neatly. He didn't need Ezra to dislike him more than he already did.

Zigzagging to avoid the booby traps across the property, Logan followed her to the edge of the swamp. The overgrown grass and weeds swished around his ankles and shins, the ground wet and spongy. Grasshoppers leapt ahead of them. The air smelled earthy, like wet grass and rotting vegetation.

His hands hung in loose fists at his sides. His palms were sore and blistered. Last night, he'd worked for hours to bury the bodies of the intruders they'd killed.

He could've left them in the woods where they'd fallen—there were plenty of dead already scattered along US 41. Or hauled them to the swamp and let the gators take care of them, like they'd done with the seven Shepherds.

But the Collier brothers hadn't wanted to leave them like so much trash. Neither had Dakota. So Logan had offered to bury them himself, alone.

He'd needed to do it. Not for the dead scumbags, but for himself. He needed to work himself to the bone, to make his hands blister and bleed, his muscles ache and burn. He needed strenuous labor to distract him, to drown out the things he couldn't afford to feel.

The digging was hard and painful, the soil soggy and threaded with roots. But it did its job. The moonshine was still in the flask, still full, ready and waiting for a moment of weakness.

He'd worked long into the night. The blonde woman he did last and buried the deepest—this close to the swamp, that wasn't far. He shoved more soil on top, forming something that slightly resembled one of those old Indian burial mounds.

It may have kept him from drinking, but the grave-digging hadn't made him feel better. It hadn't done a thing to stop the sickening waves of shame, the bitter self-loathing.

Only one thing helped with that.

He felt its pull, felt the desire to blot out the whole world and go numb bubbling up, toxic and irresistible. If he went back to it, he'd lose something critical. Of that, he was certain.

He'd sink into oblivion and never come back again.

"Hey!" Dakota touched his arm. "Logan?"

He felt the heat of her fingers like an electric shock.

He pulled away. "I'm here."

Dakota flexed her jaw, studying him again. Then her expression cleared. Whatever she was thinking, she'd made up her mind. She turned on her heels and motioned for him to follow her.

A part of him whispered that he shouldn't go. Wherever this was headed, it'd only lead to disaster and heartache for them both. But he shook it off.

Another, stronger part of him wanted to go with her. Despite everything, despite the whole world caving in on him, he wanted what he wanted.

She led him out to the old but well-made dock. The sturdy boards creaked as they strode to the small fishing boat tied to a post at the end of the dock.

She got in the boat and gestured for him to do the same.

He hesitated. "We shouldn't go far—"

"We won't." She patted the two-way radio hooked to her belt beside her holstered Springfield. "I've already let Ezra know where we'll be. First sign of trouble, we'll be right back here."

Logan stumbled awkwardly into the boat, plopping down on the aluminum bench with an unceremonious thud. It was the bow seat, she told him as she switched on the motor and directed them out into the millions of watery acres covered in endless waves of sawgrass.

He sat stiffly while she settled in behind him on the stern seat. They motored toward a channel—a clear break between the maze of grass. There were little paths everywhere, but Dakota seemed to know exactly where they were going.

Miles and miles of sawgrass as tall as their heads punctured a sea of still, dark water. Swirls of brown scum coated the surface. Clumps of trees gathered here and there like small islands, their branches draped with long, ropy vines.

Clouds of mosquitos were everywhere, buzzing and biting with that high-pitched whine. Dakota pulled a small, greenish spray bottle from her pocket and handed it to him. "Haasi's insect repellent made from crushed beautyberry. It'll last a couple of hours."

The stuff helped immensely. The swarming gnats and skeeters mostly stayed away, for a while at least.

After a few minutes, Dakota cut the motor. "Believe it or not, we're only a few minutes from the cabin. I took the long way."

Into the Fire

They floated for a while in a sea of grass, not speaking.

She pointed at a vaguely circular area filled with brown water. It looked deep. "Alligator hole. They dredge it, make it themselves. See how it's soupy, muddy? It's occupied."

"Occupied?"

"With an alligator. The monsters of the swamp."

Abruptly, the surface of the water erupted.

An enormous alligator launched itself at a tall, leggy bird dipping its bill into shallow water a dozen yards away. The alligator clamped its jaws over the bird's feathery chest and dragged it flapping and squawking below the surface.

The water churned as the gator spun with its prey. Within a minute, only a swath of bubbles revealed the bird and the gator had even existed in the first place.

"Holy hell," Logan breathed.

"Don't mess with the wildlife." She smiled at him: a real smile, soft and genuine and open, not a mask, not a shield.

It did something, tugging at some invisible string inside him.

He almost managed to smile back. "I guess not."

Desperate for a distraction, he examined the sawgrass as the boat slid past. The ends tapered to spears. Tiny, sharp teeth ran up both sides of each blade. He reached out and grabbed a stalk to study it more closely.

The clump of sawgrass cut his palm like a fistful of needles. He jerked his hand back and opened and closed it, blood welling from a half-dozen tiny cuts. He swiped his hand on his shirt.

"Everything in this swamp is dangerous," she said with a small, almost sad smile. "Scorpions hiding under logs; coral snakes, pygmy rattlers, and diamondbacks slithering through the pinelands. Alligators, water moccasins, and crocodiles in the water. Wild boars with tusks that can gut you. Even the grass is sharp as a sword."

"But you still love it."

"I still love it." She looked out over the vast expanse. "When I lived with Ezra, this is where I used to come when I needed to escape, when I needed to think."

He saw it, too. After five days out here, he truly did. There was peace, wild and untamed, but still present. A peace he wanted. He felt the longing in his very soul. "It's...something else."

She smiled wryly. "That's quite the compliment, coming from you."

Above the tangled roots of mangroves, several dozen white egrets perched, their reflections pristine against the brackish water. A thousand insects buzzed all around them. Occasional splashes indicated creatures swimming—and hunting—just beneath the surface.

Dakota said, "I think we need to talk."

42

LOGAN

Logan didn't say anything. He didn't know what to say.

Dakota stared at the murky water. "After my parents died, I learned I couldn't trust anyone but myself."

"You don't have to—"

"I want to. I think I need to." She spoke softly, haltingly, with an ache in her voice that twisted his guts. "I learned the people who were supposed to take care of me were the ones who were the most dangerous. It was a hard lesson. But I learned it. And I survived.

"After having so much of my life out of my control, I thought the way to fix everything was to control as much as I could. But that doesn't work with people. So, I'm having to learn to trust the people I care about.

"The world is terrible and broken and full of ugly and dangerous things. But it's also beautiful. Eden taught me that. She could see the beauty—could find it and name it and draw it in her notebook—and that's what kept us going. When you forget to find that thing, that's when you lose yourself, when you lose what matters.

"Something is eating away at you. I can see it. You can tell me. You can trust me."

They were sitting parallel, side by side but not facing each other. Maybe it was better that way. He couldn't bear to see the judgment in her eyes. "It's not what you think."

"A bad thing happened to you," Dakota said. "I can tell."

The sun was a white-hot circle in the sky, beating down on them. A great blue heron stood ankle-deep in the water.

Beyond it, the log resting on the muddy bank wasn't a log. An alligator, maybe twelve feet long, basking only a few yards from their flimsy fishing boat.

"I was the bad thing," Logan said.

The gator didn't move. Just stared silently back at him, a monster sizing up another monster.

Logan closed his eyes. "I was the bad thing that happened to someone else."

She raised her hand and held it over Logan's. He watched her fingers hovering over his own, hesitating, questioning. What would he do if she touched him? Did she know? Did he?

"Sometimes the bravest thing you can do is ask for help," she said.

She withdrew her hand and set it gently next to his, inches away but not touching. She was leaving the choice up to him. She wasn't going to force anything he wasn't ready for. Or didn't want.

It wasn't a matter of want. But how could he explain that to her?

"Logan," she said. "Let me in."

He'd gone too far, killing that woman. Almost killing the other two.

He hadn't been able to stop himself. He hadn't cared in the moment, but he cared now. Killing in self-defense, killing to protect the people he'd come to care about—he felt no guilt or remorse over those acts.

He'd done it before and would do it again in a heartbeat.

But killing out of bloodlust...out of anger and vengeance...wasn't that simply cold-blooded murder?

If he'd taken half a second to analyze the situation, he would've known the threat was already neutralized. But he hadn't wanted to. That was the darkness, the monster, the machine-like thing inside him that made him feel inhuman.

His stomach lurched as he glanced down at the tattoo wrapped around his forearm in a tangle of barbed wire. He rubbed the five-dot prison tattoo between his thumb and pointer finger. "I've done things..."

"Tell me." There was no judgment in her voice. No condemnation.

He remembered the night they sat together on the metal stairwell outside the hotel, when they both stayed awake to keep watch while the others slept and the city descended into chaos.

She'd opened up to him, laid herself bare, and he'd forgiven her for everything.

He doubted forgiveness was possible for him. He knew it wasn't. The person whom he most needed forgiveness from was no longer among the living.

His hands were trembling. That sick, cold feeling thrummed through his whole body.

He forgot the oppressive sun, the heat, the bugs. Everything was still—the sawgrass, the mangrove trees along the far bank—hanging limp and motionless, drained by the heat.

Tell me.

He did.

43

LOGAN

"For you!" Tomás stood outside Logan's apartment doorway, clutching an orange and gazing up at him with those huge, earnest eyes. An oversized Avengers backpack sagged from the boy's slim shoulder.

"Fruit of the day," he said with a goofy grin.

Logan leaned out and peered down the shabby hallway to the right, then the left. The exposed fluorescent light bulbs along the cracked, stained ceiling flickered and buzzed.

No one there. No one but the kid.

A big deal was going down tonight or maybe tomorrow. He didn't have time for this. Still, he managed a smile and took the orange.

"Next time, I owe you a candy bar."

"I just got *Call of Duty: Black Ops 5*. Wanna play?" Tomás folded his hands into two finger-guns and mimed a shooting battle. "Bam, bam, bam! You're so dead! I'll beat you this time for sure."

Occasionally, Tomás's mother, Adelina, asked Logan to watch Tomás for an hour or so while she went grocery shopping, to the doctor's, or had to work late cleaning houses for rich people in the suburbs.

Into the Fire

Logan and Tomás would play video games until she returned, exhausted and rubbing her eyes, but with a grateful smile. That she was a beautiful woman didn't hurt, either.

"Where's your mama?"

Tomás shrugged. "We ran out of Lucky Charms. She promised she'd stop at the store on her way home."

Logan glanced at his phone. It was already past 3:30 p.m. She'd be back by 4:00, 4:30 at the latest. The kid would be fine on his own for a while.

Tomás poked his gun-finger into Logan's stomach. "Bam! Let's play."

"Maybe later." Logan was distracted. There was too much going on. He needed to think, to focus. He plucked the orange from the kid's hand, said a hasty goodbye, and shut the door.

He tossed the orange in the overflowing trash bin beneath the sink filled with dirty dishes. He didn't like oranges all that much, though the kid seemed to think he did.

Anyway, he was too tense to eat.

He paced his narrow one-bedroom apartment, his shoes scuffing the peeling linoleum in the kitchen and worn carpet in the living room. It was less than ten long strides from the sagging kitchen cabinets to the far wall, bare and yellowed around the huge 70-inch TV screen Alejandro had bought for him last year.

Alejandro Gomez, second in command of the La Mara Salvatrucha, or MS-13, chapter in Richmond, Virginia. A stone-cold killer and ruthless leader, one no one wanted to cross or disappoint, not if you wanted to keep all your fingers.

It was Alejandro who had taken him in like his own son, had given him a role, a purpose, a brotherhood. To Logan, a fatherless boy scraping out a living on the streets, brawling for every inch of space to call his own, that was everything.

He'd fought and bled and killed his way through the ranks until he was Alejandro's righthand man, his soldier, his assassin.

So what the hell was Logan doing here in his apartment, wearing out the soles of his shoes? A cold fury burned through him. It was all he could do not to break something.

Last night, Francisco "The Snake" Torres-Amador, a rival leader of one of the regional Bloods franchises, had taken out seven of Alejandro's men in a raid of one of their stash houses. They'd stolen 1.5 million bucks in coke and destroyed the house, setting it ablaze and attracting the attention of the cops.

One of the MS-13 members killed was Alejandro's sixteen-year-old cousin.

Alejandro would never let it go. Not until he hunted down every single Blood involved and removed their limbs from their bodies, one by one, while they were still alive.

Thing was, the stash was only at the house for a day on its way to L.A. and bigger buyers. Only a handful of the local upper tier MS-13 members knew about it or its location.

Which meant only one thing.

Alejandro's crew had a mole—and Alejandro suspected Logan.

Logan cursed. The simulated gunfire and rumbling noises of Tomás's video game echoed through the paper-thin walls. The old lady across the hallway, Mrs. Costales, was cooking empanadas; the delicious scent wafted through the crack beneath the door.

Sometimes, she brought him a few, always chattering in Spanish about pairing him up with her single thirty-two-year-old granddaughter. But he wasn't hungry for empanadas now—he hadn't eaten since last night, when he'd learned Alejandro hadn't come straight to him to plan their revenge.

In fact, he hadn't heard from Alejandro at all.

Alejandro had already cut him out. Someone had been whispering toxic lies in his ear. Maybe Oscar Reyes, a treacherous, slippery eel of a man without a loyal bone in his body. He'd slaughter his own grandmother for a chance at more power.

Into the Fire

Logan had loathed him for years but had never been able to pin him down and expose his duplicity. How was he going to fix this?

Logan was an idiot for remaining here like a kicked dog, for sitting back and allowing this betrayal, letting the knife slide into his back without a fight.

If he was going down, he was going down swinging. And Oscar Reyes was going with him.

Anyone who knew anything about Logan Garcia knew he'd claw his way out of the grave just to keep on fighting. He flexed his scarred knuckles and nodded to himself. No, he couldn't take this lying down.

He grabbed his Glock from the counter, strapped on his holster, and slipped three loaded magazines into his pockets. Reyes had another thing coming if he thought—

The door burst open.

Instantly, Logan dropped to one knee, elbow braced on his thigh, pistol aimed at the doorway, ready to shoot someone's head off.

"Easy, *ese*." Alejandro laughed. "I brought you a present."

44

LOGAN

Alejandro strode into Logan's shabby apartment like he owned it. He believed he did, just like he owned Logan.

Two muscular, tattooed Latinos followed him, dragging a limp body between them. They hauled the body into the living room and dropped him, groaning, onto the carpet two feet from the muzzle of Logan's gun.

The Snake looked up at him through eyes nearly swollen shut. Logan could barely make out the tattoos of snake eyes inked on Francisco Torres-Amador's eyelids through the mashed flesh, torn cartilage, and mangled bone that remained of his face.

Francisco eased back on his heels, wincing and breathing hard, one hand clutching the right side of his ribcage. He'd likely suffered several cracked ribs. Alejandro enjoyed kicking his enemies while they were down.

Blood leaked from a jagged cut in the man's forehead and dripped onto the carpet. Logan stared at the round, red stains until his vision blurred. The empanadas cooking down the hall filled his nostrils. The muffled bang and boom of Tomás's video game filtered through the wall.

Fresh anger roiled through him.

"This is where I live," Logan hissed. "You can't come here like this. We don't do this in our own backyards!"

Alejandro only offered him a hard smile. "No? Maybe we should, *ese*. Maybe I wanted to see you two face-to-face, yeah?"

Gonzalo Rodrìguez stood to the right—a huge, hairy gorilla of a grunt who spoke little and communicated mostly with his massive fists. On the left, rat-faced Oscar Reyes held a pistol outfitted with a silencer to The Snake's skull.

A silencer wasn't silent enough. Would Tomás's video game muffle the sound of real bullets? Would these flimsy walls offer any protection at all in case things went sideways and a stray round punched through gypsum straight into Tomás's living room?

Logan rose to his feet, gun still in hand, and circled the fallen man, Alejandro's grunts on either side of him, buying himself a few moments to think.

He'd lived here peaceably for three years. He liked his neighbors. Knew them. Many of the low-income housing tenements were overrun by low-rung hoodlums and neighborhood teenage gangs killing each other over territorial scuffles.

He'd searched long and hard to find one that was relatively quiet.

It meant something to him.

Alejandro had helped him find this place. He knew Logan better than anyone, which meant he knew how to hurt him.

"Times like this, we need to prove our loyalties, *ese*," Alejandro said.

Logan glanced from Reyes to Alejandro. Reyes' grin was gleeful— and greedy.

Alejandro looked tense, suspicious, and quietly furious. He had a hairpin trigger of a temper. His retribution was swift, pitiless, and often reckless. He only questioned himself afterward, when it was far too late for the poor soul he'd already maimed and murdered.

Logan needed to tread very, very carefully.

"Just tell me what to do," he said evenly, though his pulse had skyrocketed. "I'm your brother."

Alejandro raised his brows. "Are you?"

"You know that I am."

Alejandro's lips pressed into a thin line. He waved his gun at Francisco. "Kill him. Slowly. So we all can see where your loyalties lie."

Alejandro knew Logan killed with efficiency. He was very good at what he did, but he had a distaste for cruelty, for torture. A bullet to the brain was just as effective and saved energy and ammo that could better be applied elsewhere.

Alejandro was playing with him, like a cat plays with a mouse. Testing him. But to what end?

Francisco swore at them. Alejandro kicked him savagely in the face. The man collapsed with a yelp and curled into a fetal ball.

Reyes laughed and spat on him. "Not so hot now, are you?"

"Ask him who told him about the coke," Alejandro instructed. "Shoot his feet, then his hands, then his knees, until he talks."

"We can't do this here," Logan said. "It's too dangerous."

Reyes smirked. "You better hurry, then."

"Get him to talk." Alejandro's voice went low and cold. "And you better pray he doesn't say the name of someone in this room."

"Go to hell," Francisco growled. "I'll kill you! My boys'll hunt you down and cut off your—"

This time, Logan kicked him in the stomach. "Shut up!"

Reyes pulled a silencer out of his pocket and handed it to Logan. They watched as Logan threaded the long, black metal tube to the end of his Glock.

He pointed the gun at the man's right foot, encased in the latest pair of Lebron Soldier basketball shoes. He hesitated. He was a good shot. He wouldn't miss. But the round might go straight through the foot into the ceiling of the apartment below.

He got low as he aimed so if the bullet went into the floor, it would

Into the Fire

skim the ceiling over the occupants' heads and lodge itself harmlessly in the outer wall. Hopefully.

He breathed in, focused, shut out the anxiety, the dread, the fear souring his gut. He exhaled and shot down and angled into the side of the man's foot.

Francisco screamed.

"Tell us a name," Logan said.

Francisco was too busy writhing on the floor in agony to answer.

Logan didn't have a clear shot of his other foot. Reyes stomped down on his leg, eliciting another shrill scream but it anchored him in place. Logan aimed for a larger target and shot just above the left kneecap.

Each shot sounded like a cannon blast echoing in his ears.

"Logan?" a tremulous voice asked.

Logan whipped around.

Tomás stood in the doorway. Alejandro's men had left the door propped open.

A chill went up Logan's spine. His mouth went dry. They'd left the door open on purpose. They wanted someone to hear, wanted an innocent victim.

Now they had one.

"Get out!" Logan said.

Tomás only looked at him in confusion. He held a bright orange in one hand, the plastic *Call of Duty* case in the other.

"I just wanted...I thought..." His voice trailed off, his eyes growing larger as he took in the men, the guns, the bloody, groaning man on the floor.

Oscar Reyes smiled like a shark, completely devoid of warmth or humor. "Come on in, kid."

45

LOGAN

Reyes herded Tomás into the room, pointing with his gun. "On the couch."

"No," Logan said. "He doesn't have anything to do with this. He didn't see nothing. Get him out of here."

The boy froze. One step inside the doorway, the kitchen to his left, the main apartment corridor behind him, the living room straight ahead. His gaze went wild with fear as understanding slowly infiltrated his eight-year-old mind.

Francisco wheezed through his broken nose. He raised his head and glared at Reyes. "Let me go and I'll tell you what you want. I'll tell you exactly who—"

"No." Reyes pivoted, aimed his weapon down, and pulled the trigger. The bullet punched through The Snake's left temple, just above his ear. He died in mid-scream.

Reyes looked straight at Logan. "Now, he's seen plenty. Now, he's a witness."

Logan lunged at Reyes.

"I wouldn't do that."

The ice in Alejandro's voice brought him up short. Logan

stopped himself, muscles straining, every fiber of his being longing to close his fingers around Reyes' skinny throat and wring the life out of him.

Reyes glared at him, eyes flashing in triumph, but he wisely said nothing.

One more word and Logan would kill him.

"Move, boy." Alejandro pointed his gun at the kid.

Trembling, Tomás obeyed. He shuffled to the couch and sat down stiffly, his little shoulders quaking.

"Reyes, shut the door."

Reyes had only taken a few steps toward the door when footsteps came down the hall. They'd all been so focused on Tomás that none of them heard it until it was too late.

A figure appeared in the doorway, clutching a brown bag of groceries.

Logan's stomach sank. It was Adelina, Tomás's mother. She was harried and huffing, strands of black hair falling into her face, but smiling like she always did when she came to his door. *Esta Tomás aquí?*

Only this time, the smile froze on her face, transforming into a rictus of shock and horror. "*Qué estás haciendo!* Tomás!"

Reyes reached her in one long stride, seized her arm, and jerked her inside the apartment. He slammed the door shut and turned the three bolt locks.

Adelina stumbled and fell to her knees, the paper bag slipping from her fingers. Cans, boxes, and a bag of beans spilled out. The lid of a colorful box of Lucky Charms peeked out of the fallen bag.

"Get up!" Reyes grabbed a hank of her hair, dragged her to her feet, and threw her onto the couch next to her son.

She sobbed as she pulled her son close. Tomás wrapped his thin arms around her waist and gazed up at Logan beneath his mop of black curls, those big eyes shiny with bewilderment and terror.

Logan felt like he'd been gut-punched. The boy had only looked at him with trust and adoration before. Not anymore. Now, both Adelina and Tomás saw him for the monster that he was.

"You!" Adelina cried. "I trusted you! What you do? You bring death here? To my son? *Qué has hecho?!*"

He shook his head, panic rising, clawing at his throat, his mind frantically searching for a way out of this, a way to get Tomás and Adelina out of here alive. Even as the thoughts careened inside his head, the sickening churn of his stomach told him what his body already knew—there was no escape from this.

He was as trapped as they were.

Alejandro turned to Logan. "Kill them."

"We don't have to do this—"

"We do. You do."

"He's just a kid."

"A kid who saw us murder this *perro hijueputa*. He could put us all in the joint for life," Reyes said.

"You goin' soft, *hermano*?" Alejandro said. "So soft you would disobey me? Or maybe...betray me?"

"No," Logan said around the growing lump in his throat. "Never."

Alejandro's phone buzzed. He pulled it out and scowled. "We've been burned. Someone called the cops. Gio says sirens, five blocks away."

Rodríguez cursed. It was the first time he'd spoken a word.

"Kill them," Alejandro said. "Now."

For a split second, Logan imagined firing a bullet point blank at Alejandro, punching the round directly between his hard, startled eyes. Imagined the shock of betrayal turning to rage and then despair as the man he called brother realized he was dying.

Logan could do it. He could whirl and nail both Reyes and Rodríguez in less than three seconds. Then only Alejandro would be left. With the element of surprise on his side, maybe it would be enough.

He could kill all three of them...then what? Hope Tomás and

Adelina were grateful enough to lie for him? Pray he could escape with nothing but the clothes on his back before the police arrived?

No. He couldn't.

Alejandro was his mentor, his brother. Logan despised Reyes, but the rest of them were his family. The only family he had. Without them, he was lost. Without purpose, without meaning.

As good as dead himself.

Besides, even if he took out these three, the rest of his brothers would know who'd betrayed Alejandro. They would come for Logan and they wouldn't stop coming until they killed him.

He didn't tell himself he didn't have a choice. That was the coward's justification, and a piss-poor one at that. He knew what he was doing, what choice he was making. His life for theirs.

In some distant, horrified part of his brain, he understood that Tomás's face would be seared forever into his consciousness. He could never unsee this, never undo this moment.

"Do it!" Reyes said, already moving toward the door, Rodríguez hustling right behind him, their expressions tense. "We gotta burn this place. Let's go!"

Only Alejandro remained beside him. "Where your loyalties lie, ese?" he asked, quiet and deadly calm.

"No!" Adelina cried. She reached for Logan, begging, weeping, her mascara streaming down her face, her despairing gaze piercing straight through him. "Take me, kill me. Not him. Not Tomás. *Por favor!* Please..."

He let the darkness take over. He let himself go numb and cold and hard. He shut out the screams, the cries for mercy, those desperate, terror-filled eyes.

He raised the Glock. Exhaled, aimed, squeezed the trigger.

It was a good shot. A perfect shot.

He shifted his aim to the left and slightly down. He hesitated, muzzle trembling.

"Oh, screw it." Alejandro raised his own weapon. The shot echoed in the small apartment. A muffled *pop*, and then it was over.

It was done fast, he told himself.

They didn't suffer.

The only one left to suffer was himself.

46

LOGAN

Logan stared at the placid swamp, his eyes stinging. His stomach churned. Acid burned the back of his throat. He felt sick. Disgusted with himself. Repulsed and horrified.

He tried to shake off the memories, but they lingered—dark shapes submerged below the surface, like the hulking beasts that drifted in the black waters beneath their boat.

He couldn't stand it. Couldn't stand himself. He wanted desperately to get away, to escape, to claw out of his own wretched skin and be anyone but who he really was.

He waited for Dakota to judge him, scream at him, reject him.

Hell, maybe she'd pull out her XD-S and put him out of his misery for good.

He'd topple into the swamp and sink to the muck below. The blood leaking from the hole in his skull would attract the lurking monsters, monsters that'd tear into flesh and bone with their massive jaws, devouring him limb by limb, until there was nothing left.

It was what he deserved.

He waited.

Nothing happened.

She didn't say anything. Didn't do anything. She just sat there.

The sun beat down on his head and shoulders. The silence lengthened, broken by the occasional splash of fish and the buzzing of a hundred different species of insects.

The bulge of the flask in his cargo pocket pressed against his thigh. He longed to slug it all down right here and now. To go numb. To forget everything in his past, every horrific thing he'd ever done.

Drinking would give that back to him. The forgetting. The numbness. A way to survive the crushing guilt, the self-loathing, the despair.

He formed sentences in his head, each more terrible than the last, the words like ashes disintegrating on his tongue. They clogged in his throat, cutting off his breath.

The silence stretched taut as a rubber band about to snap, until finally it became unbearable. He had to say something. He had to say it out loud.

"I killed them," he said.

"You did," Dakota said. There was no hatred in her voice, only heavy sadness, a tinge of grief. But no accusation, no judgment.

"I killed a child and I killed his mother."

"You didn't shoot Tomás."

"I might as well have," he said, that old despairing fury rising in his chest. "I stood there and did nothing, didn't I? I let it happen to save myself. It doesn't make me any less responsible. It doesn't make me any less of a monster."

"You aren't a monster," she said softly.

He didn't dare look at her. "You must hate me."

"I don't."

"You should."

"I'm quite capable of thinking my own thoughts."

"I'll leave. You can take me back to the cabin. I'll pack my bag and be out of your hair by nightfall."

"Did I say I wanted you to leave?"

"No, but—"

"I'm not going to justify your actions for you," she said quietly, staring down at her hands. "But I'm not going to condemn you, either."

He waited, said nothing, his whole body tense like he was entering a battle weaponless. There was no way to fight this thing inside him, no way to ever make the past okay.

Tomás would never grow up. The little boy with the too-big head and huge eyes, who loved NASCAR and video games, who despised oranges but loved his mother too much to disappoint her, who'd looked at Logan a thousand times with nothing but trust and affection.

Pain wracked him. With it came the shame, black and ugly, a cancerous rot eating away at him as surely as the insidious radiation. "You don't understand—"

"Yes, I do." She turned and stared straight at him. "Would you do it again?"

"Never. It doesn't matter whether it's my life on the line. I'd rather die a thousand times than hurt them—or any innocent person—ever again."

"Okay," she said simply.

"Who I am isn't who you think—"

"I know who you are."

He watched her warily. "But who I was..."

"Someone I respect once told me that we can't change the past, but we can decide whether we let it control our future."

He gave a hard, helpless shrug. "I don't know if I can do that. If I deserve to do that."

He listened to the birds chirping from a cluster of cypress trees off to their right. A large gray bird with long, spindly legs stalked in the shallows across the far bank, hunting for its prey.

A mosquito buzzed around his face. He ignored it. "I'm a murderer."

"You are, but that isn't all you are."

He waved his hand helplessly. "I almost killed an unarmed woman and a girl yesterday, in case you forgot."

"Almost. You didn't do it."

How could he say the words out loud, make it real? It was like dressing a shadow in flesh and bone, creating a monster out of smoke and dust. "I can't control it. I'm...I'm afraid of myself."

"You stopped, Logan. You *can* control it. You made the choice. Maybe that voice inside your head tells you that you can't, but it's a liar."

He cracked his scarred knuckles. The words he'd tattooed on his arm stared back at him, the accusing Latin words bristling with barbed wire: *et facti sunt ne unum.*

Lest you become one.

"I belong in prison. Four years wasn't enough. Not for this. Or maybe I deserve the electric chair."

"Maybe," she allowed. "Maybe a few weeks ago, I would've agreed with you. But things have changed. The world has changed. But you have to make that choice yourself. You have to decide."

"Decide what?"

"You can turn yourself in and waste the rest of your life in a cell. You can drown your guilt in the bottom of a bottle and waste the rest of your life in misery. Or you can stop feeling sorry for yourself, man up, and be who you want to be."

"I don't deserve a good life. Not after what I've done."

"I don't know if there's a God out there, judging us. Maybe Julio's right and God is all about love and mercy. Either way, people get what they don't deserve all the time."

"How can I ever make up for what I did?" he asked brokenly.

"You can't. Not for Tomás and Adelina. But throwing away your life won't do anything for them, either. Julio believes every life has a purpose. Maybe yours is to do enough good that someday it tilts the scales against the bad."

"Like redemption."

She shrugged. "Maybe the idea of redemption is just something religious people believe in, but I don't think so. The world needs people willing to fight for something that's good, now more than ever." Her jaw flexed. "Everything we do matters. It has too. Otherwise, nothing matters."

"That all sounds great, but not for me. Not after what I've done. I'm...not a good person."

"The worst of humanity, the truly evil people, they don't give a rat's ass whether they deserve anything. It's the decent ones who worry about whether they're good or not."

He bowed his head, his shoulders hunched. "I'm not."

"How many lives have you saved in the last three weeks, Logan? You've stuck with us, haven't you? Even after I lied to you. You risked your neck for me and Eden more than once. A lesser man would've hit the road long ago. So don't give me that crap. I didn't know who you were, but I know who you are now. I know you."

He didn't say anything, but he heard her. He heard every word.

For the first time in a long time, he saw the glimpse of a future that contained more than violence and death, more than shame and despair. Maybe there was a way. A way to merge both death and life, violence and love.

He was a man of violence—that wasn't going to change. But maybe he could harness that darkness to protect, not to destroy.

Maybe there was a way back.

It had seemed impossible, but right now, anything seemed possible. Here was Dakota Sloane, the toughest girl he'd ever met, who'd survived her own hell, who'd battled her own demons but didn't judge him for his.

He'd shown her the worst of him—the darkness, the monster without a conscience, the thing he most loathed about himself—and she hadn't flinched.

She didn't run away. She was still here. She was just one person, but she was the most important person.

And somehow, that made all the difference.

Something took root inside his chest, something he hadn't felt in a long, long time. Hope.

"Thank you," he forced out around the lump in his throat.

"Julio's the one for the deep talks." Her mouth twitched, the faintest hint of a smile forming. "I pretty much suck at this."

"No," he said, "you really don't."

Her smile widened.

Their boat drifted into a wall of cattails stretching as far as he could see in either direction. It was a maze inside, like they'd been swallowed by a labyrinth of green stalks.

Small green frogs leapt from the cattails into the water. On his left, two birds screeched and lifted off with a flurry of beating wings. Bullfrogs croaked. A majestic great blue heron made its way across the sky, gliding, its wings a slow rhythmic flapping.

It felt like they were the only two people in the world.

Dakota's hands were loose on her knees, her right knee only a few inches from his own. Her hair was up in its usual ponytail, the sun streaking the auburn strands a fiery red. A few loose strands clung damply to her cheeks and forehead.

This close, he could see the faint spray of freckles across her nose, the sardonic tilt of her lips, the curve of her jaw that gave her face that hint of softness that he loved.

He didn't hesitate this time. He took her hand.

Dakota wound her fingers through his and squeezed.

"Burn it," she said. "Burn the past. Build something new."

When he leaned in and kissed her, it felt right.

It felt like the most right thing in the whole broken world.

47

MADDOX

The door to the infirmary burst open. Reuben shouldered his bulk inside. "Enough resting!" he crowed. "Time for all my favorite things—fighting, killing, and vengeance."

Maddox smoothed the wrinkles in the fresh shirt and khakis he'd just dressed himself in. Dim dawn light spilled into the room through the opened door, but he'd been awake for hours. "I've been waiting for you."

"Ha!" Reuben guffawed. "We've been waiting for you to get off your sorry butt for, what, six days now?" His eyes glittered. "You're running out of time."

"Tonight," Maddox said. "It's happening tonight."

Reuben's gaze sharpened. "You sure you're up to it?"

"I'm fine. I'm ready."

"Great, man." He leaned in and slapped Maddox's shoulder far too close to one of the scabbed lash wounds. Maddox bit down on the inside of his cheek to keep from crying out. Hot tears sprang to his eyes, but he quickly blinked them back.

Reuben was testing him for weakness.

Maddox refused to show him any. Ignoring the pain, he squared his shoulders. The days of rest had done him a world of good. His strength was returning. He felt better than he had in weeks, since before the blast. "Let's go. We've got a mission to plan."

"Of course." Reuben's smile was wide and bright as usual, but there was a glimpse of something in his eyes, a hint of displeasure. Jealousy, maybe, that the Prophet had chosen Maddox, not himself. "First things first, though. The Prophet's got something big brewing. It'll blow your mind, man. He said it was time to show you."

He smiled back, just as wide and bright as Reuben's. "So, show me."

They turned toward the door.

Sister Rosemarie stepped into the doorway, dressed in her long dusky blue skirt, her graying hair tucked into a bun and her hands clasped demurely in front of her.

"Blessings be upon you, Reuben," Sister Rosemarie said stiffly.

Reuben flashed his teeth at her in an approximation of a smile, but they both knew it wasn't. "And you, Sister."

They'd never liked each other. Reuben hated how Sister Rosemarie insisted on speaking her mind. He preferred his women quiet, meek, and obedient, just like his father did. And Sister Rosemarie despised Reuben's brashness and obvious taste for violence.

"We were just leaving," Maddox said.

"Godspeed," Sister Rosemarie said quietly, something raw and broken in her voice. "May God show you the right path."

He didn't want to hear it. He didn't need a reminder of the heretical doubts she'd tried to implant in his head. He shoved roughly past her, pushing her out of his mind with just as much finality.

He had no need of her anymore.

He followed Reuben out the door. It wasn't ten in the morning yet and the heat wrapped him in a thick, stifling blanket.

They crossed the main clearing of the River Grass Compound and headed south toward the swamp. A gravel path took them through a thick wooded area of cypress and live oak trees to the restricted zone.

Guards patrolled the huge, fenced perimeter of the entire compound, but a second fence enclosed this area, off-limits to anyone but the Chosen.

They approached the entrance. A young Shepherd in his mid-twenties dressed in military fatigues with a wicked-looking M4 slung over his shoulder. He slumped against the fence, legs crossed at the ankles, eyes half-closed with a dazed, sleepy expression.

"You remember Aaron Hill," Reuben said breezily.

The Shepherd snapped to attention. He lifted his chin and pulled his shoulders back, clearing his throat nervously.

"Wouldn't take a nap right now if I were you," Reuben said dryly. "Not when Satan's minions could attack us at any moment. Can't have God's soldiers falling asleep on the job, can we?"

"No, sir!" Aaron had the same medium-brown skin tone, small build, and narrow features as his little sister, Ruth. Aaron still had a slight limp after a run-in a few years back with a mangrove rattler—a venomous water moccasin.

He and Maddox had played together as children, but not for many years. Maddox tried to remember what he was like, but his memories came up empty.

"What's the penalty for that?" Rueben asked.

"Five lashes to remind us of our sacred duty to the Lord, sir."

Reuben smirked. "Should we make him pay it?"

"Not now," Maddox said, already impatient with Reuben's games. "Guess you get a pass, soldier. This time."

Aaron nodded gratefully at Maddox as they passed.

Maddox didn't bother to nod back. "Where are we going?"

"Just be patient."

They entered the training arena—several acres studded with fox holes, sandbags, and shredded paper targets tacked to various trees. Maddox glimpsed a few dozen men spread throughout the arena. The sounds of gunfire, grunting, and muffled shouts peppered the air.

"They're training for combat conditions," Reuben explained.

"They're practicing short range rifle drills and close-quarters combat drills. Tactical scenarios, ambushes, guerilla warfare. You know the drill."

"I know the drill."

"We've got to be ready." Reuben spat on the ground at his feet and wiped sweat from his brow. "They'll be coming for us soon; you can count on that."

Maddox didn't have to ask who was coming for them. It'd been hammered into their brains since they could walk. Those who lived outside the compound walls were wicked, the depraved, demon-possessed enemies plotting their demise. The corrupt, degenerate U.S. government, the pinnacle of unholy Satan's power, would attempt to destroy the Chosen people of God.

With the Prophet's plans now in play, it would be sooner rather than later.

They reached the green-painted wood and corrugated metal buildings, all deep in shadow beneath the cover of a cypress dome. The trees protected them from the prying eyes of drones and satellites, if anyone ever cared to take a second look at a million miles of worthless swampland.

Inside the first building, three Shepherds sat before a bank of screens and high-tech electronic equipment. Wires and cords were coiled everywhere, attached to various blinking black boxes.

Maddox raised his brows. "I thought we just used old-fashioned written letters to communicate so we stay completely off the government's radar."

"Mostly. But we have other ways." Reuben gestured at a computer screen featuring what looked like a gameboard of squares labeled with numbers and letters. Some were gray, some were filled in with different colors. "The internet is awesome, isn't it? You can find anything on it. Literally anything. This is a website for an old board game made in the '80s called 'Acquire.' A few hundred die-hard fans get on this site and play each other in private games. The goal is building cities and managing stocks or something."

"It's actually pretty fun," said one of the Shepherds at the computer. He was a skinny guy in his thirties with big ears and an acne-scarred face. A tech nerd, not a warrior.

Reuben sneered at him. "It's not for *playing*. The square grids and the tiles with different number and letter combinations are freaking perfect for a code. Which is exactly what we did. In the game, the tiles generate randomly to each player, but Tim here hacked the site so we can choose whichever tiles we need to play for different codes. We can communicate with our people on the outside whenever we need to."

Skinny Guy grinned proudly. "And our enemies are none the wise. Even the FBI and CIA'll never figure this out."

"Yeah, okay," Maddox said, "but where are the guns?"

Reuben led him back into the woods along the gravel road. Outside the armory, several large, heavy-duty cargo trucks with raised suspension, studded tires, and armored sides were lined up in a gravel parking area. Small canons were mounted in the cupolas on top.

Reuben slapped the door frame. "These puppies have enough armor to repel a small army outfitted with RPGs."

Inside the armory, the walls were lined with shelves boasting an impressive collection of guns: pistols, shotguns, semi-automatic rifles, machine guns, and boxes and boxes of ammo. There were tactical bullet-proof vests, night vision goggles with infrared and thermal imaging, and scopes.

Reuben pointed across the room. "We got ourselves a few stinger missiles a couple of years ago. We can take down a chopper with that beast."

Maddox whistled. "How'd the Prophet get his hands on hardware like that?"

Reuben shrugged. "He's the voice of God on Earth. Nothing is out of his reach if God wants him to have it."

Maddox had his doubts, but he kept them to himself.

Reuben grinned at him. "The real answer? Donors, man. The Prophet's got believers out among the wicked heretics. Filthy-rich ones that own condos and luxury apartment buildings in Manhattan and Fort Lauderdale—all well clear of the bombs, of course. Whenever we need an influx of cash, they sell a bunch of condos and wire us another million."

Maddox tried to hide his surprise. He'd had no idea, but it made sense. No one within the compound owned property or held jobs in the outside world, and yet the Prophet never lacked for funds.

Reuben palmed a grenade and grinned. "Feels good to be on God's side of the war, that's for sure."

48

MADDOX

Maddox donned a tactical vest, loaded it with preloaded magazines and gear, and selected an M4A1 carbine for himself. He activated the optics, brought the carbine to his shoulder, and took a closer look through the telescopic sight of the scope.

The six-pound heft of it felt right in his arms. The specs were nothing to sneeze at: full auto capability at 950 rounds per minute, a muzzle velocity of 2900 feet per second, range of six hundred meters.

"Good choice," Reuben said.

"I want a team of the best."

"Don't worry, man. I've got your back. I've already assembled us a team of our best killers."

"I want twenty men."

"What?" Reuben sputtered. "For an old man and a couple of girls? Are you stupid? They're non-factors." His lip curled. "Or maybe you're just afraid? Maybe you're not ready for this after all."

Maddox didn't react to the insult. "The Prophet trusted me with this task. Me. Those 'non-factors' already took out five of ours, in case you forgot."

"Those guys were young and green." Reuben waved a dismissive hand. "This time, it's us. You and me. They'll never see us coming."

"Twenty men."

A shadow crossed Reuben's face—he didn't like to be contradicted or told what to do. But Maddox was in charge, not him. He didn't care who Reuben's father was, and he didn't care if Reuben resented him for it.

"Yeah, okay. Fine," he said finally.

A small smile played across Maddox's lips. He allowed himself to imagine the victory, the feel of the M4 jittering in his hands, spraying death wherever he chose to aim. "They aren't harmless. We won't underestimate them. But I have an idea."

"Of course, you do!" Reuben said brightly, instantly back to his jovial self. "That's why you belong among us, cousin." He raised a hand to slap Maddox's shoulder again, but Maddox deftly sidestepped the blow.

"I know, *cousin*."

"There's one more thing you need to see." Reuben narrowed his eyes at Maddox. "You sure you're ready? You can still change your mind. No shame in it, man."

The way he said it meant he thought there was tremendous shame in it. Maddox forced himself to match Reuben's fake smile. "I am."

"Then what're we waiting for?"

Maddox followed Reuben deeper into the woods, swatting at mosquitoes. Reuben took him to yet another squat concrete building, one he'd never seen before.

This one was larger than the others. Tall antennas and satellites bristled from the flat tin roof, piercing the leafy tree canopy shielding it from prying eyes. Two armed Shepherds stood motionless on either side of the single door, standing guard.

A short, squat middle-aged man of European descent stood a few feet in front of the building, speaking in low tones with Maddox's father. Maddox had seen him around the compound the last few years. He was a quiet, withdrawn man who spoke with no one but the Prophet or Solomon Cage.

Abruptly, Reuben seized Maddox's arm and jerked him behind a thick tree and screen of underbrush. He held a finger to his lips until Maddox nodded, showing he understood. This was a conversation they weren't supposed to overhear—Reuben's favorite kind.

That's our resident nuclear physicist, Franco Sorokin," Reuben whispered. "Defected from Ukraine or Bosnia or Russia or something. The Prophet's had him hard at work lately."

"For what?" Maddox whispered back.

Reuben's eyes gleamed. "The next stage."

They waited behind the brush, straining to listen and silently enduring a dozen mosquito bites.

"I'm not finished yet," Franco said. He had a harsh Eastern European accent, though his English was precise.

"That's unacceptable!" Solomon Cage said, his voice dripping with the derision Maddox knew so well. "The Prophet has already spoken. It is God's will. Everything is playing out exactly as planned. It happens in three days, or it'll be your head to pay."

Franco Sorokin bobbed his head frantically, his thick glasses slipping down his nose. He nudged them back into place with his thumb. "Okay, yes, of course. I did not mean to cast doubt."

He mumbled something in a harsh, phlegmy foreign language.

"You better not let the Prophet hear you talk like that," Maddox's father snapped.

"Oh, sorry, sorry." He bobbed his head deeper. "With God's blessing, it'll be ready."

Maddox's father sneered down at the cowering man. "It'd better be."

He turned on his heel and stalked down the narrow pathway between the trees, already pulling out his handheld radio to browbeat someone else into submission.

He didn't see Maddox or Reuben in the shadows.

The nuclear physicist scurried back inside. They waited several beats in silence before moving.

The Shepherds standing guard said nothing when Reuben strode up, Maddox trailing behind him. They didn't say anything when Reuben hauled open the door and ushered Maddox in, either.

Reuben was the Prophet's son; no one questioned him. Most of the time, Maddox hated it—once in a while, it worked in his favor.

Inside, the building was lit with harsh fluorescent lighting. A generator hummed. Maddox took it all in, his brain scrambling to catch up with what his eyes were seeing.

His heart jackhammered against his ribs. He wiped his already sweaty palms on his pants. He hadn't been sure what to expect. It wasn't this.

"Holy—" he muttered.

"I know, right?" Reuben's grin widened. "It's gonna be insane. It's gonna change everything, man. Absolutely everything."

49

LOGAN

"You don't belong here," Ezra said.

Logan looked up sharply. "What?"

Ezra Burrows stared at him with those disconcerting sky-blue eyes of his. Wrinkles creased his leathered face like lines in cement. "You heard me."

Logan wasn't sure how to respond. "Dakota invited me."

"Dakota's a smart, capable girl. But you think you're smarter, don't you?"

Logan thrust the shovel into the ground and scooped dirt into the wheelbarrow behind him, grunting with the effort. "I'm not sure what you—"

"You're after Dakota."

Heat rushed to his throat, his face. He shifted awkwardly. "Well, I don't think I'd put it that way."

In the last six days, it seemed that Logan had made zero headway in winning Ezra over. If anything, he seemed more hostile.

But then Ezra had specifically asked for Logan's help. Dakota was out patrolling the perimeter of the property, checking for any overlooked deficiencies. Julio was helping her but took a few minutes to check in with Shay and his wife.

Park was preparing a lunch of turtle stew in the cabin. It went slowly because he was one-handed. And Eden was working on memorizing her Morse code stuff after several hours of target practice with the .22 pistol and the shotgun.

After days on end with hardly a minute apart from the group, Ezra finally had Logan alone. Well, now Logan knew why. The old codger wanted to scare him off.

And he didn't want Dakota around when he did it.

"I see the way you look at her," Ezra said. "Hungry, like a wolf. You're gonna use her up and throw her out. That's exactly what dirtbags like you do."

Logan shook his head. It wasn't like that—not at all.

He remembered her kiss, the softness of her lips, the warmth of her eyes. The way his stomach had dropped, filling him with desire.

But not to use her. He simply wanted *her*. All of her—the good, the bad, everything.

"You may have her fooled, but you don't fool me, boy."

Logan went still, the shovel half-raised. His head was spinning. This conversation was getting out of control way too fast. "Just hold on a damn second."

For the last two hours, Ezra had been impatiently instructing Logan in the art of creating cartridge booby traps. Ezra placed a shotgun cartridge inside a short section of pipe attached to a square piece of board. The pipe's diameter was just wider than the shell, so it stood on its end, the primer resting on a nail. When the board was placed at the bottom of a knee-deep hole, the pressure of an intruder's footfall would push the cartridge down onto the nail head, firing the cartridge into his foot.

It was a simple, elegant trap.

They'd built a half-dozen of the things inside the coolness of the cabin, but they needed to place them in the most tactically optimal locations throughout the property. They'd spent the morning and afternoon working mostly in silence, digging holes and setting traps.

Now, they were sweating in a pocket of shade beside the storage shed, damp cloths draped around their necks, keeping hydrated with frequent refills of their water bottles.

"I know exactly what you are." Ezra pointed his spade at Logan, pinning him with that shrewd, penetrating gaze. "I know your kind."

For an instant, he thought Ezra was referring to the fact that he was Hispanic. He opened his mouth, about to rip the old man a new one.

"I see that flask you carry around with you." Ezra scowled. "You're a good-for-nothin' drunk."

Logan's mouth went dry. Now he understood. "I haven't—"

"A man who drowns himself in a bottle isn't worth the air he breathes."

"I'm done with that."

"So you're a liar, too?"

"No, sir, I'm not."

"Right." Ezra spat in derision. "You ain't gonna convince me you're anything but what you are. Maybe you can hide it. Maybe you think you can deceive Dakota. She's got a bigger heart than she lets on. That's her weakness—she cares when she shouldn't. She lets her emotions blind her to the truth. I may be old, but I'm far from blind."

Ezra's words struck him like a blow. He punched the shovel into the ground with a savage thrust, breathing hard. That familiar, sickening shame lurched in his gut. "I would never hurt her."

"Weak words from a weak man."

Logan cleared his throat, fighting down his natural inclination to get defensive, to argue, to fight back. This man was important to Dakota. She respected him, loved him like a father.

The last thing Logan wanted was to get between them.

"I know how much you care for her," he said with measured calm, though his pulse hammered against his throat. "You want to protect her."

"That girl can protect herself. I taught her how. I taught her everything she knows. I made sure she didn't need no half-baked, no good man-child to do a job she could do herself." With his good hand, Ezra mopped his grizzled jaw with a threadbare scrap of an old plaid shirt, folded the creases out of it, and hung it over the wheelbarrow handle. "Hell, she can do better than most men."

"I know that."

"You're no good for her. You don't deserve her."

"I know that, too," Logan said quietly.

He wasn't worthy of her. That was a cold, hard fact.

But she'd seen something in him. Something he had a hard time seeing in himself. Instead of despising him like he deserved, she'd called him to be someone better than he was.

And he would be. Not just for her—but for himself.

Because if Dakota saw goodness in him, it must exist.

But the shame and the anxiety twisting his gut said otherwise. It didn't matter how hard he tried to push out the words—the old man was getting under his skin.

By the triumphant flash in his eyes, Ezra knew it.

"I'll do my best by her for as long as she'll have me," Logan said haltingly, feeling like an idiot and hating it.

Ezra glared at him, staring with distaste at the tattoos sleeving his bare arms. "Losers like you don't change."

"I will." But the words sounded hollow in his own ears.

"There's darkness in you. Violence. You're the kind of man who destroys everything he touches. I heard what you did. You murdered that refugee woman, nearly killed that mother and her little girl."

Logan went rigid. He wondered who had told Ezra—was it Julio or Park? Did they judge him as mercilessly as Ezra did, as mercilessly as he'd judged himself?

Logan's throat thickened. He didn't speak. He wasn't sure if he could.

Ezra tossed the spade he was using to remove the grassy topsoil aside and wobbled to his knees. Carefully, he reached in and placed the cartridge contraption into the bottom of the hole, set it, then rose heavily to his feet.

He brushed the dirt from his pant legs, wincing as he straightened. He moved slowly, stiffly, like his joints were aching, his splinted left hand cradled close to his body.

He examined the injury for a moment, his jaw clenched like he despised the sight of his own weakness. He turned away from Logan and stared off toward the swamp. A white ibis flew low over the water, its white reflection mirrored almost perfectly.

"You should leave," Ezra said. "You can take whatever you want. I have an extra backpack. Fill it with as many supplies as you can carry. Take one of the rifles. Find yourself a life somewhere far away from here."

Logan stood, too. He stared at the old man's stooped back for what felt like an eternity. "Are you...bribing me?"

"I'm giving you an out. If you truly care about her like you say, then leave before you break her heart—which you will. It's in your nature."

Logan didn't say anything. What could he say in his own defense? Absolutely nothing.

"You know her past, don't you? What she's been through. What they did to her. If she deserves anything in this world, it's a little bit of happiness." Ezra popped his knuckles one by one. "And you sure as hell aren't the one to give it to her."

Logan stood there, swaying and dizzy from the heat, from the tumult of emotions roiling through him—remorse, shame, and hot, bitter anger at himself.

As much as he desperately wanted to believe he could be different, that he could somehow erase his past, be good enough, deserve a life and a good woman who loved him—in the deepest, darkest part of himself, he feared every word Ezra spoke was true.

50

DAKOTA

"Thanks for having us," Dakota said to Haasi.

Dakota and Logan stood on Haasi's front porch, waiting for the rest of the Collier brothers to arrive. Zane was out patrolling US 41. Tessa and Eden were feeding the rabbits while Peter and Park helped Maki finish preparing dinner.

They'd been here in the Glades for six days. Nearly a week. It almost felt like it used to, like home.

Except for the looming threat of Maddox and the Shepherds.

Dakota checked her radio one more time. Leaving the compound was a risk, but they needed allies, regardless of what Ezra thought. She hoped it would be worth it.

Julio and Ezra were on watch back at the cabin. Julio would message them the second anything went wrong. They'd brought the F-150 so they could get back fast if they needed to.

"The kids missed Eden," Haasi said. "They love having her back. Eden seems to love it, too."

Dakota swallowed a lump in her throat. Haasi was right. Eden was blossoming here. How Dakota wished this was simply a social visit, an evening of companionship with friends. Maybe that future was possible, but not right now.

Right now, they were just trying to figure out how to survive the next few days.

Dakota shifted and shielded her eyes with her hand as she looked out over the wild, weed-infested yard to the road. She heard the sound of the engines before she saw them.

Several motorcycles roared up the gravel driveway. Dakota counted six—and several carried two people. She recognized Archer's massive form as he hopped off and helped the smaller person clinging to him—a little girl.

Behind him, a woman climbed off her Yamaha, took off her helmet, and shook out her short brunette hair. She smiled and waved at Dakota.

Several kids ranging from around seven to twelve took off while Jake hollered at them to not get dirty. Boyd strode up the porch steps, holding hands with a short Asian woman with a pleasant, friendly face and a belly swollen with pregnancy.

"Meet the Colliers," Haasi murmured.

"There's...so many of them."

Haasi chuckled. "You have no idea. This isn't even all of them. A couple of the older kids stayed back at the homestead, and Zane's wife and four rambunctious boys aren't here."

The adults jogged up to the house, already sweating. Archer offered Haasi a grocery bag and winked. "We brought extra fried sweet potatoes, as promised."

She rolled her eyes as she bent to pick up the crossbow leaning against the doorframe and bring it inside. "Come on in—but you better wipe those dirty boots on the mat first."

Logan and Dakota went inside, followed by a half-dozen kids, the dog Nokosi, and the shaggy spotted goat, Dot, which Maki quickly shooed out the door. The kids were covered in dirt, all boisterous noise and gleeful smiles, including Eden.

After everyone had cleaned up, they crowded around a long wooden table that took up almost the entire length of the kitchen. An assortment of metal folding chairs, stools, and benches provided seating.

"Sit, sit. You are our guests," Maki said stiffly when Dakota stood to help.

The brothers, though, insisted on helping. Boyd and Jake helped serve the food to the kids, while Archer poured everyone lemonade. In Archer's massive paws, the mugs looked like toys.

Everyone dug into the delicious home-cooked meal of fried alligator gar featuring sides of crookneck squash, swamp cabbage, and roasted potatoes spiced with the dog fennel herbs the kids had harvested that afternoon.

Logan took a plate and stood by the screen door, his AR-15 slung conspicuously over his shoulder. Dakota shot him a look—*do you need help?*—but he waved her off.

He wanted to keep watch. It was her job to do the convincing.

Haasi introduced everyone, but Dakota couldn't hope to remember all the names and faces. The kids all had wildly unruly chestnut-brown hair like their fathers. They were giggly and restless, but good-natured. Archer and Boyd's wives—Olivia and Tamayo—were kind and friendly, peppering them with questions about themselves and what they'd endured in Miami.

They seemed like good people, which made Dakota's reason for coming even more distasteful. She didn't resent them for their happiness. They deserved to be happy. They deserved to be safe.

After they'd cleaned up the table, the kids hurried outside to fish from the dock in the backyard before it got dark. Eden went with them, the big dog, Nokosi, pressed against her legs, one hand buried in the scruff of its neck, the other avidly signing something to Tessa, who had her arm wrapped around Eden's waist.

Anxiety tugged at Dakota as Eden disappeared out the door, but she pushed it away. She had her whistle and the walkie talkie in case of emergency. And Nokosi was right by her side, protecting her. She was surrounded by allies.

After a few minutes of small talk about the state of Maki's beehives, the reproductive habits of Archer and Olivia's rabbit warren, and praise for Zander's latest batch of moonshine, things turned serious.

Haasi leaned back in her seat and folded her arms over her bosom. "You came here for a reason. Time to spit it out."

Dakota inhaled a sharp breath. "We're here to ask for...for help." The words were bitter on her tongue. She hated asking for help almost as much as Ezra did. Almost. But she was here, not him, and she was willing to beg if that's what it came down to. "Help defending ourselves from the Shepherds."

"How do you know they're still coming?" Olivia asked. "It's been days. You beat them. Maybe they gave up."

"They didn't give up," Dakota said. "Maddox plays games. His brother, Jacob, did the same thing. Maddox hated him for it, but he does it, too. It's psychological torture—the waiting, the unknown. He's wearing us down."

"For how long?" Zander asked.

Logan snorted.

"That's the question, isn't it?" Park's face was pale. Dark circles rimmed his eyes. He looked sick with worry.

Dakota felt it, too. With each passing hour, they all felt the tension strung tighter and tighter. Their sleep was restless and pocked with nightmares. The stress of waiting was exhausting. And that's exactly why Maddox did it.

"Maybe it'll be tomorrow, maybe in a week," she said. "But make no mistake—they will come."

51

DAKOTA

The table fell silent for several long, protracted moments. Everyone stared at each other, worry and tension in their faces.

"Ezra might be an ornery old fool," Archer said grimly, "but an attack on one of us is an attack on all of us. I think we should help them."

"No way," Jake said.

Zander shrugged. "He's lived here for almost thirty years. Doesn't that make him one of us?"

"Ezra made it clear he wants no part of this community," Boyd said. "Fine, we've left him to his own devices. Now suddenly you want us to put our lives and families on the line for him? Where was he when Ford was killed? Nowhere. He didn't bother to lift a finger."

"He's liable to shoot us if we even step on his property," Zander said.

"He wouldn't shoot you," Park said.

Logan snorted again.

Boyd curled his lip. "How would you know? You've only been here a few days. You don't know the man like we do."

Dakota used to, but she wasn't sure anymore.

"Those paramilitary religious freaks think they're such a big deal," Zander shook his head. "We could take them, just like we took care of the looters and thieves. We've been handling our business here for three generations, long before they ever set up shop."

"I'm sorry, but no," Jake said adamantly. "The Shepherds have never bothered us before. I'm sorry they messed with Ezra, but that's your business. Those guys are crazy. They've got more guns per person than you've got fingers and toes, man." He glanced at his wife. "I'm not getting my family killed over whatever spat's between y'all. This isn't our fight."

"You know the things that go on in that compound," Haasi said, her voice quiet but firm. "We've all heard the rumors."

Dakota's cheeks reddened, her scars itching. Embarrassment roiled in her gut.

She glanced up to see Maki studying her. The woman leaned against the counter in front of the sink, her strong arms crossed over her chest, a line between her thick black brows. When Dakota caught her gaze, the woman gave her a slight nod.

"We've heard those rumors for twenty years!" Boyd said. "You didn't feel compelled to do anything then. Suddenly everything's changed? Now? When we most need to defend ourselves from all the desperate refugees flooding in from Miami?"

"We helped you." Park leaned forward in his seat, his dark eyes flashing. "Logan and Dakota helped you drive off those looters. I heard how it went sideways. They were there to defend you."

The Colliers exchanged heavy glances. Olivia put her hand on her husband's arm. He wrapped his huge arm around her slight shoulders.

"They did save your lives," Olivia said, glancing between Boyd and Jake across the table.

"Logan joined you on patrols," Park said, the frustration clear in his voice. "We all helped cut down those trees to block the road."

Logan said nothing. He stared out at the front yard, his back rigid.

"And we appreciate it!" Jake said. "But that's not the same as asking us to fight a small army. This is different. This is a huge ask."

"I know," Dakota said, almost choking on the words. It had been stupid to come. A mistake.

"I'm so sorry," said Boyd's pregnant wife, Tamayo. "I really am."

Park slumped back in his seat with a defeated sigh.

Boyd glanced at Haasi, and his sharp gaze softened. "Look, I know you care about Ezra. He used to be a decent guy before he went all crazy hermit on us. But I have a family. We all have families. Things are about to get real for all of us. They already have."

"I'm not losing another brother," Jake said fiercely as he looked around the table. "I won't."

"You know we're right, Archer," Boyd said. "I'm sorry, but this is the way it has to be."

"You're exactly right." Logan turned from the screen door, glowering at them all. Everyone stared at him in surprise. "You have your own needs to tend to. We'll tend to ours."

Logan banged the screen door open and stalked out of the house.

52

DAKOTA

Dakota pushed back her seat and hurried after Logan. By the time she reached the porch, he was already past their truck and striding down the driveway, the stiffness of his back and the set of his shoulders telegraphing his foul mood.

He didn't want company. She knew how he felt. She and Logan were cut from the same cloth—the type of people who valued their independence and solitude.

Much as she wanted to go to him, she remained on the porch. She'd talk to him later, when he was ready.

She didn't want to go back inside. Not yet. She needed air. Her chest was too tight. She hated asking for help, hated begging anyone else to put themselves on the line for her.

But this time, she was afraid they were in over their heads.

The screen door opened and closed behind her. The scent of lemon and honey wafted in the still, muggy air. Haasi moved to stand next to her.

She pressed a small glass jar into Dakota's hands. "Here's some more poultice to take with you for Ezra's hand. If you need more, just let me know."

"Thank you," Dakota forced out, her throat thick. "Ezra thanks you, too."

Haasi laughed—a deep, hearty chuckle. "Somehow, I doubt it."

For a moment, neither of them spoke.

Haasi swatted away a swarm of tiny bugs. "That's not how I wanted things to go."

Dakota heaved a sigh. "I know."

"I'll keep trying, but I can't promise anything."

"Boyd and Jake are right. It's not your fight. But they're still coming."

Dakota turned from the road and stared out over the marshland. In the distance, a great blue heron took flight and winged gracefully across a sky burnished gold by the setting sun. It was so beautiful it made her heart hurt.

Her gut tightened. For a moment, she'd allowed herself to hope they could be a part of something greater than themselves. But when it came down to it, you could only depend on yourself.

No. That wasn't true. Not anymore. She could count the number of people she trusted on one hand, but that was more than she'd ever had before. Eden and Ezra. Julio, whose steady, reliable nature she'd come to depend on more and more.

And Logan.

She pressed her lips together, remembering the feel of his mouth on hers, his hands tangled in her hair, her whole body tingling. When he'd embraced her yesterday, they'd fit together like two lost puzzle pieces.

It was strange. She should be terrified to let her guard down, to let him in. Dakota Sloane, the tough-as-nails foster kid, falling for an ex-convict murderer. It was a match made in hell. But maybe it took seeing hell to long for something better.

Her whole life, she'd kept her heart closed like a fist. She'd had to, in order to survive. But maybe survival was something different than she'd first thought. Maybe to truly live, you had to open that fist and let things in—even if it hurt. Especially if it hurt.

Peering into the gathering gloom, she glanced toward the road again. Logan stood at the end of the weed-choked drive, his hands shoved in his pockets, anxiously kicking rocks into the brush hugging the shoulder of the road.

"He's waitin' for you," Haasi said.

Dakota's cheeks went hot.

"He sure looks tough, but he's a good one." Haasi winked. "Trust me. I can sense these things."

"Yeah," Dakota said, blushing furiously. It felt weird to talk like this, but also good and strangely comforting. The faintest smile tugged at her lips. "I think so, too."

Logan glanced back at her for a moment, hesitated, then waved.

Despite everything—the fear, the anxiety, the dread building inside her chest like an immense pressure—her heart still lifted.

The future was a giant question mark. Violence and death stalked her every move.

But she wasn't alone.

53

MADDOX

Anticipation burned through Maddox's veins. It was finally time. The mission began now. By morning, it'd all be over.

Maddox gathered his team, a group of tough, hardened warriors in camouflaged fatigues with M4s slung over their shoulders, handguns and tactical knives at their hips. He relayed their final instructions while Reuben shifted impatiently next to him. But he didn't let his cousin's insubordination get under his skin.

These were his men.

He wondered briefly what they thought of his burn-reddened skin, his hollowed eyes, the blisters healing around his lips. But he didn't care. They were signs of God's blessings—the one who should have died instantly, charred into ash, now chosen by God Himself for a singular purpose.

The men saw it. They knew it. They looked at him with a new respect. They knew what he'd been through, what he'd survived. The fact that he was still standing here was a testament to his hardiness, vitality, and courage.

With every order, his confidence and determination grew. He was strong and invincible. A nuclear bomb couldn't kill him. Neither could radiation. The lashes scouring his back only made him more formidable.

He belonged here. This was his purpose.

"Whatever you do, don't harm my sister," he said. "Kill the old man. Kill everyone with them."

Reuben flashed a knowing smile. "And Dakota?"

"I want her," he said with relish. "Leave her to me."

54

MADDOX

Maddox stepped onto the porch and banged on the front door with his free hand. He took several swift steps back into the scabby yard, raising his carbine and positioning the stock against his shoulder, ready.

His men formed a loose semicircle around him, their M4s up and ready to rip the house to shreds.

It was almost ten pm, well after dark though the air was still muggy. Bugs swarmed. Crickets chirped and frogs sang.

An old rusty truck sat in the weed-choked driveway. Lights shone from inside the house.

They were home, but no sentries were posted. No one on guard. Idiots.

Using his NV goggles, he scanned the property again, more carefully this time. At the end of the driveway, several large bushes had been uprooted and positioned to shield the drive from casual passersby.

No. Not complete idiots, then. They felt safe because their security lay elsewhere...if they were smart, maybe they'd established a patrol along US 41 to prevent fleeing stragglers from making it this far.

"Hostiles could come from the road behind us," he said in a low voice. "Gordon, Stevens, and Hastings, guard our six at the end of the driveway."

Footsteps shuffled behind him as the men obeyed. The remaining Shepherds didn't move or speak. They waited.

Maddox's heart hammered against his ribs. His veins ran cold with adrenaline. The pain and the nausea were gone. He felt no fear, only anticipation and growing excitement.

This was it. He was in charge, no one else.

He alone determined the fates of every person here.

He couldn't keep the smile off his face.

The saggy screen door slapped open. An older Indian woman with long gray hair slammed out of the house, a crossbow held firmly in her arms, the bolt aimed at his chest.

He propped the goggles on his forehead and gave a friendly wave. "Is that any way to greet a neighbor?"

The old lady scowled. "You're no neighbor of mine."

He recognized her from the house-to-house search he'd conducted three years ago in search of Eden. He hadn't liked her then, either. "You should know that rudeness irritates me. A little politeness from you would go a long way."

"I remember you, Maddox Cage," the woman said. "You and your hooligans have sixty seconds to get off my property, or I'll send this bolt right through your rotten heart."

One of the Shepherds sniggered.

Maddox frowned. "I think you have that the wrong way around, sister."

"No, she doesn't," came a voice to his right.

A second Indian woman had circled around the house and flanked them from the side. She stood twenty feet away, deep in shadows, her shotgun aimed at them.

"We have you dead to rights," the old woman said. "Maki has your righthand man in her sights. I've got you. You're both thirty seconds from being dead."

"Lower your weapons, turn around, and get out," Maki said.

None of the men moved. Reuben kept his own weapon aimed at the old woman, though Maki's gun was trained on his head.

"That isn't how this works," Maddox said calmly. "You're right. You can shoot me and Reuben dead right now. But while you're squeezing those triggers, my men'll be squeezing theirs. We don't care if we die. Every single one of my men is willing to die for our cause, including me. Somehow, I think you don't feel the same."

Something moved inside the house. Maddox shifted just slightly to the right, the muzzle of the M4 moving with him, until his sights focused on the figure behind the old woman.

"Mama?" A girl stood just inside the doorway, dressed in a long white nightgown, her raven-black hair mussed and her eyes sleepy.

The old woman gasped. "What did I tell you, Tessa? Get back in the house!"

"Come closer, Tessa." Maddox smiled. He sensed their fear. He fed off it, felt their courage wane as his strengthened. "Come right up beside your grandma. No one gets hurt if you listen. You understand? There, that's it."

"Don't you dare lay a finger on her," Maki said. "Don't you dare."

"Here's what's going to happen," Maddox said once the girl was next to her grandmother, barefoot and shaking. He aimed the carbine at her head and made sure the mother and the grandmother saw it.

"I don't want to hurt this little girl, but I need you to listen. If you don't listen, I'm going to have to do something I don't want to do. Does everyone understand?"

"Don't lower that gun, Maki." The old woman stared at him, unflinching. "I'm not scared of you."

"You should be," Reuben snarled. Beside him, Maddox could feel his cousin's body thrumming with tension—he was itching to pull the trigger. Maddox needed to keep him in line.

"Harrison," Maddox said. "You see that goat over there? Shoot it."

"No!" the girl squealed.

Harrison twisted, aimed at the nearest goat—a scruffy black-and-white creature contentedly nibbling the weedy lawn—and squeezed the trigger.

The animal never had a chance to make a sound. It toppled over, already dead.

"My next shot is the girl. Understand?"

Reluctantly, the old woman lowered her crossbow. Maki followed suit.

Reuben gestured to one of the men, who strode forward and quickly grabbed their weapons.

Maddox breathed easier. This was going perfectly.

The little girl said something, a strange word he didn't understand.

"Tessa, no!" Maki said.

A deep bark came from inside the house.

55

MADDOX

The little girl's fear transformed before Maddox's eyes—her jaw set, her black eyes flashing. "Nokosi!" she cried. "Attack!"

A blur of black and brown burst from the darkened doorway and launched from the porch. In the second it took Maddox to recognize the creature as something between a massive German Shepherd and a Rottweiler, the huge dog had already streaked across twenty feet and launched itself at a man named Puckett.

Puckett let out an unearthly howl and toppled onto his back, the huge dog's teeth latched onto his forearm. Blood streamed from his arm in rivulets and matted the dog's muzzle.

"Get it off! Get it off me!" Puckett screamed over the dog's savage snarls.

Reuben swung around, aiming his M4 at the dog's head.

"No!" Maddox held up one hand, stopping his men.

"Maddox!" Reuben said, indignant.

Maddox returned his attention to the old woman. A distraction would be all she needed to try for the upper hand. She was just a woman, but Maddox knew better than to underestimate her.

Unlike his men.

"It's ripping his arm off!" Harrison cried.

"Call off your dog," Maddox said, still calm, though he had to raise his voice to be heard. "I don't want to kill pets or kids, but I will."

The girl shook her head, but the grandma overruled her with a sharp look. The girl's shoulders slumped. "Nokosi! Release! Come here."

Out of the corner of his eye, he saw the big dog drop the man's mangled arm. Obediently, it returned to the porch, pressed itself between the woman and the girl, and faced the Shepherds. The old woman gripped its collar. The dog's hackles were raised, black lips peeled back as it growled fiercely.

No doubt, the beast wanted nothing more than to tear them all to shreds with those gleaming, blood-soaked fangs. And yet it was well-trained and disciplined enough to ignore its own primal instincts.

Maddox respected the hell out of that.

He'd always wanted a dog. His father and evil witch of a stepmother hadn't allowed it. He would've trained it to fight side-by-side with him, to rip out the throats of his enemies. He smiled at the thought.

"What are you doin', man?" Reuben asked. "Kill it!"

Maddox ignored him. Reuben wasn't in charge. The Prophet wasn't in charge. This was *his* mission, and his alone. If he wished to exercise restraint, to show mercy, that was his prerogative.

"Any hesitation, shoot the dog, then the girl," he ordered his men. "Russell, take Puckett back to the compound and bring him to Sister Rosemarie."

Russell frowned, irritated and confused, but he obeyed immediately, lifting his bleeding, whimpering comrade to his feet. Together, they limped toward the rear of the property and the boats the Shepherds had stashed in the reeds.

"What do you want?" the old woman spat between clenched teeth.

"I think I've proven I'm a reasonable man. More than reasonable. Anyone in the house needs to come out and stand beside the girl. If we go in and find anyone else inside, someone dies. And not a goat."

The woman nodded, defeated. "Come out, Peter."

A boy a head smaller than his sister with the same inky black hair and eyes shuffled out, followed by two burly brown-haired men in their mid-thirties—Maddox remembered the biker brothers. And that there were more of them.

"You crazy assholes!" The first biker spat. "You think you're so bad, scaring little girls? "Come fight me like real men."

His words didn't faze Maddox. He knew better than to rise to the bait. "That's all of you? Harrison, search the house. Thoroughly. Reuben, if we find anyone else, shoot the dog."

Reuben grinned maliciously. "With pleasure."

"No, you can't!" the girl wailed.

"Last chance."

The old woman's hard gaze faltered.

Harrison moved toward the porch.

"Wait." She raised her hands helplessly. "There's one more."

A slight Asian guy with one arm in a sling stepped hesitantly out of the doorway. Harrison gestured with his carbine, and the guy shuffled to the end of the line beside the biker brothers.

Maddox's brows lifted as recognition struck him. "I remember you from Bellview Court. You're with Dakota. What's your name?"

The guy's face contorted in fear—and outrage. "Yu-Jin Park. You killed my friend.

Her name was Nancy Harlow. She was a good person. And you shot her."

"She pointed a gun at me first."

"It was empty!"

"I didn't know that at the time." Maddox shrugged carelessly. "Oh, well."

This weak, sniveling Park guy was Dakota's friend. Someone she cared about. Maddox's heartbeat quickened. A new opportunity had suddenly presented itself.

He could work with this. Oh yes, he could.

56

MADDOX

"Thank you for your honesty," Maddox said to Haasi when Harrison had finished his search of the house. "Things will go better for you, I promise."

He ordered the girl to put the growling dog inside the house and shut the door. Then he asked for the names of his new hostages—they gave them, angrily, fearfully, but they obeyed.

He returned his gaze to Haasi, the old Indian woman. She was clearly the leader here—woman or not. "I'm here to offer you a truce. My men and I have no quarrel with you. We have no desire to hurt any of you, especially your children.

"All we ask, and it is a very small request, is that you do nothing. Remain here tonight. Tend to your property. Hug your kids and kiss them goodnight. That's all."

Haasi's eyes narrowed. "You want us to stay out of your fight with Ezra Burrows."

"It's none of your business. Keep it that way, and we can remain harmonious neighbors."

She shook her head. "You're evil. Pure evil."

"You filthy maggots!" snarled the fat biker—Zander. "We should've run you out a decade ago!"

Reuben swung his M4 at the biker. A Shepherd behind him made a disgruntled sound in the back of his throat.

Maddox needed to keep control of the conversation, or he risked losing his men's respect.

The thinner, goateed biker named Boyd placed a restraining hand on his brother's arm. "Shut up."

The distant sound of motorcycle engines reached them. Haasi's expression didn't change, but Zander's eyes widened in anticipation—and hope. He thought his brothers were roaring in to save the day.

He was dead wrong.

The rest of the Collier brothers were ambushed by the Shepherds guarding the road, M4s aimed at their heads. With their family members held at gunpoint, they had no choice but to lay down their own arms and join the other hostages on the porch. They spat and swore, full of impotent fury, but they obeyed.

"How many people do they have holed up with Ezra?" Maddox asked. "How many weapons? What are their defenses?"

"We don't know." The tallest, giant of a brother glared down at them. "Ezra's a hermit. He hates all of us as much as he does you. None of us know a damn thing."

"I know that's a lie." Maddox slanted his eyes at Park. "You've got one of theirs with you right now. If I know Dakota, she saved whoever she could and brought them along like little lost puppies."

Park's mouth tightened.

"We won't harm anyone if we don't have to," Maddox said in a soothing voice. "We didn't kill your dog, when we had every right. Eden will be safe. So will Dakota."

Haasi snorted.

"Despite what you may think, I'm a man of my word. We just want what's ours. Eden belongs at home. This is a family spat. Just

Into the Fire

help us get what we need and we'll be on our way. There's no reason to get your families involved. No reason at all."

For a long minute, everyone stood staring at each other, waiting in strained silence to see what the other side would do, who would break first. Reuben shifted restlessly, but remained silent.

Maddox waited. He was infinitely patient when he needed to be. The long game was often the most rewarding.

He took one hand off the carbine for a moment and raked his hand through his sweat-dampened hair. Several strands came free and stuck to his fingers. He wiped his hand on his pants.

Haasi was staring at him, her eyes narrowing. He didn't care whether every follicle on his head fell out. It was all part of the long game. All of it.

"I'll tell you," Zander said finally.

"Zander!" Archer said. "What're you doing?"

"I'm not letting them kill my family. Not over the likes of Ezra Burrows. No way."

"There's more than Ezra Burrows holed up in that cabin," Haasi said. "They've got a little girl in there, too!"

"So do I!" Zander shook his head, his expression strained with the weight of his choice. "I'll do anything to protect my family."

"Don't—" Archer said.

"I have to. I'm sorry." Zander stepped forward. His wild, frantic eyes darted from Shepherd to Shepherd before resting on Maddox. "They've only got six people. That's including your sister. With Park here, it's only five. Only Ezra, Dakota, and this guy Logan know anything about weapons. Logan's good, though. Don't underestimate him. He's a force to be reckoned with."

Maddox's smile widened. "That's the neighborly spirit I was looking for."

Haasi shook her head in disgust. "Shut up, Zander!"

But Zander ignored her. He was shaking, pale with fear, sweat stains spreading beneath his armpits. "They've been preparing for you. Making sandbag fortifications and booby traps in the yard. You'll have a hard time sneaking up on them. They've got a watch posted 24/7."

"I'm sure we'll think of something. The rest I can get from our friend here." He motioned at Park with the muzzle of his M4. "Park, you're coming with us. We're going to need you."

"No way." Park shook his head adamantly. "Go to hell."

"You can't just take him!" Archer took one lumbering step toward Maddox, but several rifles lifted simultaneously, all pointed his way. He hesitated, the aggression leaking out of him as he realized the precariousness of his predicament.

"You can't do this," the giant said again, but there was no confidence in his voice, no authority. Guns beat brute strength every time, and he knew it.

"We can and we are." Maddox tilted his chin at Hastings. "Search everyone. Search the house. Confiscate every radio so they can't warn anyone. Hastings, stay behind and guard them, just to make sure they keep their promises. The rest of you, mow down anyone who stands in our way."

57

LOGAN

They came in the middle of the night. Julio, who was on watch, sounded the alarm. Two short whistles.

Logan woke with a jerk, a quick gasp of air and then he was up and alert, already reaching for the AR-15 at his side.

"Intruders at the gate!" Julio shouted.

"Get your guns!" Ezra ordered, his voice hoarse with sleep. "Get to your stations!"

Everyone was already completely dressed, shoes included. Logan gathered his weapons, ammo bag, canteen, earplugs, and handheld radio, all stashed in the duffle bag beside him on the floor.

The lights were off. He fumbled in his cargo pocket for his penlight and switched it on as he hurried to his station at the front southwestern window. He hunkered down behind the sandbags and rechecked his weapon as Dakota and Eden rushed from the ham radio room, wiping sleep from their eyes.

"Where's Park?" Dakota asked.

"He hasn't come back yet," Julio said.

"What do you mean?" Dakota glanced at her watch. "It's past midnight!"

"I thought he was just blowing off steam at Haasi's place." Julio shrugged helplessly. "He wasn't dealing with the stress well."

Park had stayed behind when Logan and Dakota had headed back with Eden. Maki had promised to bring him back later. He'd mumbled something about needing to relax for a while. Logan hadn't blamed him. The tension and anxiety after six days were nearly overwhelming.

"Too late to worry about him now," Ezra said. "Eden will have to cover the eastern side at the kitchen window."

Eden pursed her lips, her eyes wide, but she nodded grimly, her shoulders straight, her head high. She signed *I'm fine* before gripping the Mossberg tightly in both hands.

She'd be okay. There was a toughness in her beneath that softness —Logan was sure of it.

Julio handed Ezra the handheld monitor that displayed the security camera's feed at the front gate. Logan left his duffle bag at his station but kept his Glock and joined Ezra, Dakota, and Julio.

Dakota pressed against his side. He felt the tension thrumming through her body, felt the dread thrumming through his own. It physically hurt to be near her. He wanted to hold her close and simultaneously destroy anything that threatened her safety.

The thought of leaving her punched a hole in his chest that left him breathless.

He pushed those thoughts down deep. He couldn't think like that, couldn't let in any distractions. He needed to remain focused, every sense on high alert.

Everything else could wait until after tonight.

He concentrated on the monitor. At the gate at the base of the drive, the motion sensor light attached to the tallest pole blared down on five figures dressed in black, with a smaller sixth person in lighter clothing between them.

Into the Fire

Though it was difficult to discern physical features from the grainy grayscale pixels, the figure was clear enough.

Julio gasped and crossed himself. "That's Park! They have Park!"

Logan's insides went cold and slippery. He swallowed.

Before anyone could react, their radios crackled. The Shepherds must be using Park's handheld, which was tuned to their frequency.

"Since you're watching us already," a male voice said, "why don't you let us in so we can talk, man-to-man?"

Dakota's face went bone-white. She pressed her lips together. "That's Maddox. He's here."

"Open the gate," Maddox said.

"We're not opening that gate," Ezra snarled into his radio.

"I have a hostage here who'd like to stay alive. He's asking—no, begging—that you comply with my request. Open the damn gate."

Logan cursed.

"We have to do it," Dakota said, her strained voice rising. "He's giving us no choice."

"It'll compromise our position," Ezra said. "It gets them too near the cabin."

Anger washed over Logan, along with a resentful, grudging sort of respect. Maddox Cage wasn't stupid. He knew his men needed to cross well over a hundred and fifty yards of open ground, where Logan and the others could've picked them off easily from their fortified positions.

With a hostage, the Shepherds could cross that deadly space free and clear.

"I'll give you until the count of three, and then I'm shooting a foot." The radio cackled with mirthless laughter. "Let me clarify. I mean Park's foot, not my own."

"He could be bluffing," Julio said, but his voice was hollow. He didn't believe it himself.

Dakota clenched her jaw. "Maddox Cage doesn't bluff."

As if on cue, Maddox reached the count of three. They watched in tense, agonizing silence as Maddox's grainy figure aimed his pistol. The gunshot cracked through the radio.

Park dropped, writhing.

"His kneecap is next," Maddox said calmly. "Don't think he'll ever walk again after that one. A one-armed, one-legged man. How long do you think he'll last out here?"

In the background, Park moaned.

Dakota turned to Ezra. "Open it, damn it!"

"If we do this, we're putting ourselves at greater risk—" Ezra warned.

Dakota shook her head, growing more adamant. "We'll improvise. We'll figure it out. We have to."

"Dakota's right," Julio said. "It's the right thing to do."

Dakota and Ezra stared at each other for a long moment, communicating things Logan didn't understand and never would, both of their expressions grim but determined.

If it were up to Logan, he'd side with Ezra, much as he hated it. Park was a nice guy, but that was all.

Dakota was his priority, not Park. He'd let a thousand Parks die bloody deaths before he'd risk her life.

But Dakota wouldn't. Maybe that's what made her a better person than he was.

Maybe Ezra was thinking the same thing. Something cracked in his gaze—a glimmer of defeat. Tension deepened the groves in his face. Finally, he relented. With a curse, he dug into his pocket, pulled out a small remote, and jabbed a button.

They watched on the screen as the dented gate swung open.

The figures started up the long driveway. Park sagged between two Shepherds, limping heavily, one foot dragging uselessly behind him.

"Poor kid," Julio said quietly.

Dakota moved quickly to the window. She pulled a pair of binoculars from the bag slung over her shoulder and peered through the window. "Something's not right."

Logan watched her. "What is it?"

"Maddox has five men with him. Only five. That doesn't make sense. He'll have more. I know he will."

"He could be using Park as a distraction," Logan said, "while a secondary force sneaks up on us from another direction."

Dakota's shoulders stiffened. She lowered the binoculars and reached for her rifle. "I think you're right."

"People, to your stations," Ezra ordered. "Remain on high alert. More hostiles could come from the woods on the east or west perimeter, or from the water. Looks like they're outfitted with automatic weapons. 5.56×45mm NATO rounds, probably. Maybe armor-piercing. Automatic rounds are gonna chew through the walls eventually, ballistic-resistant or not. Take them out before they can focus concentrated fire at us. I'll be in the sniper's nest."

Everyone nodded tightly.

Dakota took the front southeastern window, Eden the kitchen, while Julio took the rear. Ezra lowered the stairs in the hallway and climbed into the attic. With the four gun ports drilled into the roof, Ezra could lend sniper fire in any direction.

Adrenaline surged through Logan's veins as he moved back to his station at the front of the house. He checked and rechecked his guns, made sure his ammo bag filled with preloaded magazines sat by his side.

Everything was ready, or as ready as it was going to get.

This was it.

He breathed deeply, that familiar cold calm settling over him. His rifle was a solid, comforting presence in his arms, like an extension of his own body.

His vision sharpened, his senses taking in everything.

The night was windy. The trees stirred restlessly, and no stars were visible behind the thick, dark clouds. In the distance, heat lightning flickered. The faint smell of fried squirrel stew still lingered in the air. Soon it would be dust and bullets and blood.

This was his thing. What he was good at. The only thing he was good at.

Time to make it count.

Not everyone was going to live through the next several hours. Maybe not everyone in this house. If Logan had his way, he'd kill every damn Shepherd in existence before that happened.

For Dakota, he'd kill them all.

58

EDEN

Eden watched in growing dread as Park staggered between the Shepherds. They dragged him up the long dirt driveway, three more Shepherds marching behind him, their guns trained on the cabin.

She'd left her post at the kitchen to better see what was happening. She crouched beside Logan at the western living room window, her thighs already starting to twinge in protest, her shotgun lowered.

Logan had pushed her behind him, both of them kneeling, his own focus still laser-centered on the hostiles outside, his rifle balanced against the window frame.

"That's far enough!" Logan shouted when the Shepherds were twenty yards away. Instead of picking the Shepherds off in the open fields surrounding the house the way they'd planned, the enemy was right in their midst.

Maddox raised his hand, and his men halted beside him.

Eden stopped breathing. There he was, right in front of her. Maddox. Her brother.

His lean, wiry body sharp as a knife blade, that angular arrogant face, that mocking smile. His features were gaunt from the radiation sickness, his eyes bright and feverish.

The last time she'd seen him, he'd held a knife to her throat.

She felt like he was staring straight at her, could see her through the window, see the dread knotting in her gut, her heart throbbing with fear. Like she was still the scared little girl she used to be.

She wanted to shout at him, to scream as loud as she could, until he was forced to hear her, to pay attention. *You aren't going to win*, she whispered in her mind instead, her teeth gritted. *Not this time.*

Eden forced herself to look away from Maddox and examined the Shepherds with him. They barely squinted against the harsh white light blaring from the sensor lights attached to the cabin's eaves on all sides. They stood still and ready, the wind whipping their dark clothes, weapons in hand, silent and menacing.

Her heart plummeted. These weren't the baby-faced boys the Prophet had sent the first time. These were the real Shepherds of Mercy. The chosen ones, the army of God. Strong, well-trained, wearing bullet-proof vests with tactical gear and NV goggles perched on their foreheads, all armed with heavy-duty submachine guns.

The wind rustled the long grass. Along the perimeter of the property, the trees creaked against each other. Somewhere, an owl screeched. Outside the pool of light, darkness crouched, thick and heavy with shadows.

And then she saw it. Park was doing something with his arm. It was slow and subtle, and he was clearly trying to disguise his movement, but she noticed. Her breath caught in her throat.

She needed to tell Dakota, to warn her. But she couldn't speak a damn word.

Across the cabin, Dakota was focused on her targets outside the window.

Eden whistled softly.

"Not now," Dakota said.

Into the Fire

Eden whistled again. She needed to get her sister's attention. It was important.

Dakota risked a quick glance at her.

Eden met Dakota's gaze, took one hand off her gun and jabbed her finger at her own forearm, her eyes widening in emphasis. She signed the letters P-A-R-K.

Dakota shook her head, confusion in her eyes. She looked back at the Shepherds.

Silently, Eden willed Dakota to see what she saw.

Between the hulking Shepherds holding him up, Park slumped, barely hobbling on one foot, his face a sickly yellowish-white. He was bruised and bloodied, his lip split, his jaw already the color of a bruised banana.

His sling was gone, his broken arm in its cast held close to his chest. He held his left arm tight against his chest, too, like he was hugging himself to help with the pain.

"Open the door," Maddox said loudly.

"Not going to happen!" Dakota shouted back, returning her attention to Maddox.

She was crouched behind the sandbags, the rifle balanced and aimed out the window. "Give us Park, and we'll let you go with your asses intact."

Maddox grinned. "Oh, Dakota. How naïve you can be. You think I came all the way here to leave empty-handed?"

A big, thick-necked blond Shepherd pushed forward and seized Park's arm. His face was broad, his eyes dull with malice. It was Reuben Cage, the Prophet's own son. He was a vicious bulldog of a man, the kind who enjoyed cruelty but hid it well behind a veil of jokes and jovial, white-toothed smiles.

Eden's pulse quickened, her mouth going dry.

Between the two of them, Maddox and Reuben would happily kill every person here without blinking.

Reuben pressed the muzzle of his gun against Park's left temple.

"Enough games. Open the damn door or he dies, and we shred your little house with a thousand bullets."

"Don't...do it," Park managed between his split, swollen lips.

Reuben slammed a savage punch into Park's gut. Park doubled over, groaning. But he was still moving his good arm. There was something there, in his hand. Something Dakota needed to see.

Eden motioned again, trying to get Dakota's attention.

"What is it?" Logan whispered beside her.

She pointed out the window at Park and pointed to her own hand, trying to mime what she meant, but she only had one free hand with the rifle balanced in the other.

Logan shook his head, baffled.

They didn't understand her. Frustration built in her chest, mingling with stress, adrenaline, and fear. She'd give almost anything to be able to speak. To save Park, to *do something*.

Instead, she was absolutely useless. And Park was running out of time.

59

DAKOTA

Dakota kept her sights on the spot between Maddox's eyes. She lifted her head and peered through the window, taking in the entire group, trying to see what Eden was telling her.

All the Shepherds were focused on the cabin, their submachine guns trained on the door and windows, except for Reuben, who still had his pistol pressed to Park's head.

Everything was the same. She saw no new threats, no new opportunities.

"We'll die before we give you anything," Logan said.

"You don't have to die," Maddox said. "Give us Eden. Give us Dakota. That's all we want. We'll leave the rest of you in peace. You have our word."

Reuben sneered. "If you don't, we'll burn this craphole to the ground with all of you inside."

"Go to hell," Logan said.

Above them in the attic, Ezra said nothing. He was completely silent, waiting for the right moment to surprise the hell out of them. Dakota knew he was boiling with fury at these hostiles daring to threaten him on his own land.

The old man wanted nothing more than to shoot them all, Park be damned.

He wouldn't wait for long. The window to save Park was rapidly dwindling. The plan was already shot to hell and the battle hadn't even started yet.

Eden made another sound, a cluck of her tongue.

Dakota forced herself to scan the Shepherds again, searching for whatever she was missing. Big, burly men. Savage expressions. Weapons aimed, but no fingers on triggers. Not yet.

"I'm not an impatient man," Maddox said, raising his voice over the wind, "but I'm running out of patience."

And then she saw it.

Beside Reuben, Park was moving. He was still half-bent, his hands pulled in close to his chest. At first, she thought he was clutching at his stomach. But he wasn't.

Something glinted in the light as he straightened and slid an object out of his cast. He gripped it in his good hand. She squinted to make it out—the pocketknife she'd given him. He must've hidden it inside his cast before the Shepherds had gotten to him. Smart.

Dakota's pulse surged. This was what Eden was trying to show her. Park could create a distraction. If they could take advantage of the moment of confusion and simultaneously shoot all five Shepherds without hitting Park...

There was still a chance to get him out of this alive.

"Take Reuben, the bulky blond one. I've got Maddox," she said to Logan in a low, tense voice. "Eden, you've got the bearded one on the end. Be ready."

Logan grunted in response.

For a moment, Park gazed straight at the cabin. He couldn't see Dakota, not with the sensor lights blaring, but she saw him clearly—his pale round face, his mouth working in a silent cry for help, his eyes desperately pleading.

He was clearly terrified, but he was going to act anyway.

Into the Fire

"Screw this." Reuben clicked the safety off his handgun.

Park flicked the pocketknife open and gripped it in his left hand. Shifting slightly, he thrust the blade into Reuben's right side just below the bottom edge of the bullet-proof vest.

With a howl of enraged pain, Reuben staggered backward, stumbling against the Shepherd closest to him, both their guns wavering wildly.

Her nerves strung taut, Dakota zeroed in, finding Maddox in her sights. Maddox ducked, already moving. She didn't have time to aim properly, to exhale, to focus. She squeezed the trigger.

The bullet zinged past Maddox's head. A miss.

"Kill them!" Park cried. "Just do it!"

Maddox pivoted swiftly. In one smooth movement, he pointed the muzzle at Park's head and pulled the trigger.

"No!" Dakota screamed.

Park crumpled to the ground. Blood bloomed across his slackened face, soaking his dark hair. He didn't move. He didn't get up.

He was dead.

Dakota froze in horror, her sweaty finger still on the trigger. Just like that, Park was gone.

He was dead because of her. She'd failed him.

Ezra didn't freeze. From the sniper's nest, he rained bullets down upon the Shepherds.

A cacophony of booms shattered the air as both sides let loose in a furious exchange of firepower.

Reuben's body jerked as several bullets thwacked into his vest. He dropped to his knees.

The Shepherd beside him glanced down at Reuben. Another boom thundered from above Dakota. A hole appeared in the center of the Shepherd's forehead. He slammed backward, the rifle flying from his fingers, dead before he hit the ground.

Ezra didn't take prisoners.

The bearded Shepherd on the left side got off a quick volley.

Rounds struck the cabin in a wide arc. Dust and shards of concrete sprayed everywhere.

Dakota ducked. It took everything in her not to curl into a ball on the floor behind the sandbags, her hands over her ears, and collapse into tears.

Her whole body was shaking, her ears ringing. She kept seeing the wide desperation in Park's eyes, the spray of blood, his body lying there, unmoving.

She sucked in a sharp breath and shot a quick glance at Eden. The girl was crouched, aiming and firing out the window with her shotgun even as tears streamed down her cheeks. She was crying, but she was defending the cabin just the same.

Her heart swelled with pride—and fresh determination. *Get it together, Dakota!* If she didn't get her crap together right now, someone else was going to die. Maybe they all would.

She couldn't afford to think about Park. She couldn't afford to think about anything but keeping Eden and everyone else alive.

Cautiously, she raised her head.

More gunfire shattered the night air. The bearded Shepherd's body jittered. His head snapped back, and he collapsed like his bones had turned to water.

She didn't know if the rounds came from Ezra or Logan, or Eden. It didn't matter. Three Shepherds were down.

She searched for Maddox again, scanning the bright white yard. He was running straight for the cabin, crossing the small space far too rapidly. She squeezed the trigger—missed.

Aimed again quickly, fired, and struck him low on the right side, but still on the vest.

He stumbled.

Automatic rounds tore into the wood window frame two feet above her head. *Thunk, thunk, thunk.* She was forced to duck, eyes squeezed shut as slivers of wood sprayed around her.

By the time she raised her head, Maddox was on his feet, Reuben staggering behind him. They both made it around the east corner of the cabin before she could re-aim and fire.

Distant thunder rumbled. A few seconds later, lightning lit up the sky.

"We've got company!" Julio shouted from the back bedroom. "At least a dozen hostiles, coming from the swamp!"

60

DAKOTA

"You help Julio and Ezra at the back," Logan said. "I'll keep these two from breaching the front."

Dakota gave a terse nod and scurried from the living room, through the kitchen and hallway to the rear bedroom's fortified window.

She took up her position, adrenaline coursing through her veins. She quickly squeezed off a burst of three shots, taking out one Shepherd at the knees who'd dodged out from behind the henhouse wall to shoot at her, then swinging her aim back and forcing a second behind the treeline a hundred and fifty yards away. Spent shell casings spat out, bounced around.

Above her in the attic, Ezra fired and took out two more. Then another dropped and didn't get up. They were taking them out one by one, but it wasn't easy.

The Shepherds were approaching with skill, moving forward in spread-out groups of four, while four remained behind to offer covering fire. They stayed close to a straight line toward the cabin from the dock, trying not to stray into the parts of the property that hid the booby traps.

Into the Fire

Her heart sank. Park had told them about the traps. She didn't blame him. It had nothing to do with bravery or cowardice. Under torture, most people would give up their grandmothers after the first couple of broken fingers.

But Park hadn't remembered the location of all the traps. Neither could the Shepherds in the dark, under the onslaught of stress, panic, and oncoming fire.

One of the Shepherds strayed a few feet to the right. He jerked and stumbled as his leg disappeared into a hole. Dakota couldn't see his face, but she imagined it contorting in agony as the spikes punctured the man's boot and lanced deep into the flesh of his foot.

The Shepherd went down hard, struggling to pry his leg free. His companion bent over him. She zeroed in on the fallen man. Squeezed the trigger. His head snapped back.

His companion sprang up, about to dart away, but it was too late. She shifted her sights a smidge up and to the left. Squeezed the trigger two times. The first one missed. The second grazed his shoulder.

A third round punched through his throat. Not her bullet—Ezra's. No matter how old he was, he was still a crack shot.

Two less Shepherds to worry about.

A dozen yards closer and to the right of the shed, another Shepherd went down as he activated a tripwire. Before she could aim, Ezra nailed him in the head with a single shot.

Three down.

She aimed at another hunched, loping figure and squeezed off a burst of shots. Her rifle clicked. She ducked back down behind the sandbags and reached into the duffle bag for another magazine.

The ear-splitting rat-a-tat of automatic gunfire shattered the air. One of the motion lights on the eastern side of the cabin winked out. Then another.

The Shepherds were intentionally shooting out the security lights. Now they could use their NV goggles to give them an advantage. They didn't need the light. Dakota, Logan, and Ezra did.

Ezra's property plunged into darkness. Thunder rumbled. The wind shook the trees. The attackers were almost impossible to see in between the flickers of lightning.

She squeezed the trigger again and again, shooting into the dark, hoping she was doing damage. A growl escaped between her gritted teeth. She emptied the magazine, removed it, and loaded another from her bag.

This was stupid. She had to be smarter. She scanned the treeline, searching for muzzle flashes to expose their locations, her eyes dry and gritty from lack of blinking.

Eternal minutes passed. She aimed and fired at the occasional muzzle flashes, but she had no way of knowing whether she'd hit her target. It was difficult to make out the ones stalking closer without firing.

Over the barrage of gunfire, as a bullet found its mark or one of the booby traps crippled another victim, she caught the occasional scream of agony. From her count, they'd killed seven or eight Shepherds, but there were at least ten more.

There were simply too many of them. Even with Ezra's enormous stash of ammo, they would run out. They couldn't compete with the automatic fire strafing the cabin again and again and again.

Slowly, inexorably, the Shepherds inched closer and closer.

61

DAKOTA

From behind Dakota came a groan, followed by a series of heavy thuds.

She risked a quick glance back. Ezra had half-climbed, half-fallen down the attic ladder. He was crawling toward her on his hands and knees, more slowly than she'd ever seen him move. He'd aged another decade in the last thirty minutes.

He raised himself to his knees and gingerly pressed his hand to his right shoulder. His fingers came away wet. A wide splotch of blood stained his plaid shirt, spreading from his collar to his shoulder and beneath his armpit.

"You're bleeding! You've been hit."

"I'm fine...I just..." He tried to raise his arm and grimaced, his face going white.

"Sit down. Rest." She tried not to show her dismay. She was concerned for his welfare, but they were also horrifically outmanned. The loss of a shooter was nothing short of catastrophic.

Julio was helping as much as he could. So was Eden. But the weight of this battle rested on Logan and Dakota's shoulders now.

Rounds struck the wall above the sandbags. She flinched and

ducked. Flecks of dust drifted onto her head and shoulders as she ejected the AR-15's empty magazine and slapped in another one.

She checked on Eden with a quick glance to her left. The girl was crouched less than twenty feet away, below the kitchen window in front of the sink. She still held the shotgun, but her head was down, her knees drawn up to her chest, her whole body trembling.

She'd gotten off several shots, but the constant barrage of bullets was too much for her.

"I'm taking her to the shed bunker," Ezra said.

"No. It's unsafe—"

"It's unsafe here. Their firepower is...unexpected. I didn't know, I didn't..." He stared her bleakly, his voice threaded with exhaustion. "She'll be utterly safe there. Not even these rounds can penetrate the walls. There's a lock on the inside with a keycode. They won't be able to get in. You know that."

"Ezra—"

He crawled closer, moving stiff and gingerly, his breathing labored. Blood dripped on the floor beneath him. "I'm useless to you," he said, his voice heavy with resignation.

It cost him to speak those words, to admit it. Pain, self-disgust, and defeat shadowed his gnarled features. With his wounded shoulder, he couldn't hold the weight of a rifle or properly aim a pistol. He hated it, but he knew it.

"I can get her there. You can't focus when your attention is divided. Without me in the sniper nest, you need to be able to move between stations, to adjust on the fly. Let me take her."

Dakota raised up, peered through her sights, and scanned the dark yard. No movement.

"A stray bullet could kill her. You can't protect her and take out these fools. I've got her." He gripped Dakota's arm with his good hand. "Trust me."

She tasted drywall dust in her mouth and the metallic tang of blood. She'd bitten her own tongue. The stench of gunpowder filled her nostrils. Another round thudded into a kitchen cabinet two feet to the right of Eden.

She did trust him. With her life, and with Eden's. Wounded or not, she trusted him more than anyone, knew without a shadow of a doubt that he would protect her sister with his own life.

"What about you?"

"The bleeding isn't bad." He grimaced. "It just hurts like a mother, and I can't hardly move it. But I'll be fine. Eden can put some Quik-Clot gauze on it. You worry about defending this place. Come and get us when it's over."

She nodded tightly. Quickly, she twisted and glanced up over the sandbags into the yard. "Looks like they're all in the back. I don't see anyone out front."

"Then we need to go now." Ezra raised the radio with his splinted left hand. "Logan, can you clear a way to the shed?"

The handheld crackled. "We'll keep 'em pinned in place. Give me sixty seconds, then go."

Ezra crawled for the doorway, his head down, huffing from the effort, and the pain. "Come on, girl!"

Eden glanced at Dakota for confirmation. Her heart in her throat, Dakota nodded. There was no time to say anything or hug goodbye. *I'll never leave you. Never, ever.*

Ducking low, Logan ran into the room and headed for the kitchen window so he could cover their escape. "Go! Go! Go!"

Just like that, Eden was gone.

Dakota turned back to the task at hand. The Shepherds were too near the house. They were almost inside. She had to keep them distracted and pinned down so they didn't notice Eden and Ezra fleeing the cabin.

Dakota couldn't afford to close her eyes, but she sent up a quick prayer to Julio's God anyway. *Keep them safe. I'll do anything. Anything.*

62

LOGAN

Logan focused on providing covering fire from the kitchen window as Ezra and Eden escaped through the crawlspace Ezra had fashioned, shoving aside the rug and the fake tile in the bathroom and squeezing down below the floor.

The remaining Shepherds were focused on infiltrating the rear of the cabin. Behind Logan, Julio clambered up the ladder to replace Ezra in the sniper's nest. "Pin them down at the back door," Logan called.

"Got it," Julio said tightly.

A few eternal moments after they disappeared into the bathroom, they reappeared. Dark, shadowy forms moved behind the saw palmetto as Ezra punched through the flimsy, grassed-over hatch and slithered out, followed by Eden.

"Logan," Dakota said, her voice urgent, desperate. Dakota didn't say another word, but she didn't need to. He heard every ounce of her fear in the way she said his name.

Logan scanned the dark yard, eyes straining for any movement, for a muzzle flash. Ezra and Eden dashed across the fifty yards of open

Into the Fire

ground to the shed, two dark shapes in a sea of black. Behind the shed, the trees waved and bent in the wind.

Logan aimed and took out the motion sensor security lights before they could switch on. That strategy went both ways. It took several shots and who-knew-how-much roof damage, but he hit the general vicinity enough times that the lights were good and shattered.

Through his scope, the taller shadow of Ezra stumbled, then righted himself and kept going, Eden a fluttering shape at his side. His gait was uneven, favoring his right leg. He limped across the yard, one hand on Eden, keeping her close.

Logan swung the rifle and peered through the scope, searching for potential enemies. Every muscle in his body was stretched taut. Sweat dripped down his temples. They couldn't run fast enough. *Come on, come on.*

Movement. A dark shape crouched between two of the huge cisterns. A Shepherd.

Logan fired three quick shots. *Click.*

The figure disappeared behind the closest barrel as Logan ejected the spent mag and fumbled one-handed in his bag for a new one. Only one loaded magazine left.

He swore under his breath and slapped it in.

Lightning flickered in the clouds, illuminating the entire property. Ezra and Eden were frozen in the sudden strobe of light as Ezra wrestled to unlock the door.

The figure behind the water barrel reappeared, the long barrel of a submachine aimed at Ezra's back. No way the attacker could miss.

Logan didn't have time to aim. He squeezed off two shots, then two more. He held his breath, rigid and frozen, finger on the trigger, forced to wait desperately for the next lightning strike to determine Ezra and Eden's fate.

Had he hit his mark and saved them?

Or had he failed? Were the two people Dakota loved most dead?

Gunfire shattered the air. The stench of gunpowder scorched his nostrils. Thunder rolled and boomed.

Lightning emblazoned the sky, highlighting the sharp outline of Ezra standing before the opened shed door, stooped over a large form on the ground at his feet, Eden shoved protectively behind him.

The pistol wavered in the old man's hand as he fired a single shot into the Shepherd's skull. Logan had missed. Ezra hadn't.

But it had cost him. The old man dropped the gun and slumped against the door, his shoulders quaking. Everything went dark again.

In the next shuttering flash, Eden was holding him up and pulling him inside. In the next, the doors were closed.

They'd made it.

Logan didn't have time to feel relieved.

A nearby shriek of pain rent the air. One of the intruders was trying to climb inside the bathroom window; the razor wire must've torn into his hands.

The Shepherds had reached the cabin's back door.

63

LOGAN

They fought for what felt like days. Logan's muscles ached. His eyes burned. He had no clue how much time was passing, minutes or hours.

It was still dark. Outside, the thunderstorm boomed and crashed above them. Scattered gunfire punctured the air.

The slide of his Glock locked back. His AR-15 was already empty. He had no more loaded magazines. He was completely out of ammo.

"They're at the back, about to break in!" Dakota said, moving fast and low from the back bedroom to the living room. Her ponytail sagged against her back, damp strands clinging against her smudged cheeks and forehead. Her eyes were wide, her pupils huge. "Any more ammo?"

"No." Logan pressed himself against the fridge in the kitchen, hoping it'd provide the cover the flimsy interior walls couldn't, and peered around the corner into the empty hallway. His mouth was gritty with dust. His pulse roared in his ears.

"There's more in the shed. But we can't get there—" Her tense expression brightened. She ducked low, scurried over to the couch, reached beneath it, and pulled out a Remington 870 pump-action shotgun and a box of shells. She tossed them both to Logan. "Ezra's secret stash. There's a Glock 19 taped underneath the cabinet next to the fridge. Ammo, too."

"We can't keep them out," he said, breathing hard.

"I know. But if we're going out, we go out fighting."

Logan gave her a tight nod, longing to say so much more, but there was no time. He cared nothing for himself; his only concern was Dakota.

Already, the rear door was splintering off its hinges. The door was intentionally made the weakest entry point for a reason. The Shepherds would be forced into the narrow hallway, vulnerable and exposed. A twelve-foot funnel of death, Ezra had called it.

Ezra had planned to lift the trapdoor in the ceiling and take them out one by one from his elevated position. But Ezra had gotten himself shot.

Julio was up there, but he wasn't nearly the sharpshooter Ezra was. He'd probably end up getting killed. Logan wasn't willing to put Julio's life on the line any more than it already was.

Time for a new plan.

He fed five shells into the mag tube from the bottom, his hands trembling against his will, making him clumsy and slow, then dumped the remaining shells into his cargo pocket. He pushed off the safety.

"I hear something," Dakota said.

He couldn't hear anything through his earplugs other than the boom of gunfire and the crash and thud of the Shepherds bashing through the back door. They'd be inside within seconds.

A dull, distant roar sounded from somewhere, but he didn't have time to consider the source.

The back door collapsed beneath the onslaught, and the first intruder shouldered inside. With the stock firm against his shoulder, Logan ducked low and peered around the corner, aimed at the first moving object he saw, and squeezed the trigger.

The first man's thigh exploded in a spray of red. He staggered back, falling into the man behind him, who struggled to throw him off. Logan unleashed three shots on them both, pumping the action as quickly as he could.

Boom. Boom. Boom. The sound was deafening in the narrow confines of the cabin. He had his earplugs in, but the blasts still rang in his ears. The third man ducked into a bedroom, but not before Logan sent two rounds into his back.

Logan shifted for the fourth man, who raced down the hallway toward him, firing wildly. Logan darted back behind the fridge, crouching as he pumped the action, his heart jackhammering against his ribs.

The fourth man rounded the corner of the kitchen, M4 aimed slightly above Logan's head.

Logan squeezed the trigger.

Nothing.

The Shepherd smiled.

Logan threw himself forward and jammed the barrel of the shotgun into the shepherd's crotch. The man grunted, stumbling as he squeezed the trigger, a half-dozen shots zipping over Logan's head and slamming into the upper cabinets ten feet behind him.

The Shepherd regained his footing. The M4's muzzle swung toward Logan's face, less than six feet away. Logan's heart contracted. This was it, then. This was—

The crack of a gunshot resounded, booming through the small room. The man's head snapped back. He crumpled to the floor.

Logan stared at the man's bloodied body, stunned.

Across the living room, Dakota crouched behind the side of the couch closest to the wall, her forearms braced against the arm of the sofa, her Springfield in both hands.

She rose and tucked the pistol in her holster. "That was the last round."

With the empty shotgun, he nudged the mangled body of the

Shepherd who'd gotten the drop on him. He couldn't quite believe he was still alive. "Thanks for saving my ass."

"You're welcome." She managed a weary smile that pierced him to his very soul. "Hurry up and get us a few of those M4s."

He bent and grabbed the carbine from the closest dead man's hands, checked the magazine. It was empty. He swore and threw it aside.

Heavy footsteps thudded down the hallway.

"More coming!" Dakota cried.

Too late to go for the other carbines in the hallway. Back to the shotgun.

He fished more shotgun shells out of his pocket and tried to load it as quickly as humanly possible. His fingers were trembling with nerves. The first shell clattered to the floor. He fed the second correctly.

Before he could chamber it, four more Shepherds burst from the hallway, M4s bristling.

64

LOGAN

"Nobody move!" one of the Shepherds shouted.
Logan froze.
Behind him, Dakota expelled a sharp breath.
A bulky, bearded Hispanic man shouldered into the room behind the four men. "Hands up!" he barked. "On your knees!"
Slowly, Logan and Dakota raised their hands as one of the Shepherds relieved them of their weapons—including Logan's knife, which he tossed across the room—and swiftly patted them both down. He forced them to their knees, cuffing Logan painfully upside the head as he did so.
Logan glared up at them.
Dakota's expression tightened in a rictus of hatred. "Abel Flemmings."
The man's mouth creased into a facsimile of a smile, all white teeth and gleaming malice. "Ah, Sister Dakota. How we've missed you."
"Screw you."
"Still as sweet, I see. I swear I never knew what Maddox saw in you." Abel shouldered his carbine and turned to a tall, slim Caucasian

Shepherd with an acne-scarred face. "Let Reuben know we've got them. There's one more hidden somewhere. Find him and kill him, along with this one." He gestured to Dakota. "The girl, we're saving for Maddox."

Logan gathered his strength, every muscle tensing, readying himself. If he could draw their attention to him, maybe Dakota could find a way to escape.

It was a snowball's chance in hell, but if it was a chance at all, he'd take it.

He leapt to his feet and launched himself at the nearest Shepherd, a muscular, bald black man. Action beat reaction every time. They weren't expecting an attack from an unarmed man.

By the time their brains registered the fact that he'd moved, he'd already seized the bald man's head in a vice-grip. He jerked it in one direction, then violently back again with a sickening twist. There was a hiss and a snap, and the man went limp and dropped heavily to the floor.

"What the—" Abel cried.

Growling, Logan whipped around and lunged for the next Shepherd. The Shepherd staggered back, nearly tripping over a chair leg to avoid the blow, his gun swinging around but not fast enough.

Logan went in low like a battering ram, tackling the man, bashing his head so viciously against the floor, the guy was unconscious before he knew what was happening.

"Stop, or she dies!" Abel screamed, his face purpling with rage.

Abel's pistol was unholstered and pressed against Dakota's forehead.

"Don't listen to him!" Dakota cried. "Do it!"

Logan released the man's deadweight and clambered slowly to his feet, his legs lead, dread squeezing the air from his lungs. "No."

"On your knees!"

Logan sank obediently to his knees, despair rising up inside him.

The remaining two Shepherds kept their weapons trained on him.

Into the Fire

Abel pivoted, took two swift strides, and jammed the pistol against Logan's temple, a deranged look in those small, beady eyes. He wanted to kill Logan. He was going to do it.

Logan refused to close his eyes or to cower. He stared back at death with all the fury he could muster.

This couldn't be the end. Not after everything they'd survived, everything they'd bled and fought for. They'd outlived a freaking nuclear bomb—now these scumbags were the victors?

He refused to accept it.

But it didn't matter. Death didn't give a damn what you did or didn't accept, what you wanted or desired or despised. It came as much for the undeserving as it did for the deserving.

Logan deserved it as much as anyone. After everything—Tomás, the bomb, the radiation, the gangs—it was finally here for him.

Abel sneered. "Time to die, you—"

A cacophony of bullets exploded around them. The two Shepherds collapsed. Blood sprayed everywhere. Screams and shouts echoed from outside the cabin.

Abel half-turned, gaping, a look of astonishment on his broad, flat face.

A second later, his head exploded.

Stunned, Logan dropped to the kitchen floor, his hands over his head. He could only hope Dakota had managed to do the same.

The shots had come from outside the cabin. What the hell was going on?

Heavy footsteps stomped down the hallway toward them.

Instinctively, Logan twisted onto his belly and army-crawled through dust and splattered blood, clambering over the bald man he'd killed, heading toward the cabinet.

The Glock. If he could reach the gun...

He jerked open the wooden door and fumbled for the pistol tucked inside the holster duct-taped to the cabinet ceiling. He flipped onto his back, ignoring the jolt of pain, finger already on the trigger as he aimed—

"Don't shoot!" Julio shouted from the attic above them. "Friendlies on their way!"

Logan hesitated. He removed his finger from the trigger just as Archer Collier lumbered into the kitchen, a semiautomatic rifle cradled in his huge arms.

Jake, Zane, and Haasi crowded in behind him, all armed.

"Hey!" Zane's face went slack when he saw Logan's Glock aimed straight at them. "We're the good guys."

Logan just stared at them, his brain unable to process how quickly everything had changed. Ten seconds ago, he'd believed he was a goner.

Now, four dead men lay at his feet, and he was surrounded by allies.

"Dakota?" he asked.

"I'm here," she said in a strained voice. "I'm okay."

The adrenaline leaked away, leaving him dizzy with exhaustion. He bent at the waist and dry-heaved, spittle trailing from his lips.

Archer glanced around, grimacing as he took in the bodies and the bullet-riddled cabin. Splinters of wood and shards of glass and ceramic crunched beneath his boots.

He gave a resigned shake of his head. "Well, hell. Ezra's gonna be pissed about the mess, that's for sure."

65

SHAY

"Talk to me," Shay said. "Distract me."

She and Hawthorne were waiting in the American Airlines' Admirals lounge for Hawthorne's uncle, General Pierce, to get out of a meeting. The general had asked them to meet him, sounding strained and more worried than usual.

As if there wasn't plenty to worry about already.

Several soldiers in ACUs and military buzz-cuts hurried past their lounge chairs, gesturing emphatically to each other. Dozens of official-looking people in stuffy-looking suits strode back and forth, hurrying from one crisis to the next.

It was far more chaotic today than usual, and that was saying something.

Hawthorne squeezed her hand and gave her a mischievous grin. "I can think of a few distractions, but I'm not sure that's what you mean."

Heat rose up her throat and bloomed in her cheeks. The memory of their last kiss tingled on her lips. "I'm not against public displays of affection, but um, maybe not here."

He gave a hearty laugh. "Also noted. I'll definitely remember that later. I guess for now I'll have to resort to boring methods of distraction."

"Nothing about you is boring," she said, her whole face burning.

"I sure hope not." He winked at her. He shifted in his seat, dug around in his pocket with his free hand, and pulled out a package of bubble gum. "Before I forget."

"Thank you. Bubble gum is my favorite." She released his hand to take the package and open it. She pulled out a stick and stuffed the rest in her pocket for later.

Hawthorne tapped his temple. "I know. I remember these things."

"Storing up brownie points?"

"Whatever works."

"Oh, it's working." She popped a stick in her mouth and relished the burst of fresh, fruity strawberry-banana-punch flavor. "What I *meant* was, tell me about what you're doing. Tell me we've caught these scumbags, or are about to. Is it really Iran who did this to us?"

"I wish I had better news." His eyes dimmed as he sat back in his seat. "The short answer is we don't know yet. Some things are classified and well above my paygrade, but I can tell you the FBI has been scouring that van in Chicago, the one with the bomb that didn't go off. They're taking it apart piece by piece. They found sand and shell fragments lodged in the tire tread and the wheel wells."

Shay's eyes widened. "Shell fragments? Like seashells?"

He nodded.

"That sounds like Florida."

"Yeah. Florida or Alabama, along the gulf coast. The tech guys said it was a shell from some kind of blue crab found only on the panhandle, or something. Anyway, the van was registered to a vehicle rental company out of Panama City that turned out to be a shell company." He shot her another wry, tired grin. "No pun intended."

She rolled her eyes good-naturedly.

"Sorry, can't help myself." He cleared his throat and grew serious. "Our tech experts did their thing. We know the shell company is regis-

Into the Fire

tered to a shipping corporation based in Malta, with strong ties to Japan and China. They've also contracted with Russia, Ukraine, and the Middle East."

"Including Iran?"

"A little, but not as much as Russia and Ukraine."

She chewed her gum thoughtfully. "So maybe it isn't Iran."

"We're working on it. But nothing is as it seems. On the global stage, with nations vying for power and dominance and America at her weakest, the stakes couldn't be higher, and our allies smile at us with knives held behind their backs.

"These are new wars like we've never seen. Proxy wars and shadow armies, where the invasion is through cyber attacks, data breaches, and information warfare, all seeded with propaganda, subversion, and misdirection."

"A nation can lose a war before she even knows she's in one," Shay said.

"Exactly." Hawthorne nodded. "We'll get to the truth. The real truth. We have to. And then we'll nail them—hopefully with a nuclear missile." He rubbed his head absently with his free hand, looking tired but determined. "Everyone's working together on this—ATF, CIA, FBI, Homeland. We're the best in the world for a reason."

The door to the conference room opened and several middle-aged men and women strode out, hurriedly shuffling papers, murmuring to each other or staring angrily down at their tablets, all of them hollow-eyed and exhausted. Several assistants scurried after them.

These people were sheltered from the worst of it—the administrators and officers, liaisons and planners. They all boasted important titles: disaster relief coordinators, community response teams, public assistance directors, hazard mitigation, unmet needs, recovery logistics.

How many times had they visited the mobile medical tents or set foot outside the base? Since Governor Blake had ordered everyone but essential personnel into the FEMA camps, maybe there wasn't anyone out there anyway.

Maybe Miami was a ghost town of radiation, rubble, and roaming gangs.

She hated thinking like that—like a cynical pessimist. Everyone here was working their butts off to save Miami and every other struggling city.

Miami would get back on her feet, just like America would.

They had to.

66

DAKOTA

Jake wiped sweat and specks of blood from his face. "Well, that was one hell of a fight."

Dakota recovered her pistol from the dead Shepherd. With shaking fingers, she reloaded her magazine from the extra 9mm rounds hidden in the cabinet. She hated to be weaponless for even a second.

She spun in a slow circle, sucking in ragged breaths and gripping the handgun so tightly she couldn't feel her fingers. *One, two, three. Breathe.*

She hardly recognized the cabin. Her only home had become a war zone. Dust and debris mingled with splatters and puddles of blood like red paint, bullet holes pockmarking the walls, the floor, the ceiling. Spent shell casings were scattered everywhere.

Her gaze lowered to the bodies. She toed the inert form of Abel Bowers. He lay contorted on his side, legs and arms splayed awkwardly, his dead eyes wide open. "Is it over?"

"It's over," Archer said. "I promise."

"What about the soldiers outside? What about—"

"We got them." Haasi raised her crossbow triumphantly. "They're all dead. The dirtbags never saw us coming."

"Did you check all the bodies to make sure they're dead?" Logan picked up one of the dead Shepherds' carbines, checked to make sure it was loaded, and moved to the front living room window. He peered out at the storm outside, still on alert.

"I counted seventeen carcasses out there and in here," Zane said proudly. "And I killed three of 'em myself."

"It was a pleasure killing Maddox Cage, I'll say that," Archer said.

Dakota turned to him, her heart surging. "Are you sure you killed him? You sure it was Maddox? It's dark, and with the storm—"

"Damn sure," Archer said. "Drilled a bullet through his deranged skull at twenty yards."

Maddox Cage was dead. He was finally dead.

Dakota closed her eyes for a moment, waiting for the relief to thrum through her veins, for the *knowing* to settle deep in her bones, for it to be real.

It didn't come. All she felt was exhaustion, every inch of her body aching, the tension still like a knot in her belly. Maybe it would come later.

Or maybe he would always haunt her, even in death.

"I want to see," she said, whirling toward the door. Everything lurched and she lost her balance, almost stumbling. She righted herself. "I want to put another damn bullet in him just to make sure."

Haasi reached out and pushed down Dakota's pistol so it was aimed at the floor. "It's okay, honey," she said. "You will. But maybe you should rest a minute, first. You're not looking so good."

Her ears were ringing. She tasted acid on the back of her tongue. Her pulse wouldn't stop thudding against her throat. She nodded dully and leaned against the nearest wall.

She kept feeling like she was missing something important, like her brain was too muddled to think clearly. "Julio?" she croaked. "Where's Julio?"

"Right here." Julio clattered down the attic stairs, shell-shocked and covered in dust, but alive. A round had skimmed his right ear, lopping off a quarter-inch of flesh. Blood dripped down the side of his neck and soaked the collar of his shirt, but he insisted he was fine.

"I can fix that right up." Haasi looked around. "Where's Ezra? And Eden?"

"Safe in the shed," Logan said. "I made sure of it."

"He was shot in the shoulder, though," Dakota said, worry building in her chest. "It wasn't bleeding too badly, but—"

Someone pounded on the front door.

Everyone jumped. Several guns aimed at the door simultaneously. Logan, watching at the window, remained unfazed. "It's Maki."

"Boyd's hurt!" Maki called from the other side of the door.

Logan unlocked the multiple deadbolts and stepped aside as Maki stumbled in, Boyd's arm draped around her shoulder. Dark red blood leaked from a torn gash in his upper right thigh.

"One of those scumbags nicked me with a lucky shot," he grumbled, wincing as Maki lowered him carefully to the couch.

"Damn it, Boyd!" Archer went pale. "What'd I tell you about playing the hero?"

Boyd rolled his eyes as he grimaced. "It's a flesh wound. I think. Tell me it's a flesh wound, Haasi."

Haasi held her crossbow in one hand and fisted her free hand on her hip. "I can do no such thing. We need to get you to my place so I can examine it."

Archer sighed. "Just tell us if he's gonna live."

Haasi eyed Boyd with pursed lips. She leaned her crossbow against the couch, knelt next to Boyd, and untied the bandana from around her neck. "Let me see."

Boyd's ruddy face went fish-white beneath his beard. He gritted his teeth against the pain as Haasi wrapped the bandana around his thigh above the bullet wound to staunch the bleeding.

She frowned. "Since you're not gushing like a hose, it missed your femoral artery. You'll live. Probably."

"Told you that you weren't gonna die," Maki said.

Boyd leaned gingerly against the couch cushions. "See? Leave it to Maki to always see the bright side."

Maki only scowled harder at him.

"You saved us." Dakota couldn't pull enough air into her lungs. A giant vise squeezed her chest. She felt lightheaded, dizzy with relief. "I didn't think you would come."

Jake shrugged. "I for one wasn't planning on it, until those arrogant scumbags invaded Haasi's home and threatened us all."

She glanced at Boyd, then all of them. They'd all earned her gratitude tonight, that was for sure. And her respect. "I'm sorry I dragged you into this."

Haasi stood, wiped her hands on her pants, and put one hand on Dakota's shoulder. "Evil has a way of spreading beyond its boundaries. People think you can contain it, but you can't. The evil in that place would've spilled into our lives sooner or later. It's not your fault."

"What happened at your place?" Julio asked. "How did they get hold of Park as a hostage?"

At the mention of Park, everyone's smiles faded. Guilt pierced her. Park had paid the ultimate price—and it wasn't even his fight.

Soberly, Jake explained the earlier events of that night. "Maddox Cage offered us a devil's deal. He'd let us live if we stayed out of the fight with you. If we didn't, he'd kill our children."

Haasi picked up her crossbow and slung it over her shoulder. "They confiscated our radios and left a man with a submachine gun to make sure we kept our end of the bargain."

Julio managed a weary smile. "I see that went well."

"Maki pretended to cry," Zane said. "She got the moron to go right up to her to see what was wrong. She whispered something and he leaned in close—you know, the beautiful damsel-in-distress thing. He never saw it coming. She jumped up and punched him in the face! Then she kneed him in the crotch, grabbed his gun, and cracked his skull with it. She had him unconscious in two seconds flat."

Into the Fire

Maki blushed and turned her face away, but a faint smile tugged at her mouth.

"Guys?" Boyd attempted to lean forward but fell back against the couch cushion, his ruddy pallor going a pasty shade of white. "As much as I appreciate this post-battle party, I've got a chunk of lead puncturing my thigh. My leg isn't feeling so good, and neither am I..."

Zane and Jake rushed over to their brother. "He can ride on my bike with me," Jake said, "but we need to get him back so Haasi can work her magic."

"Bring Ezra over so I can take a look at him." Haasi was already moving for the door. "Boyd, get your ass off that couch."

After they'd left, Julio looked out the shattered window. "I'm going to find a place to bury Park."

"Let me get Ezra and Eden, then I'll help you," Dakota said.

Julio half-turned to her, unconsciously touching the gold cross at his neck. His shoulders were hunched, blood leaking from his ear, but his gaze was firm and unyielding. "I want to do this myself. You go be with your family. I've got it."

"The shovel is still out by the hen house." Logan still stood by the window, tensed and silent. Greasy sweat matted his unruly black hair to his skull, little curls clinging to the sides of his face. Sweat, dirt, and blood smeared his cheekbones. His expression was stony, a haunted look in his eyes.

It took everything in her not to go to him right then.

Julio nodded without a word and slipped out the front door, his boots crunching over shards of glass and ceramic, chunks of drywall, and spent shell casings.

Dakota needed to go, too. She still needed to check the bodies on her way to Eden and Ezra. She couldn't wait to tell them it was over, that Eden was safe.

She longed to wrap Eden in her arms and feel the warm softness of her, to see that sweet, bright smile lighting up her sister's face. She'd hug Ezra too, no matter how ornery he got. He didn't have a choice.

She wiped her brow with the back of her arm. Every inch of her body was caked with sweat, dust, dirt, and blood. Her jaw ached from clenching it so tightly. Her muscles protested with every movement. She was so tired she could sleep for a week.

But it didn't matter. None of it mattered.

They'd won.

67

SHAY

"There you are!" General Randall Pierce barreled out of the conference room and hurried toward them. "I was hoping you'd stop by."

Shay was in the middle of blowing a huge bubble with her gum to impress Hawthorne. She popped it quickly and swallowed it, nearly choking as she scrambled to her feet.

General Pierce enveloped her hand in a vigorous handshake. In his mid-fifties, General Pierce was a formidable black man with short, wiry gray hair and a graying beard. He was as tall as his nephew but at least a hundred pounds heavier, solid as a slab of concrete, and imposing in every sense of the word.

He was the State Coordinating Officer for the Joint Field Office at the EOC—the Emergency Operations Center—which made him in charge of basically everything related to the blast and the recovery efforts in southern Florida, according to Hawthorne.

"So nice to see you again, sir," Shay said.

Without preamble, General Pierce swiveled to Hawthorne and embraced him in a giant bear hug.

"Sir?" Hawthorne grunted. "Not that I don't enjoy this, but...I can't breathe."

General Pierce released his nephew and stepped back with a sigh. "All this death. I just needed to be reminded that there's still life, too."

Hawthorne grinned weakly, still recovering his breath. "However we can help, sir."

Shay liked General Pierce. He was affable, but also frank—what you saw was what you got with him. Genuine warmth sparkled in his dark eyes, though they were lined with stress and fatigue, and his short, wiry hair seemed more gray than the first time she'd met him.

Two burly, suited men passed close by them, heading down the long corridor, their faces sullen as they muttered under their breaths. They trailed a fast-walking balding man with ram-rod straight posture wearing an expensive, pale-blue seersucker suit.

General Pierce scowled as soon as they were out of earshot. "Don't trust those guys as far as I can throw them. Something squirrely about 'em. After several decades of honing your B.S. meter in public service, you learn to sniff out the cream from the..." He glanced at Shay. "Well, I'll leave that to your imagination."

Hawthorne winked at her. "We appreciate that, sir."

"Who are they?" Shay asked.

"The skinny one strutting like he's got a stick up his butt is the liaison to the governor's office, Alfred T. Forester. Always insists you say that damn 'T', too. He's Governor Blake's mouthpiece, and a giant turd if you ask me. Instead of doing everything he can for the victims, he's quibbling over jurisdiction, fund allocations, and politics. As if anyone in Florida gives a damn about Blake's re-election."

"And the other two?" Shay asked.

"His minions, I suppose. Not sure exactly what they do other than follow him around and mutter angrily in his ear." The general watched Alfred T. Forester strut around the corner, trailed by his muscled entourage. He rubbed his eyes and gave another weary sigh.

"You wanted to see us?" Hawthorne asked.

General Pierce turned back to them, his expression solemn. "We were waiting on the last report from NOAA and the National Hurricane Center, hoping against hope we wouldn't have to do this..."

"What?" Hawthorne asked warily.

"The hurricane. Overnight, it strengthened into a category three."

"Oh boy," Hawthorne said. "That's not good."

"It's worse. A high-pressure system is forcing the storm from its original path toward Cuba into a northward curve. The scientists from the NHC called it a Bermuda High or something. They threw around a lot of terms—subtropical ridges, vertical wind shear, beta drift—but the result's the same."

Shay's gut tightened. Her palms went damp. "Tell us."

"The order comes from the top. We're evacuating."

"Who's 'we'?" Shay asked. "What about the mobile hospital tents? All those sick and injured people—"

"They'll be dead if we don't move. Hurricane Helen is projected to hit Miami dead-on sometime between tomorrow night and early Monday morning."

"So there's still time," Shay said with a wild, desperate hope. "It could still shift and make landfall somewhere else, or miss Florida altogether."

General Pierce shook his head heavily. "It could. But the meteorologists say it's unlikely. That was the spirited discussion we just had. Governor Blake, through the mouthpiece of Alfred T. Whatever-his-name-is, insisted we couldn't take the risk. If the hurricane hits us as a Category 3, the resulting catastrophe would be utterly devastating to morale, not to mention our military assets and at-risk civilians. In this case, I fear I must agree with him."

Shay chewed anxiously on her thumbnail. She wasn't worried for herself. She'd go wherever she was needed. But all she could think of were the thousands of injured and dying patients, how difficult it'd be to move them to safety so quickly without causing further harm.

She thought of Dr. Webster and her friend Nicole, giving everything she had to keep those patients alive, even though her husband had been killed in the blast, too.

Her stomach clenched in dread. Dakota, Logan, Julio, Park, and Eden were stuck out there in the swamp—with no idea a killer hurricane was bearing down on them. What would happen to them?

"Where is the evacuation point?" Hawthorne asked.

"FEMA's set up a massive tent city south of Orlando, somewhere near Celebration. Maybe they'll take over Disney World. With them, who knows? According to reports, it can house several hundred thousand people. Greater Orlando is supposed to have some open beds in nearby hospitals, too."

"Okay," Hawthorne said. "That doesn't sound too bad."

"We're requisitioning every bus, chopper, plane, and transport vehicle within a fifty-mile radius to transport refugees. Evacuations begin at zero six hundred hours. I wanted to give you two an early warning."

Beside her, Hawthorne stiffened. "Just civilians?"

"Civvies first. But everyone goes."

"But we're investigating leads here," Hawthorne protested. "And we're making significant headway against the Blood Outlaws. We've already regained Hialeah, Gladesview, Brownsville, and we're pushing hard into Little Havana—"

"Everyone goes," General Pierce said with finality, his voice forceful, eyes flashing. "No exceptions."

Hawthorne was just as tall as his uncle, but the general loomed over him, every inch radiating power and authority. There was no arguing against him. You obeyed this man. No wonder he was a general.

Hawthorne pursed his lips unhappily but squared his shoulders and gave a sharp nod. "Yes, sir. We'll do what we need to do."

"I know you will." The general's satphone beeped several times. He laid a huge hand on Hawthorne's shoulder, his fierce expression gentling. "If I don't see you beforehand, we'll meet up in Orlando. Stay safe, son. My sister'll murder me if I let anything happen to you."

General Pierce turned to go.

Before she could think better of it, Shay grabbed his arm. "I apologize, sir, but what about my friends? Logan and Dakota. They went into the Everglades."

"I'm afraid there's nothing we can do for them." He looked down at her, genuine sadness and regret in his eyes. "We already have an impossible task before us. It'll take every ounce of our manpower and then some to evacuate the entire EOC, the thousands of injured from the local and emergency hospitals, not to mention the FEMA camps. For every person outside of those parameters, it's every man for himself."

"We have to warn them, at least," Shay said. "I've tried calling several times today. They're not answering."

"They have a ham radio, don't they?" Hawthorne said. "I'm sure they already know."

"That's not good enough. Do they know they need to evacuate? Can they even get out? We have to do *something*."

General Pierce gave a weary shake of his head. "I'm truly sorry."

"God help us," Hawthorne breathed.

"God help us all," the general said.

Shay and Hawthorne watched him stride away, his broad shoulders hunched, his head low, as if he were already braced for the coming storm.

68

LOGAN

"We did it." Dakota turned to Logan, her eyes bright and shining, triumphant. "We actually did it."

Logan looked down at her, at the tilt of her jaw, the soft slope of her cheekbones, the faintest spray of freckles beneath the smudges of dirt. It didn't matter that she was covered in soot and grime and splatters of blood, that her clothes were a mess or that she held a pistol she'd just used to blow a man's head off.

She was radiant. The smile she gave him was full and genuine and unguarded.

It struck him like a punch to the gut.

Ezra was right. He could never give her what she needed, what she deserved. It would hurt her, but she was better off without him. She was better than he was, in every way. And nothing he could do would ever change that.

The world was broken. So was he.

He'd done what he came to do. She'd saved his life, so he'd saved her family. He'd kept the promise he'd made to her back in the theater. Her sister was safe. He was finished.

He didn't belong here.

She moved for the door, then paused. "I'm getting Ezra and Eden, but first I need to check the bodies. I want to see him dead with my own eyes." She reached out and touched his hand. "Come with me."

He flinched from her touch. He was empty, hollowed out. Only the darkness remained inside him.

He felt it, pulling at him, promising him a sweet release, a place without pain, without this feeling like his beating heart was being torn wide open right in front of him.

"Logan? Are you okay?" Dakota squinted at him, a faint line appearing between her brows. Strands of her auburn hair stuck to her cheeks.

It took everything in him to not brush them behind her ears. Not to lean in close, slide his hand behind her neck, and tilt her mouth up toward his.

He wanted to kiss her. He wanted to wrap her in his arms and never let go, to feel the warmth of her body pressed against him, both their hearts beating in tandem. He wanted more than that.

But it didn't matter. A man like him could never have something like that.

His nerves were exposed, raw. Exhaustion tugged at him as the adrenaline leaked away, leaving nothing but a bleak despair. He had to end this. "I'm leaving."

"What?"

"I'm leaving tonight. My bag is already packed and ready."

She stared at him. "What are you talking about?"

"I fulfilled my end of the bargain. I said I'd protect your sister, and I did. Now, I'm done. I'm leaving. I want to leave."

She took a step back. Shock registered on her face. She blinked, shaking her head. "No. No, that's not true, and you know it."

"Yes, it is."

The impact of his words sank in. Her expression changed from confusion to disbelief to something like grief. She opened her mouth, closed it.

He had to go. He couldn't stand this, couldn't bear the stunned, betrayed look in her eyes. His heart splintered inside his chest. Every word he spoke was bitter as ashes on his tongue. "I have to go."

"Logan—"

He turned away from her. "I'm sorry."

69

DAKOTA

Dakota holstered her pistol, pulled out her penlight, and hurried out into the storm. Rain slapped her face. She almost stumbled over the first body—just a shadowy lump in the darkness. Body number one.

Ezra and Eden were waiting for her. But she needed to check the bodies. She had to. The scars on her back prickled, like her body *knew* what was waiting.

She needed to see him, to make sure it was finally over.

She started in the front yard and then made her way around the property, circling the opposite side of the cabin to the back, slowly making her way toward the shed.

Rain plastered her hair to her temples and dripped down her face. Her clothes were soaked almost instantly and stuck to her skin. She forced herself to focus despite the ache throbbing in her chest.

Logan is gone.

It didn't make sense.

They'd won. Against all odds, they'd defended the cabin and defeated the Shepherds. Their allies had come to their aid. Maddox Cage, her nemesis, was dead.

With over two dozen Shepherds lost, the Prophet would think twice about attacking them again. He would slink away in defeat. She was sure of it.

She wanted it to be true so badly that she already half-believed it was.

Their victory had cost them. The cabin was in tatters. Park was dead. But she still had the people that mattered most. It was selfish and ugly, but it was the truth.

She should feel elated, jubilant, on top of the freaking world. At least for tonight. They should've had time to celebrate, to acknowledge how close they'd come to losing everything.

She and Logan should've...

But she couldn't finish the thought. It was too painful.

There was no 'she and Logan', not anymore. Because Logan had chosen to leave.

She knelt to examine the fourth and fifth bodies, shining her penlight into their faces, blinking against the water in her eyelashes. Some of the dead were rough, their heads, torsos, and limbs riddled with buckshot and bullet holes. Some lay flat on their stomachs, and she had to kick them onto their backs.

She counted each one, carefully studying their features. They looked almost alien in death, bloodied and bloated, their NV goggles distorting their faces.

Some she recognized; some she didn't.

She rose and continued her search. Seven, eight, nine. Still no Maddox.

After all of this, after all she and Logan had been through, he'd chickened out in the end. Not from an unwinnable fight, not from a battle where he was outmanned and outgunned—but from mere human connection.

Dakota knew better than anyone how much connection could cost a person. How something so simple and easy for some people could be an insurmountable mountain for someone else.

He still blamed himself. He thought what he'd done marked him for life, made him unworthy of a chance at happiness.

He was dead wrong.

She should go after him, after she saw to Ezra and Eden. She should—

But no. He'd made his choice. She wouldn't beg. Besides, he'd taken Boyd's motorcycle. He was already long gone.

She forced herself to shove those painful thoughts down deep. Later, she'd grieve for what might have been. Right now, she had responsibilities. She had people who were depending on her.

Ten, eleven, twelve. Anxiety twisted in her gut as the count grew higher and higher.

She was in sight of the storage shed. The fighting hadn't been heavy here. There were fewer bodies.

Fifteen, sixteen, seventeen. None of them Maddox.

Her breath hitched in her throat. Dread coiled in her gut, tighter and tighter.

Maddox wasn't here. If he wasn't here among the bodies, then he wasn't dead.

And if he wasn't dead, then where had he gone? He wouldn't have left the battle at the cabin without a reason, without a purpose...

Unless...

Unless he knew Eden was no longer inside.

She raced for the shed, her legs like pistons, terror pumping through her veins. The wavering penlight highlighted the rain, the dead, the slick black grass.

She banged on the slick metal door. "Ezra! Eden! It's me! Let me in!"

No one answered.

She lifted her fist to bang again and froze. On the door right in front of her, about chest high—a red, palm-sized smudge, streaked by the rain. A handprint terminating in a long, bloodied smear.

Please, no. No, no, no!

"Let me in!" she shouted.

She gripped the wet handle. It turned beneath her fingers. It wasn't locked.

Panic clawed at her. Her lungs constricted. For a moment, she couldn't suck in a breath, couldn't call out, couldn't do anything.

The rain pelted her. The wind whipped her hair, her clothes. She forced herself to turn the handle and push. The door swung open. The shed light spilled out in a dim halo.

Dread pooling in her gut, she took in the interior of the shed, spanning the neatly stacked shelves full of years' worth of preparations, the single bulb hanging from the ceiling, the cement floor smeared with a trail of more blood.

Eden wasn't there.

Just beyond the door, Ezra lay in a crumpled, bloodied heap.

70

DAKOTA

It was like falling into freezing water. The absolute shock of it. She couldn't breathe, couldn't think, couldn't move.

"Dakota," Ezra said hoarsely.

The sound of his voice snapped her out of it. She staggered inside and collapsed to her knees on the floor beside Ezra. With the penlight clenched between her teeth, she pushed aside his plaid overshirt.

The white T-shirt beneath was drenched with blood. She jerked it up with clumsy fingers, searching frantically for the wound.

"You're okay," she said, "you're gonna be okay."

Ezra took in a ragged, gasping breath. He looked up at her, defeat in his eyes. "Not...this time."

She lifted the soaked fabric from his chest, blood slicking her hands. He'd been shot twice—once in the upper right shoulder, and once in the center of his chest.

His shoulder was packed with QuikClot gauze and didn't look like it was bleeding much. It was the chest wound that sent panic jolting through her veins.

Blood pumped from the hole, the edges a foamy pink. The hole made a horrible sucking sound as he struggled to breathe.

The bullet had punctured his lungs.

Dakota's heart plummeted. The panic threatened to crush her. The shoulder could heal, but the chest wound was nothing Haasi's poultices could fix. He needed trauma doctors, an ER, emergency surgery.

They were in the middle of a million acres of swampland, hours from the nearest hospital. And even if that hospital was operational, it'd be overwhelmed with bomb victims.

There was no 911 to call, no ambulance on its way, sirens wailing. She'd never felt so utterly isolated.

"No," she moaned. "No, no, no!"

"Eden, she...They took her."

Dakota barely registered the words. She'd known the second she'd opened the door and Eden was gone. It was too horrific to take in. Her brain wouldn't accept it, not with Ezra bleeding out right in front of her.

"I was wrong," he said.

She rocked back on her heels, shaking her head in helpless despair. "Don't say that."

"We should've worked with the others. I should've asked for...help."

"Not now. This isn't the time."

He ignored her. "I made mistakes."

"We have to—"

"Dakota." He gripped her bloody hand in his weak, gnarled one. "I'm dying."

"No!" She didn't accept it. She refused.

He coughed. Blood speckled his thin bluish lips. "Dakota—"

"I said no!" She shook him off, found a clean stack of folded towels on a nearby shelf, and pressed one against the wound to apply pressure. "Don't talk like that. You're too ornery to die. You can't die. Hold this here while I find something to help you."

"Dakota, it won't matter—"

Into the Fire

"Just do it!" She yanked his hands up and placed them over the towel, pressing hers over his. "Do it."

His eyes flashed—a glimmer of his stubbornness shimmering through the pain—but he obeyed.

She had to keep it together, had to *think*. She struggled to recall his lessons from so long ago. "You have a sucking chest wound. If we don't seal it, the lung will collapse."

And after that, worse things happened, like coma and death.

If only Shay were here. She knew so much more than Dakota. She'd know all about restricted blood vessels, decreased blood flow, how to prevent shock. With her calm and practiced hands, she'd do a better job, too.

But Shay wasn't here. Haasi wasn't here. It was up to Dakota to save him.

"We need a plastic Ziplock bag, right? Or a credit card?" She searched the shelves frantically for the medicinal section, scanning the neat, orderly rows of canned vegetables, fruits, and beans; the sealed containers labeled with oats, flour, and other grains; the water purification tablets and jugs of bleach; the matches, batteries, and boxes of ammunition.

There it was, near the top center of the right side, the white label inscribed with his elegant, impeccable handwriting. She leapt up, fumbled for a pair of sterile gloves.

She searched for the large gauze pads and the QuikClot combat gauze to stop the bleeding, knocking over boxes of bandages and bottles of pills as she grabbed a roll of medical tape, too.

She dropped them beside Ezra and turned to kitchen supplies, found the neatly labeled plastic bin, and yanked it off the shelf. It fell to the floor with a thud. She already had the cover off, tossing out aluminum foil and trash bag boxes until she found the Ziplock stack.

Ezra didn't yell at her for making a mess of his precise, systematic storage. Her throat tightened. At that moment, she would've given anything for a stern lecture. But the only sound was the wet hiss and rattle of his breathing.

She returned to him, blinking back the sudden wetness as she sank to her knees. She ripped open the gauze and used it to wipe the blood from the wound. It was useless. There was too much. It was everywhere—slick on his skin, his clothes, her gloved hands, the floor.

"Breathe out as much as you can."

Too weak to fight her, he complied.

When he'd exhaled as much excess air as he could, she placed the Ziplock bag over the bullet hole, making sure there was at least two inches of plastic on all sides of the wound. She used several layers of medical tape to seal it on three sides, wrapping it fully around his ribs to keep it in place.

Leaving the fourth side open created a one-way valve to let the air escape through the hole. The suction of trying to draw air into the wound would pull the dressing against it and act to seal the chest cavity, so Ezra's lungs could expand normally.

That was the working theory, anyway. With her luck, she'd screwed it up somehow.

"Okay," she said. "Okay. Just keep breathing."

He closed his eyes, opened them again. "I need to tell you...I made a mistake."

"You shouldn't talk."

He sucked in a wheezing breath. "All the things you learn on your deathbed...and no one to tell them to."

If she smiled, she would shatter into a million pieces. "Shut up, Ezra."

"You sound just like Izzy used to."

"Stop talking. Save your strength."

"Don't be a stubborn ass like me." His face contorted in pain—and remorse. "When Izzy passed...and then you left..."

She understood him, understood everything he was trying to say. He'd been dead wrong, but she knew why he'd made the choices he had, maybe better than anyone. He was contrary and bull-headed. More than that, he was afraid.

His wife's death had broken his heart. When Dakota and Eden arrived in the dead of night, disheveled and desperate, he'd risked everything he had left to let them in.

But then Dakota abandoned him, and what was left of his heart shattered. He couldn't allow himself to trust again, to let anyone in—even when he knew better. Even to protect his own life.

She'd almost made the same mistake.

Almost.

"Shh," she said softly, her eyes burning. "I know."

"You're better than that," he mumbled. "You're better than me."

It took everything in her not to break down sobbing.

"You can get her back...you can end this."

Dakota went rigid. "Not without an army. Not without you. How could I possibly try?"

"You don't need me...you know how."

She shook her head fiercely. Her eyes burned. She didn't cry. She was too enraged to cry.

"You should be proud of her," he said. "She agreed to go with them if they left without killing anyone else...and let you be. She traded herself."

All the oxygen was sucked out of the room. "What?"

"She wrote it down on a piece of paper, asked me to say it to them. She said Maddox would honor it, and he did...for whatever reason, he did. It was...the bravest thing I ever saw. She was...still afraid...she did it anyway."

"She just went with them?" Dakota asked, stunned. Fresh rage slashed through her, mingling with the grief. For an instant, outrage blotted out everything. Bitter, disbelieving rage—and betrayal.

Oh, Eden. No, no, no. How could she? Eden was weak. She was compliant and meek, passive and gullible. She always had been.

Maddox stood outside that door and enticed her with honeyed

lies, and she'd believed him, let herself be led astray like a lamb to the slaughter.

And now Ezra would die for it.

"After everything we've been through, everything we've sacrificed—"

"No," Ezra said. "You have it—wrong. She did it...for you."

She stared at him, bewildered. She couldn't think straight. His words didn't make sense. "What do you mean?"

"She gave herself up...to save you, girl."

Dakota rocked back on her heels. "No. She got you shot—"

"I was already...shot." He breathed heavily, his eyelids fluttering, his face ashen. Blood soaked the cement beneath him. "It was too late for me...she did it for you."

Dakota was speechless. Her lungs constricted, like a giant fist was slowly squeezing, squeezing the life out of her.

Only twenty minutes ago, she'd been triumphant. She'd thought they'd won.

Then everything she'd worked so hard for had been ripped away in an instant. She'd lost Logan. Ezra, a man she loved like a father, was dying. She hadn't kept Eden safe like she'd promised.

She'd survived a cult, torture, a damn nuclear bomb. Only now did she finally feel like the whole world was collapsing around her.

Ezra fumbled for her hand and closed his fingers around hers. "Stay...with me."

"Ezra, I—"

He shook his head weakly. His skin was dead-white. His chest hardly moved. He was barely clinging to consciousness. When that slipped away, so would he. "Just...stay."

"I'm sorry. I'm so sorry. I messed up. I did everything wrong. I—"

"No, girl. You did everything...right."

It would be too hard, too unbearable to say all the things she longed to say—that she was bereft beyond words, that she loved him, had loved him since that first day he found her and Eden in the shed, the day a lonely old man made the choice not to shoot two desperate little thieves, but to save them instead.

"Don't leave me," she whispered. "Please don't leave me."

He didn't answer.

She squeezed his hand, squeezed all the grief, sorrow, and regret into his bony fingers until the death rattle finally subsided, his hollowed eyes drifted closed, and his hand went limp in her own.

71
DAKOTA

Dakota remained beside Ezra. She didn't know how long she stayed, but she'd promised. She'd promised him.

She slumped against the shelves, ignoring the ache in her shoulders and spine and the soreness of her tailbone from the concrete floor. She held Ezra's hand and stared through the doorway out into the night and thought about nothing.

She was numb, brittle, a breath away from shattering into pieces.

Ten minutes passed—or maybe it was ten hours. It felt like ten lifetimes. Julio found her at her vigil, crouched over Ezra's body, damp and shivering. He called her name, then said it again.

She looked at him, blinking, slowly coming back to herself. "Julio."

"I'm here," he said gently, wrapping a blanket around her shoulders. "I'm right here."

His palms were blistered. Black dirt smudged his fingernails. She'd forgotten where he was, that he'd been busy with his own vigil, burying Park.

"I'm sorry," she said, "I'm so sorry..."

"Oh, honey," Julio said, touching her shoulder, offering her comfort. "It's not your fault."

Julio asked where Logan was, but she couldn't answer that. He tried to get her to come inside, but she wouldn't leave Ezra.

Together, they wrapped his body in another blanket and carried him through the wind and rain into the cabin. They passed the dead bodies and left them to rot.

They'd have to burn Ezra's body, she thought dimly. He'd always wanted to be cremated. *Who wants to feed the worms and the maggots once they're gone?* She heard his voice, deep and grizzled and clear as if he were standing right in front of her.

For tonight, they laid Ezra gently on the couch. Julio said a prayer over him while Dakota stood numbly in the wreckage of the cabin, staring at the blood stains on the living room floor, the dust and debris scattered everywhere. The air stank of gunpowder and death.

Julio pulled the satphone out of his pocket, righted a tipped-over chair, and sat at the kitchen table—the scarred wooden table Ezra had built with his own hands, the table she and Eden had spent countless hours at, talking and laughing and living.

"It's Shay." He stared numbly down at the phone. "She tried to call."

Dakota barely heard him. Sounds were tinny and far away. Her earplugs were gone, but she didn't remember taking them out.

Her head felt full of cotton—her heart like it'd been ripped out of her chest still beating.

The walls were too close. The dusty air clogged her throat. *One, two, three. Breathe.* Everywhere she looked, she saw memories of Ezra, saw glimpses of all the things she'd had and then lost. She'd failed, utterly and completely.

Ezra was dead.

Eden was gone.

Logan had abandoned her.

Her chest contracted, squeezing until it felt like her ribs might crack. She had to get out of here. She had to *breathe*.

She fled the cabin, stumbling over the shards of glass, splinters of wood, and chunks of drywall and slammed open the front door, Julio calling her name behind her.

72

LOGAN

Logan drove the Harley down the center of US 41, swerving around the occasional abandoned vehicle. The powerful engine rumbled beneath him. The straps of his pack dug into his shoulders.

The beams of his headlights pierced the dark, highlighting the glistening road, the wet black leaves of the trees hunched on either side of the highway. The anti-fog visor on Boyd's helmet kept his vision relatively clear.

The rain drenching his clothes and running in rivulets down the back of his neck soothed his heat-baked skin. In a while, his soaked condition would pose a problem, but for now, he didn't care.

He hadn't ridden a bike in years, but he remembered how. He eased back on the throttle, braked gently, and avoided leaning to adjust for the rain-slicked road. The bike wasn't the problem.

With each passing minute, with each mile stretching between him and the cabin, his heart clenched like a fist, tighter and tighter. He stared ahead, numb and mindless.

It would be dawn soon. The sky lightened almost imperceptibly. It didn't matter. Nothing mattered. Mile after mile roared by. Twenty, thirty, forty.

Logan blinked. The headlights illuminated a lump in the middle of the road directly ahead.

Adrenaline spiked through his veins. He swerved hard to miss the body and almost collided with a black sedan parked on the left side of the road, obscured in the rain and darkness. He barely missed the opened front passenger door.

He forced himself to ease to a careful stop a hundred yards past the sedan. He twisted around and peered into the night. It was too dark, the rain pouring too hard. All he could make out was dark wavering shadows. He couldn't see the body.

Should he go back and roll it off the road? Why bother?

Dead bodies were part of the landscape now, another inescapable aspect of the apocalypse bearing down on them all. There was no ignoring it—pretty soon, the dead would be as common as roadkill.

He removed the helmet. Rain slapped his face. The wind howled; the trees swayed. Above him, lightning forked in jagged, sky-splitting streaks.

He pulled out his flask, unscrewed the cap, and lifted it to his lips. He'd already downed half the flask. He swallowed another burning draught, felt it slide sweet and aching down his throat.

It was a good burn, a welcome burn. The familiar warmth of oblivion, beckoning to him. It was doing its work, transforming the chaos in his head to a dull thudding nothingness.

How easy it would be.

He could turn the bike around, aim it at the hulking shadow of the black sedan. He could end this all, end everything.

No more nightmares of Tomás. No more taunting demons in his head. No more unendurable shame.

His grasp tightened on the flask.

An image of Dakota flashed through his mind, cutting through the numbness. The defiant tilt of her jaw, the fierceness in her eyes. Dakota's hand reaching for him, her fingers threading through his own.

Ezra had seen who he was. Dakota saw who he could be.

What the hell was wrong with him? What kind of man was he, wandering around feeling sorry for himself? Running away from the one person in the whole world who knew of the worst in him, yet accepted him anyway?

Who the hell cared what someone else said? Other people had been judging him his entire life—for his ethnicity, his tattoos, his failures. He was about to throw everything away because of the words of a bitter old man, an old man who'd chosen isolation and loneliness over a life—messy and sometimes ugly and painful, but real.

Logan chose to live. To do better, to be better.

He was a fighter. The scrappy kid who clawed his way up from nothing, who survived the streets, who faced grown men twice as large as he was with tenacity and grit. That's who he was, who he would be again.

The flask slipped from his fingers. It tumbled to the asphalt and lay on its side, the remains of the moonshine dribbling out, mixing with the rain puddles. He left it there.

Everything he cared about was back the way he'd come.

Everything he loved.

73

DAKOTA

Dakota ran out into the pre-dawn darkness. Thirty yards from the cabin, she stopped, half-bent, heaving and gasping. She forced herself to straighten, to raise her face to the sky. Rain splattered her cheeks, dripped down her neck.

She felt disorientated, lost, and so, so alone. The pain was inside of her, an immense pressure against her ribs, a howling void with no end, no bottom. She pressed her fist over her heart.

"I can't do this!" Dakota screamed at the storm, wind whipping her hair, tears leaking down her cheeks.

If God was up there, she longed for him to hear her, to answer her, to provide comfort or tell her what to do. Something. Anything.

"Where are you, God?" she shouted, her voice cracking, sobs wracking her body. "Where are you? How can I do this alone?"

There was no answer but the howling wind, the crashing thunder.

A twig cracked behind her. Dakota whirled, pistol cradled in both hands, aiming at the intruder's center mass.

Slowly, she lowered the gun.

"You're not alone," Logan said. "I'm right here."

SNEAK PEEK OF DARKEST NIGHT

The rain had finally stopped, but the morning brought a gray, gloomy haze, like the sky was in mourning, too. After a restless hour trying unsuccessfully to sleep, with Logan remaining awake and vigilant just in case, Dakota had risen early to take in the extent of the damage.

Or maybe she just needed some time to think.

She walked among the bodies, searching for Rueben, Maddox's cousin and the Prophet's son. In her panicked search last night, she'd only been looking for one face.

But Rueben wasn't here either. Maybe once he and Maddox had kidnapped Eden, they'd decided to cut their losses and flee, abandoning their remaining men to death.

Whatever noble titles they anointed themselves with, they were still the same despicable cowards.

The humid air clung damply to her skin. Crickets trilled and frogs sang to each other. Birds twittered and chirped.

And the flies. Hundreds of them, buzzing around the bodies. The stench of blood and excrement stung her nostrils. She wiped her forehead with the back of her arm and kept going.

They'd have to take care of these bodies, and soon. Maybe burn them. Or roll them into the swamp and let the gators have them.

So many dead. So many young, wasted lives.

Who would these men have been if they hadn't been raised in fear and hatred? If they hadn't been steeped in superstition and twisted ideology from the moment they were born?

Who would she have been? And Maddox? If neither of them had been sucked into the Prophet's vortex of evil? If Eden, Sister Rosemarie, and the other innocents like little Ruth had never been tangled in his web of lies and deceit?

But the questions were pointless. She had no power or control over the beginning of it all. The only question now was whether she could end it.

The shed doors were still hanging open, the single bulb shining. Dakota couldn't bear to look inside yet: at the shelves full of Ezra's precious stash, all the things he'd so carefully stored away to save them.

A radio spat static.

Instinctively, she jerked to attention, adrenaline shooting through her veins. Dropping the shovel, she tugged her pistol from her holster and held it in the low ready position, scanning the clearing, searching the shadows deep in the trees.

The static came again. It didn't come from out there. It was close by.

More crackling. She tilted her head, following the noise.

She crept to the first body, fallen next to one of the cisterns not five yards from the shed, and nudged it with her toe. The radio attached to the dead body's belt crackled.

She bent, picked it up with her left hand, and dialed up the volume. She pushed the button for a moment but didn't speak.

She knew deep in her gut who it was. Let the bastard go first.

The radio spat and crackled. "Dakota Sloane, is that you?"

"Go to hell, Maddox."

He chuckled dryly. "You always were a scintillating conversationalist."

"You killed Park."

"He got in the way."

"You killed Ezra."

"He had something I wanted."

"No!" Anger bubbled up, obliterating her grief. "I did! You should've come after me instead!"

"Trust me, I wanted to. Eden convinced me otherwise. You should thank her. I'll pass it along."

"Why are you doing this?" She clutched the radio so hard her fingers ached. "Jacob hated you. Your father despises you. Eden is the one who loves you. And you kidnapped her, killed her friends, and took her back to the monster who wants to enslave her!"

"I saved her!" he shouted. "I'm saving her soul."

"You're too smart to spout that crap. Or to believe it."

"I know what's best for her. I know what's best for you." He was quiet for a moment. "You love me, Dakota. You *need* me."

"I hate you," she forced out. "I hate you with every fiber of my being."

He laughed darkly. "You wish you did. But let's be honest. You don't. You can't. There's too much between us."

She swallowed the lump in her throat. "I do hate you."

"I wish I could hate you, too. I wish I could, but for some damn reason, I can't. Do you know that? Can you understand? I think you do. I think you know exactly what that feels like."

She did know. Because once upon a time, Maddox was all she had. He was the lifeline that kept her sane in the sadistic, insane world of the River Grass Compound, where a girl could be beaten and branded for reading.

She had been weak, small, and invisible. Only Maddox saw her.

Only Maddox made their grim existence bearable with his cynical attitude, sarcastic jokes, and that mocking smile of his. Out on the boat, exploring the Glades, they'd escaped the harsh rules and restrictions, the constant threat of violence, the shame and humiliation shoved down their throats in the guise of religion.

She had loved him for it.

Then he changed. To gain the approval of his father, he'd turned on her. Turned into whatever he was now. Cruel. Ruthless. Vengeful.

But there was still that thread of the past that connected them, a slender but indestructible filament that she couldn't sever, no matter how much she wished she could.

"I don't understand," she lied. "I never will."

"You and I aren't that different."

"We're nothing alike," she spat into the mouthpiece, wanting to crush it into pieces, imagining it was Maddox's windpipe instead of a stupid radio. "You're insane."

"You only wish that I was insane. You hate that you understand me better than you understand yourself."

She did hate it. She hated it even more that he was right. "Your father abused you. He forced you to abuse me, taught you it was good."

He hesitated. "You clearly don't understand the concept of mercy."

The scars on her back burned like they were on fire. "It wasn't mercy, what they did to us. It was torture. Once upon a time, you knew that."

"You sound bitter, Dakota. Are you bitter that you lost to me?"

"I haven't lost yet."

"No?" He gave a mirthless laugh. "It sure looks that way from here."

"You can still do the right thing, Maddox," she said. "You can still turn this around. Let her go."

"I won't." The arrogant confidence in his voice faltered—for just a second, just a little, but it was there. She felt it as much as heard it. "I don't have a choice."

"You clearly don't understand the concept of choice."

He snorted. "I always did like that about you. You were the only one in the whole damn compound with the guts to speak your mind."

She turned back toward the shed, forced herself to stare through the opened doors to the dark stain in the center of the cement floor beneath the single bulb, the blood almost black in the light.

She'd thought if she gave everything, it would be enough. It wasn't.

Now Park and Ezra were dead, and Eden was gone.

Nothing would bring Ezra back. She'd failed him. She'd thought she was strong enough, tough enough to defeat whatever came at them.

How wrong she was.

A dark sucking energy surrounded her, a black hole. She trembled with anger, with sorrow, with pain so deep it was endless. She could fall forever and ever and never strike the bottom of her grief.

But there was anger there, too. A fierce, smoldering rage.

She wasn't finished yet. She wasn't dead. She thought she'd given everything, but she was wrong about that, too.

There was always more. As long as she was alive, as long as she still had breath in her lungs and blood in her veins, there was more she could give.

A fish-crow cawed hoarsely from somewhere. Low scudding clouds shrouded the bruised purple sky, and the early morning air was wet and suffocating. Her footsteps squelched in the mud as she turned away from the shed and headed back toward the cabin.

She was done with this. Done with him. Done with this manipulative cat-and-mouse game he wanted to play.

She didn't want to play. She wanted to burn everything to the ground.

Dakota raised the radio to her lips one final time. "I am coming for you, Maddox. I'm going to kill your father. I'm going to kill the Prophet. And then, I'm going to kill you."

The End

ALSO BY KYLA STONE

Point of Impact

Fear the Fallout

From the Ashes

Into the Fire

No Safe Haven

Rising Storm

Falling Stars

Burning Skies

Breaking World

Raging Light

Labyrinth of Shadows

Beneath the Skin

Before You Break

Real Solutions for Adult Acne

ACKNOWLEDGMENTS

Thank you as always to my awesome beta readers. Your thoughtful critiques and enthusiasm are invaluable. My stories and characters are better for it!

Thank you so much to Fred Oelrich, Mike Smalley, and Wmh Cheryl. Huge appreciation also to Michelle Browne, Jessica Burland, Sally Shupe, Jeremy Steinkraus, and Barry and Derise Marden.

A big thanks to Debbie Butz for suggesting the name of Jake for the last Collier brother. I appreciate you!

To Michelle Browne for her skills as a great line editor. Thank you to Eliza Enriquez for her excellent proofreading skills. You both make my words shine.

And a special thank you to Jenny Avery for volunteering her time to give the manuscript that one last read-through and catch those pesky typos. Any remaining errors are mine.

To my husband and my kids, who show me the true meaning of love every day and continually inspire me. I love you.

And to my loyal readers, whose support and encouragement mean everything to me. Thank you.

ABOUT THE AUTHOR

I spend my days writing apocalyptic and dystopian fiction novels.

I love writing stories exploring how ordinary people cope with extraordinary circumstances, especially situations where the normal comforts, conveniences, and rules are stripped away.

My favorite stories to read and write deal with characters struggling with inner demons who learn to face and overcome their fears, launching their transformation into the strong, brave warrior they were meant to become.

Some of my favorite books include *The Road*, *The Passage*, *Hunger Games*, and *Ready Player One*. My favorite movies are *The Lord of the Rings* and *Gladiator*.

Give me a good story in any form and I'm happy.

Oh, and add in a cool fall evening in front of a crackling fire, nestled on the couch with a fuzzy blanket, a book in one hand and a hot mocha latte in the other (or dark chocolate!): that's my heaven.

I mean, I won't say no to hiking to mountain waterfalls, traveling to far-flung locations, or jumping out of a plane (parachute included) either.

I love to hear from my readers! Find my books and chat with me via any of the channels below:

www.Facebook.com/KylaStoneAuthor
www.Amazon.com/author/KylaStone
Email me at KylaStone@yahoo.com

Printed in Great Britain
by Amazon